# ARTERIAL
## bloom

EDITED BY

## Mercedes M. Yardley

FOREWORD BY LINDA D. ADDISON

PUBLISHED BY CRYSTAL LAKE PUBLISHING
WWW.CRYSTALLAKEPUB.COM

ISBN: 978-1-64669-310-8
Cover & Interior Design by Todd Keisling | Dullington Design Co.
Proofread by Paula Limbaugh, Guy Medley, Andi Rawson, and N.M. Scuri

"In the Loop" by Ken Liu was originally published in *War Stories,* edited by Andrew Liptak and Jaym Gates, Apex Book Company, 2014.

"Dead Letters" by Christopher Barzak was originally published in *Realms of Fantasy,* 2006.

Crystal Lake Publishing – Tales from the Darkest Depths
www.crystallakepub.com

Join the Crystal Lake community today on our newsletter and Patreon!

# WELCOME
## TO ANOTHER

# CRYSTAL LAKE PUBLISHING
## CREATION

Join today at www.crystallakepub.com & www.patreon.com/CLP

# OTHER ANTHOLOGIES BY CRYSTAL LAKE PUBLISHING

# Table of Contents

# FOREWORD
## - Linda D. Addison -

Before I met Mercedes M. Yardley in person I knew her work, not just excellent fiction, but constructive essays on writing and other subjects that touch her heart. Spending a weekend with her at a convention I discovered an intelligent, caring, talented, and fun human. This book is her first step as an editor in the anthology arena.

I've been in more than thirty anthologies and only a handful didn't have a theme. People like themes: it gives them something to identify with quickly (an anthology of *Goldfish Who Transform Into Demons* or *Terrifying Stories Using the Word "Red"*, etc.). What would possess a first-time anthology editor to do a book without a clearly defined subject? The book you're reading proves that the editor is in rhythm with some dark, wonderful magic!

I don't know how Yardley did it, but there is such poetry and unease in these stories. Even though each one is different in voice, story concept, characters, their openings put me on the edge of my seat, pulling to the next page. The stories cover a wide gamut of surreal, apocalyptic, miracle cures (not), beyond dysfunctional families/relationships, surviving loss (personal and world-level), and aggressive life forms.

There are titles that seem innocent and titles that definitely let you know no innocence will survive. The protagonists are courageous humans, serial killers, monsters, planets (yep, I said *planets*), objects and fire. I know some of these authors, excellent authors who shine in this anthology, others are new to me, but somehow they each have some poetic prose in their piece.

Everything that exists starts as an idea and comes into existence through working imagination into reality. One day I will sit with Yardley to listen to the first time she conceived of doing this book, to try to understand how she enticed the authors to create such beautiful darkness, with endings that made me shudder in wonderment.

Life is a crooked road, unexpectedly branching from first breath to last, seasoned with joy and loss; breaking us sometimes, strengthening us other times. Looking back over my life so far, I would say the theme of mine has been to survive and thrive; there is no one way to describe it.

I stopped after reading each of the stories in this anthology to sit and marvel over the language, story, characters, and endings that set my imagination on fire with their graceful horror. These stories, like life, actively branch into somber, unexpected beings, things, and places. Now it's your turn, go on, flip the page and enter these ravishing shadows that Yardley has gathered...

# ARTERIAL
*bloom*

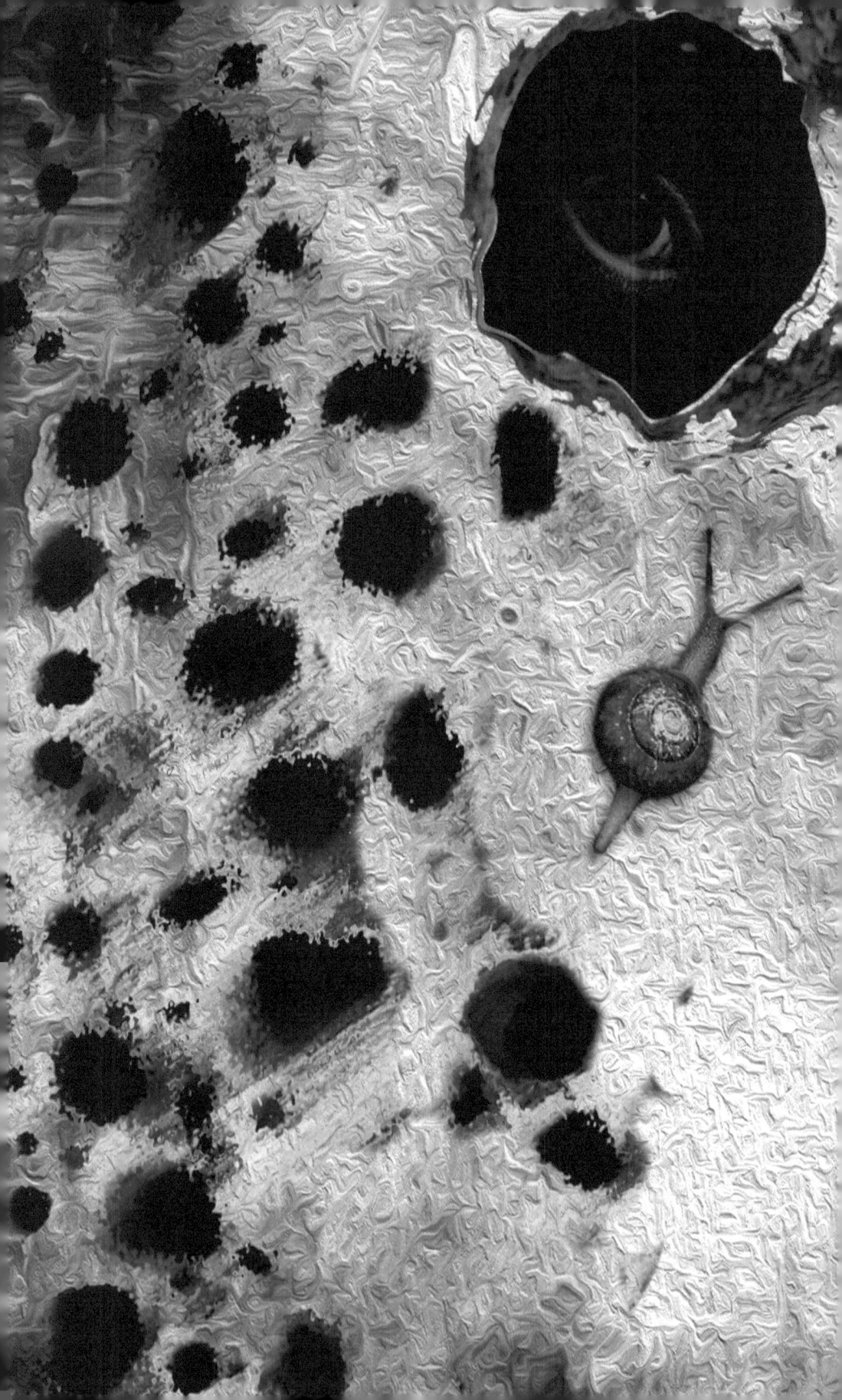

# THE STONE DOOR
### - Jimmy Bernard -

t was a clear day, with a hot sun shining down on the valley. The house built here was small, but the sisters didn't need a lot. They each had their own bedroom, and out back were vegetable gardens and a chicken coop. The only sound came from Billie riding the wooden bicycle. Its entire frame rambled, and she often worried it might break, though the chain running to the lever in front of her was still strong, which mattered most.

"I think I've found a way," Charlotte said. She was twelve, and the youngest of the three. Billie was sixteen, and Agatha, who still slept after her night shift, was fourteen. Charlotte sat at the table, bent over a pile of papers filled with sketches.

"No," Billie said.

"Just hear me out," Charlotte said, as she came to stand beside Billie holding a large piece of paper in her hands. Billie didn't look; she just stared at the chain running from the bicycle toward the lever built above the stone door laying in the hill. A large weight stood atop the door which was being held down by the spinning chain. A chain that only spun because Billie had been cycling for four hours already.

"I don't want to hear it. I never want to hear it again, not after last time."

"Last time was a mistake. This can work," Charlotte said. Billie pointed at the clock.

"My shift is done. Get ready to take over." Charlotte put her plans on the table. She took a drink of water before coming to stand next to the bicycle. Billie started cycling faster, then she lifted her right leg over the frame, while Charlotte placed her foot on the pedal.

"Ready?"

"Go," Charlotte said. And just like that Billie was off, and Charlotte had taken over. The weight didn't even budge.

Billie walked to the table and sat down, rubbing the soreness out of her legs.

"We need to use sticks," Charlotte said.

"Take a good look at that weight. Do you really think a few sticks can hold that sucker down?"

"Yes, if we can use them to board up the door. It's worth a try."

"I'm done trying," Billie said. She stood up and went to the house.

"Don't wake Agatha, but if you do, tell her about my idea." Billie left Charlotte atop the bike and headed to her room. She had one more shift coming up, from six to ten P.M. She'd have to prepare dinner, so Agatha and Charlotte could eat, but that could wait. First, she needed a moment to herself.

She lay down on the bed and closed her eyes. The rumbling of the bicycle was still buzzing in her ears, like an incessant bug. Birds chirped outside, and Agatha snored in the other room. It was just the three of them, nobody else. The woods surrounding their valley had several wild animals living within it, but they didn't dare come close to the stone door. Because that's the only sound that mattered. It was all Billie listened for. Sometimes she'd stop hearing the bicycle, and her heart would skip a beat. But then she'd look out of the window and see Charlotte or Agatha going at it. And the door was still locked, keeping it inside.

Maybe she'd walk down to the river before dinner, enjoy some alone time. Billie went outside and Charlotte turned to her.

"What if we use the sticks to create a counterweight?" Charlotte said.

"You keep thinking about that. I'm heading out to the river."

"What about dinner?"

"It'll be ready, don't worry," Billie said as she walked away.

"It better be! I'm not covering for you again," Charlotte called after her, turning her gaze back toward the door. A shiver crept through her tiny body. Yes, a counterweight had to work. All they needed was a cage filled with rocks.

As Charlotte occupied her mind with her latest idea, Billie walked toward the river. It came out of the woods and flowed down, only to disappear among the trees once more. The water was clear and cool, with smooth rocks visible at the bottom. The sunlight reflected off the surface, creating untouchable diamonds. Fresh air filled the entire valley, but here it was cold like it could only be near water. The running sound of it drove the noise of the bicycle out of her head. It was beautiful here, yet her fears remained. Because no matter how tranquil the river was, or how good Charlotte's ideas were, that door could not open. Not again, at least.

Billie looked at the scars that ran from her elbow to her wrist. There were others that ran across her legs though she kept those hidden. Tears came to her eyes as Billie tried to forget everything. She hated these scars. They were symbols of what happened here once that door opened, and they would never allow her to be carefree.

Billie sat down and put her feet in the water. She often imagined jumping in and going under. The river could take her into the darkness of the forest, and whatever lay beyond. But she'd find no happiness there either, for the stone door would always be in the back of her mind.

After a while, she went back to cook dinner. Billie ate, keeping the rest of the food on a small fire.

"Want me to go wake Agatha before I start?" Billie said, after finishing her meal.

"No, let her sleep. She looked pale this morning," Charlotte said.

"Pale? How pale?" Billie said.

"Don't worry. A good night's sleep was all she needed. I bet she'll be jumping out of bed and eating all the food in no time."

"I hope so. Let me put this away and we'll switch." Charlotte nodded, puffing and sweating profusely.

"I think we need to oil the chain again. It sounds strained," Charlotte said.

"The chain's fine. It doesn't need oil for another month."

"Can't we do it earlier, just to be safe?" Charlotte said. Billie switched seats with her and stared at the stone door.

"Alright, we'll do it tomorrow." Charlotte thanked Billie and went back to the table. They kept to themselves for two hours. Charlotte drew her ideas out on paper, and Billie rode the wooden bicycle. Then, when the sun was already setting and the first of the cool air was coming, Billie leaned back on the saddle.

"Go wake Agatha. She's slept enough and needs to eat before starting her shift." Charlotte walked into the house and left Billie alone. Her gaze remained fixed on the door, as the sun cast an orange glow over the valley, illuminating the evening beauty of their home.

"We've got a problem," Charlotte cried out from inside the house. Billie turned around.

"What is it?" she said, momentarily forgetting to cycle. The chain stopped spinning, and the weight lifted ever so slightly. Suddenly, something massive slammed against the stone door, followed by a high-pitched shriek. Billie shook and started cycling faster than before. The chain started spinning again, and the weight dropped back down.

"What was that?" Agatha said, standing in the doorway. Billie's heart raced and her lips trembled. The weight was back in place, but she kept on going fast, just in case. She closed her eyes and counted to ten. Her nerves slowly calmed down, and Billie took a shaking breath.

"Nothing, I just slipped."

"Well, don't do it again," Agatha said. She grabbed a plate of food and sat down at the table. Billie glanced at her. Agatha looked pale, there were dark circles underneath her eyes, and her nose was runny.

"Will you tell me what the problem was already?" Billie asked. Agatha rolled her eyes.

"She's sick," Charlotte said, coming out of the house with the medicine box in her hands.

"I'm fine. I've got a cold, that's all." As Charlotte and Agatha argued, Billie laughed. She'd nearly allowed the door to open. She ran her fingers over the scars on her arm. That one lapse in attention had almost been enough to add fresh scars. All because these two didn't get along.

"Will you shut it?" she lashed out. Charlotte and Agatha stared at her.

"What crawled up your ass and died?" Agatha said.

"You two, and this stupid bike, and that door, and your ideas that never work," she said, pointing at Charlotte. "Answer me this, Agatha: can you do your night shift?"

"Yes."

"No," Charlotte said. She frowned and crossed her arms. Billie knew she was upset, but right now she couldn't care less. She had little more than an hour to go before finally getting some rest. The last thing she needed was emotional drama or worries about Agatha not making it through her shift.

"I can do it. I'm not sick."

"We can't risk you becoming too weak to ride the bicycle," Charlotte said.

"I'm stronger than both of you, I can handle it." Charlotte groaned and turned to Billie, who still had her eyes fixed on the weight.

"It's your call," Charlotte said.

"Let her ride. What else is she going to do?" Billie said.

"Exactly. Now get out of my face." Agatha stood up and went back inside. Charlotte followed her but stopped at the door to look back toward Billie.

"My ideas might not work, but at least I haven't given up." She went inside, leaving Billie alone for the last hour of her shift.

Soon, she'd sleep. If she was lucky she could dream of visiting the ocean. It had to be long ago, back when Mom and Dad were still alive. Charlotte had been a baby, and Agatha barely two years old. But Billie had been old enough to remember it. Though she couldn't always tell if they'd actually gone there or if it was just a dream. This house and that door had been their reality for so long it felt strange to think of a life beyond any of it. She didn't even remember how they'd come to live here. She remembered Mom and Dad, just as she remembered their cries when the door opened and the thing inside took them. It was one memory she pushed back as deep as possible, yet it always found a way out.

"She's just worried," Agatha said. She stood next to Billie, holding a tissue to her red nose.

"Charlotte thinks too much. She's always mulling over one thing or another. It drives me nuts," Billie said.

"What do you expect? You remember what happened last time."

"I try to forget." The sisters were quiet for a moment, allowing the rumbling of the bicycle and the chain to fill the void of conversation. "Are you going to manage?"

"Do I have a choice?" Agatha said.

"I can take over half of your shift."

"You need sleep." She glanced at the small shed beside the house. "Are the torches ready?"

"I'll check before going to bed," Billie said.

"Thank you." Billie looked at the clock and saw her time was up. Agatha knew as well, and the girls switched places.

"If you need anything, call me," Billie said.

"I will, just check the torches, please. I like knowing they're ready." Billie did so right away. She opened the shed and saw three torches leaning against the wall. Some sheets and a canister of oil stood next to them, along with matches to light them up if need be. It had been seven months since they'd last used them. Seven months of peace and security.

"Goodnight," Billie said, before going inside. She went up the stairs and found Charlotte brushing her teeth in the bathroom, already wearing her pajamas and averting her gaze. Billie joined her sister and put a hand on her shoulder.

"Get off," Charlotte said.

"Your ideas aren't stupid. I shouldn't have said that." Charlotte spit and glared at Billie.

"I'm just trying to find a way out of here."

"I know. Me too," Billie said, thinking back to their last supply run. The village wasn't far, and they'd been building a railroad line last time. If she was lucky, the tracks would be finished by now. Billie hugged her sister and wondered if she could truly leave them behind. She could board a train and ride it until she reached the ocean. Then she might find a nice house along the beach and live there. Though it would never get better, Billie knew that. No matter how far she ran, or how beautiful her beach house was, she'd always remember her abandoned sisters. And whatever happiness she found would be buried underneath a new door, visible only to her.

Her life was here, and there was no escaping it. If she wanted happiness, she'd have to build it atop that door.

Billie went to bed and fell asleep, dreaming of the ocean. In her dream, she didn't hear the rolling of the waves but instead the spinning of the bicycle. The wheels turned round and round, pulling the chain that kept the weight in place. Then the sun disappeared, and only darkness remained. There was no beach, no happy life beyond. There was only a door, and a monster waiting on the other side.

Billie shot awake. She sat upright in her bed, trying to figure out what this creeping feeling of dread was that crawled up to her. Something was wrong, but what? Had Agatha become too sick to ride and had Charlotte taken over? Or had Billie slept through her own shift? No, that wasn't it, it was still dark outside and her shift wouldn't start until morning. Then what was it?

In the silence of night, she thought of what might've spooked her so, but then it hit her. The realization made her jaw drop and her lips tremble. Her heart pounded in her ears, like the pounding footsteps of a coming killer.

There was an absolute silence outside.

Billie crawled out of bed and tiptoed toward the window, where her worst fear became reality. The stone door was open. The bicycle lay toppled over on the ground, with neither of her sisters in sight. Yet worst of all was that door, and the darkness that lay behind it. It was out, and now the monster was somewhere in or around this house.

Drops of sweat rolled down her back. Fear rooted her to the ground. Her legs became weak, and she nearly fell to her knees. The darkness of night curled around her chest and choked the air out of her lungs. This couldn't be. What had gone wrong? Had something happened to her sisters? Were they even still alive? All these thoughts raced through her head, along with a whisper begging her to move. If she stayed here, she was dead. She had to get down to the shed to light the torches. It was the only thing capable of driving the monster back, if only for a few seconds.

Billie took a deep breath and tried to steady her nerves. Then she went to her bedroom door. She pressed her ear against it but heard nothing on the other side. What if the monster was in the hallway outside? Billie pushed the thought away and lowered the handle. Each creaking sound made her stop and listen. She pushed her lips together, trying to keep her teeth from chattering.

She opened the door and peeked outside. Shadows rested in each corner, and every potted plant or piece of furniture made her jump. Charlotte's bedroom door stood open, showing a dark room. Billie thought she saw something sitting by the bed, but she couldn't be sure. What if it was that thing? What if there were invisible eyes staring back at her?

Billie pushed through her fear and stepped out into the hallway. Should she go check on Charlotte? But Billie already knew the answer to that question. Charlotte never slept with her door open. She must have heard it escape and was probably heading toward the shed right this second. Maybe she could deal with it on her own? But no, Billie had to check. What kind of sister would she be if she let her youngest sibling deal with this horror all by herself?

She walked toward the top of the staircase and stared down. A dark hole, with the faint light of the moon falling through a window, waited below. And still that silence remained. Where was this thing? And where were Charlotte and Agatha? Billie took a step down, and then another. Each step asked more and more of her as she plunged into the unknown. The living room wasn't terrifying during the day, and normally, not even at night. Yet it was now. The open staircase allowed her to look out over the entire living room. Each piece of furniture looked black and menacing in the darkness. Billie crouched down, searching for a new shape; one not meant to be free.

A deep thud came from the kitchen. Or had it come from above her? Sitting halfway on the stairs made it hard to tell where the sound had come from. All Billie knew was that she nearly peed her pants upon hearing it. Had the monster been in Charlotte's room after all? If so, it would find her on the stairs and she needed to move. But what if it was down there?

The wind blew and pushed against the windows. Billie got up and descended into darkness. She had to make it outside, yet she couldn't take the front door. They hadn't maintained the hinges in years, making the door cry out each time it opened. No, Billie needed to go out the back door. Unfortunately, that meant crossing the living room.

It won't be hard, she told herself. After all, this was her living room. She walked through it every day, and it held no secrets anymore. She shouldn't be frightened of her own home.

Billie moved slowly. She saw the dark silhouette of the dining table, along with the chairs. In the corner stood a potted plant, with a lamp beside it. Moonlight fell through the windows in the back. She was nearly there, just a few more steps.

Something sighed behind her. Billie spun around quickly, her entire body tensing up. Her eyes were open wide, taking in the living room. She saw the couch and the small cabinet beside it. But then she saw something new. A shape not meant to be there. The thing opened its eyes, and two white holes appeared in the night. It sighed again, and stood up, its slender form nearly reaching the ceiling. It had twisted legs, like a giant praying mantis. Its arms were long and ended in sharp claws. But the worst part of it all was its head, hidden still by the darkness of night.

Billie stepped back and lifted her hand toward the door. The thing followed her movement with its gaze. Part of her wanted to call out for help, while another wanted to curl up into a ball and cry.

Her hand touched the doorknob, and she yanked it open. As soon as Billie turned to run outside, she heard heavy footsteps pound through the living room. The monster shoved the table and chairs aside as if they weighed nothing. She ran across the grass and toward the shed. Billie opened the door and stopped. The torches were gone. Charlotte and Agatha must've taken them all.

"Help by the shed!" Billie screamed. She knew her sisters had to be close by, and right now they were her last hope.

The monster was still coming, and without those torches Billie had no chance of surviving it. She hesitated for a second, then jumped into the shed and closed the door. She pushed her back against the wall and held her breath. Everything outside was quiet. The monster's footsteps had stopped, and now only Billie's terrified heartbeat remained to accompany her.

But then she heard another sigh that grew into a screeching cry. A claw raked across the wood, and tears sprang to her eyes. She thought back to Mom and Dad, and how they'd died so long ago. And now it seemed her turn had come. At least her sisters would live.

Her foot touched something. She reached down and found a book of matches. The monster's claw pulled back and slammed into the shed, nearly shattering the wood. She grabbed the matches and wiped her tears away.

"Come get me!" she screamed, as she kicked open the door and struck the matches. They ignited into a large flame that illuminated the monster's face. It had lifeless eyes, and a mouth that opened to reveal hundreds of tentacles, each tipped with razor sharp teeth, squirming and slithering toward Billie's flesh. But Billie wasn't done. She shoved the matchsticks up and burned the monster's chest. It let out a high-pitched shriek, and lashed out at her, cutting open her chest. Billie cried out in pain, dropping her matches at the same time. She fell back into the shed and took in a shocked breath. She pressed one hand on her wound and held the other up in defense. Blood streamed through her fingers, yet there was no pain. She only felt a warm calmness fall over her.

The scent of blood drove the monster wild, and it let out a hungry cry. Its tentacles stabbed her leg as they wrapped around it. The monster turned and dragged Billie through the grass toward the door. It should've hurt, but she felt nothing. She only saw the stars shining down on her. It actually made her smile. It had been so long since she'd seen the beauty in darkness. She'd always stared down at the door, instead of the wonderful world surrounding it.

The monster released her leg, and Billie looked down. Agatha and Charlotte stood next to the bike, reattaching the chain. The sisters saw Billie and balled their fists.

"Let her go," Agatha said. They both lifted their torches and stepped forward. The monster lifted its claws as it screeched at them. It grabbed Billie's leg and dragged her closer to the door. But the sisters weren't giving up. They ran forward, waving their torches at the monster's face. It lashed out and struck them both, but they got up and back at it right away.

The monster cried out, this time in pain and fear, and retreated to the door. It reached for Billie, but Agatha kicked at its head. She closed the door, while Charlotte got onto the bicycle.

"Good job," Billie wanted to say, but she couldn't. Somehow the words wouldn't cross her lips. Her vision became blurry, and she saw Agatha looking down at her. She was talking, but Billie heard nothing, and that made her happy. For the first time in a long time, not hearing anything made her smile. There was no threat, no duty, only the stars above and the river in the valley.

# DOG (DOES NOT) EAT DOG
## - Grant Longstaff -

When we ran out of East, Reece and I stood on tarnished bronze sand and watched the Everstorm rage over the cobalt ocean before us.

"We missed the boats," Reece said.

"Must have," I lied.

We had chased their rumours for three days, whispers of ships bound for somewhere less toxic. I hadn't believed it. Like the sketchy accounts of planes and trains before, I knew it would be hopeful propaganda. But Reece had asked if I wanted to try for the coast and I had said yes. Fed his delusion.

Reece stabbed the crowbar he carried deep into the wet earth. He stared at the dark horizon, searching for the vague shapes of distant vessels silhouetted against the stark white veins of lightning. There was nothing out there. I watched as he dug his teeth into his cracked lips to still their trembling, trying to bite back tremors of frustration, swallow the swell of anger.

"Fuck," Reece looked at me, eyes bloodshot and watery, like those of a drunk. "I thought..."

I wondered, if we had found an entire fleet of ships, where Reece thought they might go that would be safe, but knew better than to ask.

"I'm sorry," I said.

Reece turned to the ocean and screamed, the muscles in his throat as rigid as iron. He fell to his knees, clawing up handfuls of dull sand, heaved in another breath to cry out. He screamed until his voice cracked. Until deep, tired howls scraped the anger from his throat and lungs. Finally, all he could do was cough up pink bile.

Once Reece was still, I took careful steps towards him and gently touched his shoulder.

"Fucking liars," Reece said.

"Who?"

"Them. From last night."

"They were only—"

"We should go back and kill the bastards."

"What?" Reece looked up at me, cold rage in his glassy eyes, and shrugged. I tried to smile, convince myself he was joking, but it felt crooked on my face. "It'll be dark soon. We need find somewhere to—"

Reece waved an arm to shut me up. I did.

After a moment Reece stood up and pulled the crowbar from the sand, then started back up the shore. I was caught between two storms—Reece raging ahead, thunder and ocean crashing at my back—unsure which worried me more.

It was dark coincidence which had brought us together.

Four days earlier I had stepped out from a looted pharmacy window in the city and there was Reece, simply waiting for me. He was leaning against a burned-out car, patiently tapping the crowbar against his thigh. We looked each other over, mapped the cruelties of the other's survival, traced lines through our memories to the last time we had seen each other.

Reece was the first to smile.

"I thought it was you," he said. "But I followed you just to be sure."

"What are the chances?"

"Fuck knows. How long has it been? It must be..." Reece trailed off.

"Three years. Give or take."

"Three years," Reece shook his head.

It had been late September. A time before the bombs. Reece and I had sat on the terrace of The Telegraph in the baking heat of an Indian summer drinking pints. We were celebrating Reece's promotion. It had been the last time the two of us were together. A memory from the world before.

"What about Clare?" Reece said.

The fingers of my right hand found the gold wedding ring on my left and completed thirteen rotations for each year Clare and I had spent together.

I looked at Reece and shook my head.

I followed the footsteps of my old friend over the beach and found him crouched amongst the tall grass. Instinctively, I dropped low and crawled towards him. On hearing my approach, Reece tilted his head and pointed the crowbar through the scratching blades towards the road.

A motorhome was angled across both lanes. The windshield was shattered. The flimsy door to the living area banged open and closed in the wind. A scrap of dirty white cloth tied to the aerial on the roof twisted and flapped madly. *A sign of peace.*

I pointed to the roof.

"It could be a trap," Reece said.

I blew out a hot breath and I shook my head, annoyed he might be right. I pressed myself closer to the earth, grass scratching my face and arms. Reece shrugged off his backpack and pushed it towards me.

"What are you doing?"

"There could be stuff in there we could use. Wait here."

"What—"

I grabbed for Reece, but he was already out of reach, clambering through the wild vegetation, crowbar held out in front of him. Once he met the road, he waited for a moment then bolted for the van. He pressed his back to it and nodded. I saw his mouth move but couldn't make out the words over the swell of the wind. I guessed it was a warning to anyone still inside. A moment later he vanished into the camper.

I watched the black space of the door, the stretches of tarmac to the north and south, the dead fields beyond. Nothing moved. Alone, I listened to the waves and storm, wondered what secrets they spoke to one another.

A minute passed. Two. Eventually, Reece leaned out of the door and gave me the thumbs up. I gathered up our packs and made my way to the motorhome.

"Let's get what we can and get out of here before it's dark," Reece said. His breathing was heavy, eager.

"There's no one in there?"

"No," Reece looked over his shoulder into the darkness inside the van, then back down at me standing in the road. "Not alive anyway."

I flicked my eyes to the steel tip of the crowbar hanging by his knee, searching for dark spots on the blue paint. *Clean.* Relief and guilt pulsed in my guts.

"How did it happen?" I said.

"Radiation, by the look of it. I don't know why it still bothers you."

"Because it never ends."

A murky light spilled through the windows and dirty skylight in the van. Directly through the door was a small dining table, scattered with well-worn paperbacks. To the right was the cockpit. Reece was hunched to the left of the door, pulling old rags and a bottle of cleaning product from the unit under the sink.

"Is this shit flammable?" Reece held up a bottle of bleach.

"I don't think so."

"Fuck."

I edged beyond Reece, towards the gloom of the sleeping area and the shape beneath the blanket which lay there. Thin, yellow curtains covered the windows and cast the mounds of sheets and pillows in an eerie light.

"You don't want to see that," Reece said behind me, "she's a mess."

I reached for the sheet and pulled it back, revealing the gaunt face of an elderly woman. Rings of dried blood circled her nostrils and blackened veins crawled up her neck. I eased the sheet down over her face and, noticing her exposed hand, lifted it to her side. Her fingers moved freely, a faint heat in her palm. I had survived long enough to know the sweet heat of decay which clung to the back of your throat all too well. The woman couldn't have been dead long.

"Come on. Help me search the rest of this heap of shit," Reece said.

I nodded and twisted the ring, counting the rotations, trying not to think too deeply. Survival after life before wasn't black and white, but a scale of grey. Worrying about where I fit onto it wasn't helpful. I gave the woman a final glance and then began to search through the van.

The daylight was almost gone by the time we finished searching the motorhome. Reece and I sat at the table opposite one another, splitting the items between the two of us to better carry the meagre load. Tinned food, a box of matches, a Tupperware container filled with batteries. Around my neck I wore a pair of small binoculars which I had found in the bucket of the passenger seat, tucked under a worn paperback on birdwatching. Reece picked up a bottle of whiskey he had found wrapped in a blanket, his face glowing.

"I didn't know you liked whiskey," I said.

"Needs must."

"If you say so."

"Come on. What the fuck is wrong with you?" Reece laughed.

"Nothing," I said, thinking of his madness on the beach less than an hour before, now utterly forgotten. "Just tired. Must be the sea air."

"No time for sleep, we're celebrating tonight."

Reece's teeth flashed a lunatic smile in the shadows of the growing dark.

We walked in the charcoal light, squinting at the unreliable shapes of burned-out buildings rising out of the gloom, looking for somewhere secure enough to spend the night. Before the bombs were dropped, before the Everstorm blotted out the sun, the place had been a wonderful seaside town. Now all that remained were the shattered husks of old hotels and the carcasses of the occasional bungalow.

"We should have stayed in the camper," Reece rubbed the back of his head and pulled at a clump of matted hair, clearly agitated.

"It might have attracted the wrong kind of attention."

"Fuck them."

"I'm sure we'll find somewhere," I said. Simple words I hoped would placate him.

Our friendship had never been easy, but it required more tact and diplomacy than I fully remembered. The end of everything had not been kind to Reece. Before the years pushed us apart, I was a diplomat constantly wrestling with his antagonistic philosophies. Now I followed in the shadow of a dictator, afraid to do anything else.

The ruined priory stood out on the headland, a fractured tower of beige brick against the slate sky, looming on the cliff over a small bay.

"What about that?" I said.

"Seriously?"

"It's almost dark. Get ourselves hunkered in the right spot we'll be out of the wind."

I waited, watching Reece mull it over.

The ancient walls had endured centuries of storms and survived wars. Their foundations were solid. It was safer than the flimsy shell of a bed and breakfast, less conspicuous than the camper. Surely he could see that.

"Fuck it," Reece shrugged, "let's do it."

I moved between the graves which pocked the land, the pale headstones guiding our way through the darkness towards the priory. Occasional lightning forked offshore and washed the landscape in momentary light, the ragged walls flashing in and out of existence ahead. We came to what once was a steeple, the two sides which remained stretching up into the dark, stopping the wind dead.

"Here's good," Reece said.

Twenty minutes later we were sat on our dirty sleeping bags, a tiny fire smouldering in a hollow in the soft dirt between us. The weathered stones muted the nook, dulled the storm and ocean. Only a thin shriek of wind pierced the narrow window arches high above.

With the fire almost out, I sprinkled a handful of dead grass into the softening orange embers and watched the light swell. The night wasn't cold, but the glow of the flame was comforting in the pitch-black world, and I was not yet ready for the dark.

Reece leaned over to his backpack and pulled out a dark square.

"What's that?" I asked.

Reece held the object close to the flames. A small book. A robin on the faded cover. I recognised it from the campervan.

"Fucking birdwatching," Reece said.

He opened the book and tore out the first page. A second later the paper was curling in the fire, the light intensifying as the page blackened to nothing.

"We don't need to burn it," I said.

"What else are we going to do with it?"

When the politicians started throwing bombs at one another, like children throwing clods of mud, the birds were the first to suffer. Too frail to survive the toxic storms, entire flocks crashed from the sky.

"Maybe she kept it to remember them," I said.

"Seems pointless given the circumstances."

I touched the binoculars still hanging around my neck. How many hours had she watched the sky? Perhaps it gave her hope to search the endless grey above. If the birds could survive, then so might we. I saw her lying dead, the traces of poisonous radiation on her face. It was only a matter of time before all of us fell.

Reece tore out another page, let it flutter down into the flames. I watched as the birds burned, their colours turning to ash. Not satisfied with their extinction, Reece was determined to extinguish even their memory.

"How long has Clare been gone?" Reece said.

It was the first time Reece had spoken her name since we met days earlier. I stopped turning the gold band on my finger, looked up from the mesmerising fire reflected within it.

"Two years. She died before all of this."

"You never told me."

Reece twitched at my words, at the truth they delivered. An artifact from the years of silence.

"Sorry," I said. It felt inadequate.

"Why didn't you tell me?"

I shook my head. How could I begin to fill the void which had stretched between us?

"We hadn't spoken in so long—"

"So fuck," Reece unscrewed the top of the whiskey bottle and threw the cap into the darkness behind him, his intentions made clear. He tipped the bottle to his lips and took a long drink. "What happened?"

"It was cancer. She—"

"Between us."

There it was. Reece's truth. The world, and everything in it, frantically whirling around him. I stared at Reece over the glowing embers, his face washed in flickering shadows. I wished I no longer recognised him, but my own truth was the bleak knowledge that I had only ever been dust skirting around his sun.

"It was always on your terms," I said.

"What?"

"Everything. All of it. I tried. But you were always busy, or it didn't suit."

"So now it's my fucking fault?"

"No," I swallowed a mouthful of anger, "I didn't say that."

"Well what the fuck are you saying?"

Reece nipped the hair at the back of his neck, his face an animal snarl leering over the fire. I turned away and took a shaking breath. Wrapped my trembling fingers around my knees to still them as I carefully constructed a response.

"Reece, people always mean well, but sometimes life just gets in the way. Friendships can fade, but it doesn't mean there was ever any malice from either party." I dared to look at him again. "Maybe we both should've tried harder?"

"Maybe you *should've* fucking told me."

Reece stood and took another long drink of whiskey—his wide, barren eyes never leaving mine—and disappeared into the shadows.

I sat in the exposed glow of the fire and fought the urge to pick up my backpack and leave. I wanted to run, but Reece was out there in the darkness somewhere. A predator watching its prey. A cold burn of fear swelled in my lungs. It was safer to stay. At least for the moment.

The sound of an engine cut through my scheming. It was distant, but closing in fast. A moment later Reece burst from the shadows.

"Put the fucking fire out!"

I stamped at the low, orange flames and we were swallowed into the black.

We stood on the cliff edge overlooking the small bay, watching a pair of headlights cut through the night, navigating the bends of the coastal road. They were almost out of sight when the lights stopped abruptly, then moved in sweeping arcs, before jerking awkwardly as they negotiated the slipway down to the beach two hundred feet below us. The car stopped near the shore.

I raised the binoculars still hanging around my neck.

"How many of them?" Reece said.

"I can't see. You don't think they'll see us up here?"

"Too far away."

A minute or so later we saw figures moving, shadow puppets against their makeshift lights, folding in and out of the dark wings at either side of the illuminated stage. A large fire burst into life. The metronomic thump of music, punctuated with excited squeals, carried to us on the pummelling wind. Reece and I sat down, silently observing the dancing shadows from the rafters.

"Did you see the way that fire went up?" Reece said.

"Yeah."

"Must have some kind of fuel." I heard him take a swig of whiskey. "How many are there?"

"Four."

"Four," Reece repeated. A series of cheers crashed into us on a gust. "What the fuck are they doing down there?"

"It sounds like they're making in the best of it," I smiled.

"Fucking idiots."

"They're young. We were once like them."

"What? *Stupid?*"

"Young enough to know everything. Let them have this."

"They best learn what this world is really like."

Tendrils of spite smothered Reece's words. Anger clung to his skin like a fungus. Malicious spores blossomed on the tissue in the warm darkness of his skull. His growing anger was terrifying.

Reece passed the bottle of whiskey. I raised it to my mouth, making sure the liquid inside sloshed audibly, but was careful to only wet my lips. I wanted—needed—a clear head.

"Come on," I said.

"Sooner or later. They'll learn."

"You ok to take the first watch?" Reece said.

We had barely talked since returning to our makeshift camp, the earlier friction seeming to linger amongst the thick stones. The only indication I was not alone was the occasional swill and glint as Reece lost himself in the bottle of whiskey.

"Yes," I said.

"Good. Wake me when you get tired." Reece was drunk. His voice syrupy with alcohol and fatigue. "You think those kids came looking for boats?" He laughed.

"Maybe."

"There are no boats," Reece laughed again. "Fucking nowhere to go."

"No."

"The radiation, it'll get us all soon."

I listened to the storm, the thunder, the waves, hoping their rhythm would soon soothe Reece into sleep.

"Out of her misery," Reece said.

"What?"

"Dying anyway. Put a pillow over her face. Bitch still put up a fight."

"Who?" My throat tightened.

I watched shades of oil and lead twist together as Reece shifted in his sleeping bag, curling himself into a ball. I listened as his breathing slowed and deepened as he was pulled into his slumber.

"Who?" I asked again.

"...Birdwatcher."

The night turned bitterly cold.

I lay in the dark, my body aching with exhaustion, muscles frozen with terror. I turned my wedding ring thirteen times, repeating the ritual over and over, willing myself to move. Instead, I thought only of Reece's admission, of what he was capable of. I saw the woman struggling, her arms grabbing dumbly at him as he bent over her. Imagined her dying whimpers, his growled threats warning her to stop fighting.

*"Time to go, sweetheart."*

I snapped up, her voice lingering in the confusion of waking. I caught her name in my mouth.

*Clare.*

I heaved in deep breaths and squinted at my watch. Hours had passed. *Shit.* I glanced in Reece's direction and was able to discern the rise and fall of his laboured breathing. There was still time. I pulled on my boots and rolled my sleeping bag. I checked the contents of my rucksack, taking inventory by touch alone. A minute after waking I was ready to leave.

I took a final look at Reece. There was no coming back from this. I felt weightless. Unshackled from a burden I was unaware I carried. I matched my breathing to his, afraid a misplaced breath would expose my betrayal, and crept towards the black archway in the ashen wall which towered into the night sky.

"Where you going?"

The hairs on my head prickled at Reece's voice. I stopped inches from the pitch darkness which promised my freedom.

"Taking a leak." The tendons in my throat quivered, distorting my voice.

Sensing movement, I squeezed my eyes closed. Braced for the impact. None came.

"Me too," Reece said. "Go take a piss. Once you're back you can get your head down for a couple of hours."

"Sure."

Ten minutes later, I was wrapped in my sleeping bag, weeping silently, the weight of imperceptible chains taut against my cold bones.

I awoke into what passed for daylight, light which somehow managed to seep through the constant knots of cloud overhead, a dense gloom which cast no shadows. I sat up and looked around the clearing, over the decayed walls and low foundations which mapped out the entire sanctuary. Reece was gone. His backpack and sleeping bag neatly stacked against the wall.

"Reece?" I whispered his name, my voice lost on the wind. "Reece."

Nothing. I was alone.

Urged by Clare's voice, the faintest echo from a dream, I gathered my things.

It was dread which crawled across my skin when I found Reece.

I had left the ruins of the priory and was navigating a makeshift path between the headstones when I saw him standing on an outcrop of rock, naked from the waist up, staring out over the ocean and into the Everstorm.

"Reece?"

Reece turned. His face and chest were soaked in blood. The waist of his jeans absorbing the streams slowly trickling down his front. Liquid, as dark as treacle, dripped from the crowbar hanging at his side and congealed on the rock.

"You're up," Reece said. A single white eye peered out of the gore, his other was purple, swollen closed.

"What have you done?"

I dragged my feet over the uneven ground until I could see the beach. I saw the dark shapes in my watery vision, raised the binoculars. There were four bodies, lying in vast pools of dark crimson.

"They have stuff we could use," Reece said.

"Oh God. Christ. What the fuck have you done?" I moved away from the edge of the cliff, away from Reece, my entire body convulsing.

"Before I," Reece stopped, spat out a wad of blood. "They mentioned boats. Leaving from Hull they said."

"You—" I couldn't still the tremors in my throat.

"Bad news is we'll have to walk it."

"-killed them."

"The big fucker threw the keys into the sea."

Reece took a step towards me.

"Stay away," I said.

"What the fuck is wrong with you?"

"They were kids."

"You really think so? You don't think they put up a fucking fight when I went down there?"

"You didn't *need* to go down there."

"When are you going to realise the reality we're living in? We're all fucked."

Reece laughed. A hideous noise at the end of the world.

"What happened to you?" I said.

"The world has gone to shit. It's dog-eat-dog out here."

"It doesn't have to be."

"Fuck you." Reece turned towards the priory. "I'll get my stuff then we'll start south."

"No," I said.

The wind died. No wave crashed. No thunder cracked. The world suddenly still. There was never silence in these dying days, but for a single moment there was something close to it.

"What?" Reece clawed at his neck.

"No."

"Where will you go?"

"North."

"There's fuck all there."

"Exactly."

Reece ran his tongue over his teeth, chewed his split lips, pulled at his beard. Perfect rage was all that remained inside him and it was desperate to be free.

"Be careful out there," he said.

"What? You're going to…"

*Kill me.* I was numb.

"Your hippie shit about how we can all get along?" Reece smirked. "It's a nice idea, but it never helped before. It won't now." Reece moved closer and tapped the crowbar against his chest. "This world belongs to people like me. You're *dead* out there."

I lunged forward and smashed a fist into the side of Reece's face. He went down, landing on his side. I stepped back and shook my fist to relieve the crunch of pain in my knuckles. Reece turned his face up to mine. It was a mad, bloodied mess. Fork lightning crashed into the ocean behind us and I watched as it fractured the landscape reflected in Reece's single, open eye.

"I didn't think you had that in you," Reece said.

He made a low, gargling sound. Laughter. I caught bile in the back of my throat.

"Fuck you," I said.

"We were friends once," Reece struggled to his feet, "so I'll give you a head start. I owe you that."

The fist in which he held the crowbar twitched. I took slow steps away until my heel kicked the base of a gravestone. I moved to put it between us, my eyes never leaving him.

"What happened to you?" I managed.

"How long have we known each other?"

"What?"

"Eighteen years?"

"Yes, I—"

38

"Okay. Let's make it an even twenty. *One Mississippi.*"

"Wait," I raised my arms—pleading for mercy, sanity—and continued to back away.

"*Two Mississippi.*"

"Reece, this isn't you."

Only, it was. It always had been. The man who was forever angry at the world had finally found a place in it.

I turned and fled.

"*Three Mississippi.*"

I powered through the ancient burial ground without direction, fuelled only by the terror burning through my veins.

"*Four Mississippi.*"

Electricity split the sky overhead and the world was suffocated by screaming thunder.

I didn't hear my old friend count five.

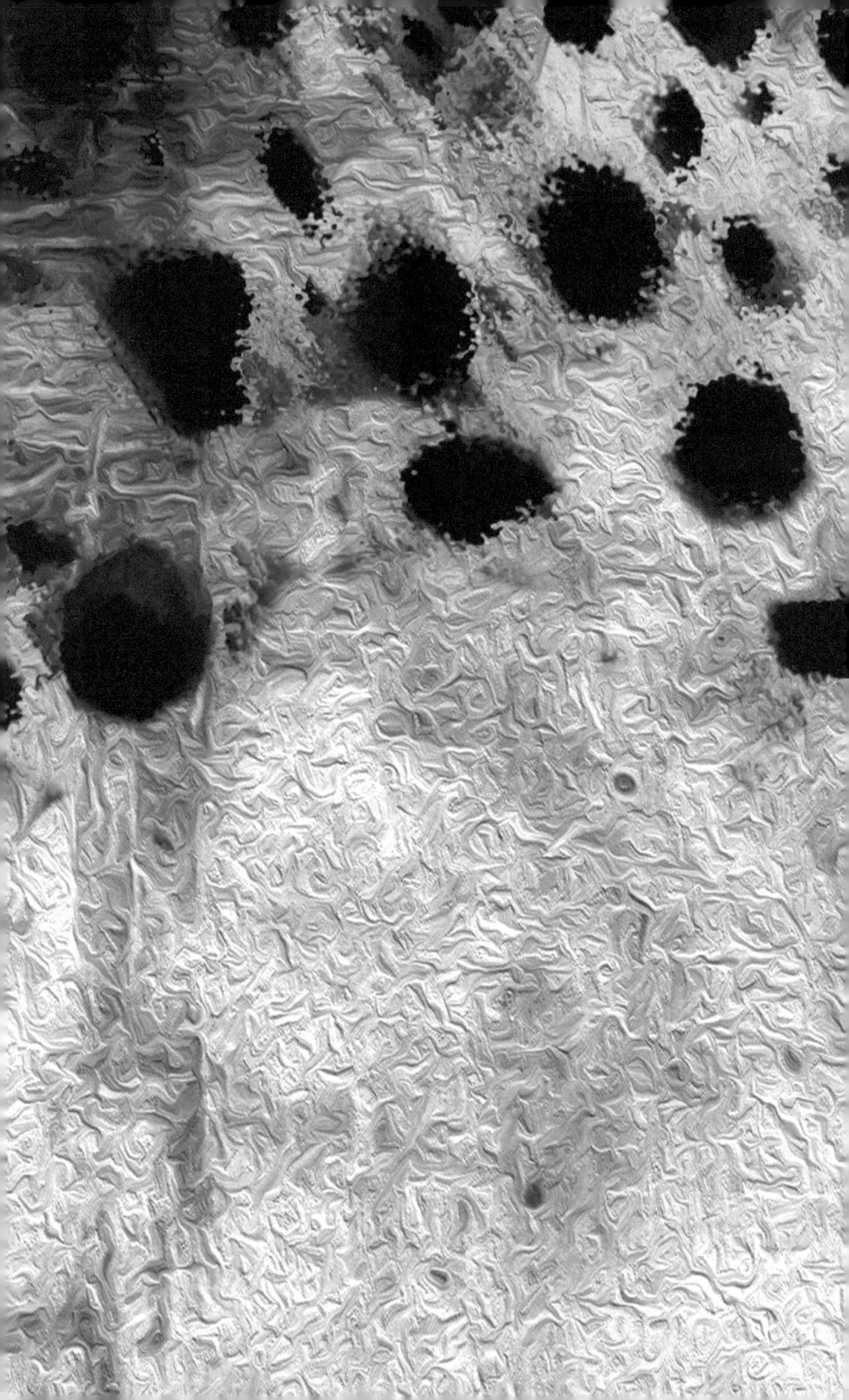

# KUDZU STORIES
## - Linda J. Marshall -

The window was open a crack. Jenny waited for the perfect weather night, chilly so he wouldn't be suspicious when she turned off the air conditioner, brisk to make the mosquitoes hide under the moldering leaves, but still a hint of summer so the vines would grow.

Her sleeping husband moaned as Jenny leaned over him and felt outside the bedroom's window ledge. Crickets silenced their singing, tree frogs ceased their chirping. She heard the kudzu growing. Far away an alligator boomed like an overgrown bullfrog. The husband muttered and shifted. Jenny froze until he settled. His mouth fluttered with soft snores, each breath puffing out cheap beer, cheaper cigarettes and the scent of sex with someone else. She reached a little further into the night. Around her hand it latched like a baby grasping fingers. She eased the kudzu in, unwound the tendrils from her soft skin, picking at it with shell pink nails. It bloomed with dangling purple racemes that smelled like grape popsicle. It grew as she watched, trying to twist around the tiny diamond chip that topped the engagement ring bought at a pawn shop. She laid the vine across her husband's neck.

Jenny knew the myth to be true, that kudzu was the vine that ate the South. She saw it cover stop signs, houses, whole forests along The Great

River Road which was a gravel two lane that nobody else drove but her. It covered crypts, forgotten on top of Crowley's Ridge. The dead lay high above the river's floodwaters only to be drowned in vines. She was surprised it didn't bridge the two-mile-wide river and connect Arkansas to Mississippi like conjoined twins.

As it latched on to his Adam's apple and twirled around his throat, he reached up and scratched, then settled his hand next to his head. His pinky dug loess, the glacial dirt of the Ridge, from his ear. That task done, deeper sleep took over. She lured another shoot through the window and wrapped it around his wandering hand.

The wildlife sang and peeped again only to be silenced when she stretched outside one more time to touch her finger to the shoot. Somewhere down by the river a thrashing and gurgling of water ghosted up with the fog. Her husband stirred at the sound. "That old alligator's caught something," she said. "You're safe up here."

A breeze coursed in bringing the scent of decay and mildew and grape popsicles. Frogs and crickets grew quiet then loud, quiet then loud. The gator harrumphed. She laid her husband's other hand over his chest, so the vine would reach and wove it through his fingers. Sliding gently out of bed, she turned off the nightlight inside the ruffled dusty rose skirt of her Southern Belle doll lamp. She turned and touched the lengthening kudzu.

"Goodnight," she said. "I love you."

"I love you, too, Amanda," her husband answered in his sleep.

"I was talking to the plant," Jenny said as she left the room.

The window was open a crack. Clarice's husband, Roy, sat up in bed.

"They're coming," he said.

He had forgotten to button up. His plaid nightshirt draped below his bony shoulders. Clarice pulled his flannel top up where it was supposed to be. "It's the wind rustling through the kudzu," she said as she buttoned him. Her bare foot touched something wet. Looking down, she saw a rivulet of lymph trickling from his pajama legs, down his ankle and into the grain of the wood floor. "I'd better wash that and tape on a patch of gauze."

"They're firing cannons."

"That's that old alligator, somewhere down by the river bellowing. You know how it goes boom all night long."

Thinking it was a diabetic ulcer, she drove him to the doctor in the morning. Instead of an ulcer, it was shrapnel. "Why was this never taken out?" the doctor said. "Is it a war wound?"

War? The only war Roy talked about was the Battle of Helena. Over and again he told her about the phenomenon of the fog. The Union soldiers looked down from Crowley's Ridge and saw thousands of feet marching toward them, not a torso to be seen. The eerie rebel yell spiraled through the dense fog like banshees warning of death. The feet began to run toward the ridge, seeming to carry nothing above but the ghostly cry. Clarice's house was on the edge of Crowley's Ridge. She often saw Roy stand there on early mornings when the fog of the Mississippi River drifted across the flat Delta, looking for the feet, the thousands of feet.

"War?" she said to the doctor. "Were you in a war?" she said to Roy.

"It was so cold," Roy answered.

"Call the VA. See if they can help you figure out if he's a veteran. This shrapnel needs to come out."

Armed with his name and Social Security number, Clarice discovered her husband was in a war, one he never mentioned, not even when his leg leaked sixty years after the fact.

The VA doctor said, "Korea. He was at the Frozen Chosin. No wonder there's still a chunk of metal in his leg."

Clarice gazed around the cold white room. Roy sat on the examination table, only in boxers and an old-fashioned string undershirt. He shivered. The doctor called out the door for a blanket from the warming box.

"I didn't know any of it," Clarice said. "Why didn't he tell me? Why didn't the army take it out?"

"Some men don't talk about the Frozen Chosin until the end of their lives. Some never bring it up. Almost 8,000 American soldiers froze to death there, more than were killed in the battle. A lot gave up and walked off into the snow to die. They don't...they can't bring themselves to talk about it."

"But the shrapnel. Why? I know there were medics."

"It was thirty-five below zero at the Chosin Reservoir. Doctors couldn't cut away their clothes. The skin would have frozen solid, then rotted with gangrene when it thawed. They plowed on with bullets and shrapnel gutting them, or laid down in a snowdrift and let life go."

"Why not later?" It was a plea blanketed in exasperation. "Why wasn't he operated on later?"

The VA doctor picked up Roy's records, tapping them on the desk. Clarice thought it looked like punctuation to end a conversation. "It was weeks before they were rescued. The ones that lived, their wounds grew over while they waited. If it didn't bother them, why take it out? Nobody expected any of them to live to be ninety-five."

Roy slid off the table and dropped his blanket. "They're coming," he said.

"Who's coming?" the doctor asked.

"Hawthorn's Arkansas Infantry Regiment. Always and again," Clarice answered for Roy.

They scheduled Roy's surgery in two weeks. That gave Clarice time to get worked up over the two-hour drive to the VA hospital, two hours where Roy would bicker and get confused, and want to go to Vicksburg instead of Memphis and complain about the car air conditioner. Dreading the logistics of getting him to Memphis and into the hospital, she wondered how she'd keep him from escaping somewhere along the way (Tunica, halfway to Memphis, always attracted him because of the neon animated signs advertising casinos. She once came out of a rest stop to see him trotting across a cotton field toward a spinning guitar in the sky.) She was afraid of big hospital parking lots, scared of the beggars in the city. She couldn't let him ooze to death because she feared losing her car in acres of asphalt. Could she talk to him about parking situations or if it was right or wrong to give a beggar two dollars? How could he have been in Korea and never mention it?

While she planned, Roy sat in on the green wicker settee in the screened-in porch that overlooked the steep ridge that flattened into cotton fields. The bolls glowed white in the moonlight. In another week, crop dusters would spray herbicide, leaving the leaves brown, the cotton ragged, looking like death at the foot of the kudzu. Crowley's Ridge, when the Union soldiers defended it, was pitted, eroded, sloughing off mud, cut with ravines. Now it was a sea of green, determined, grasping vines that didn't quit until reaching the chemical-drenched cotton fields.

"I don't understand," Roy said, "why it is so cold. Why the water is frozen so hard the rebels crawl across it at night and slit our throats."

"It's not cold, dear. Just a little cool. Do you need a sweater?"

"It's July 4th, 1863. Why is it so cold?"

"No dear, it's almost autumn. It's like a steam bath here in July. You're thinking of Korea, winter in Korea." She sighed and watched moths bat themselves against the screens, hopelessly doing the same thing over and over. "It was North Koreans who crawled over the frozen water."

Roy stared down the steep incline of Crowley's Ridge, lit up with street lights below. She heard him breathing, the breath getting faster. "My friend walking behind me, he said, 'What's that coming up over your boot?' It was my own blood, freezing and working its way out. I couldn't feel it. So cold. It looked like a cherry snow cone. I'm freezing to death and all I can think about is that I look like a cherry snow cone. By the next day, my friend, his name was Jerry, was dead. Laid down in a frozen rut of mud and died."

"Why didn't you tell me?" The moths pounded against the door, flinging themselves for a light they would never reach. "Why did you keep this to yourself?"

He turned his head to look at her. "I told you all the time. We lay in rifle pits waiting for them to come up Cemetery Hill. You froze to death...no, it was July. That was Jerry. Marmaduke brought troops from the west and south. You could only see feet. Feet and feet and feet. By the end of the day, thousands had frozen."

Clarice sat down on the settee next to him. "When you get the shrapnel out, you'll feel better. Your mind will..." She looked for the right words. "...come back."

"Where did these vines come from? It's supposed to be mud."

"It's kudzu, planted to stop erosion back in the thirties. You know that." She went into their bungalow. When she came out with some sweet tea, Roy stood at the door.

"If Vicksburg falls, we will have control of the entire Mississippi River, cutting the Confederacy in half. We've kept Helena for two years now. The

Communists..." Roy shook his head like he was slinging something out of it. "The Confederates...the Chosin...the Frozen Chosin. We were the Chosin ones." Clarice saw him look toward her, but she knew he saw something beyond. "There was an oak-clad gunboat on the Mississippi, The Tyler. But the river was frozen. It was so cold. But it was July."

"Get off your feet, dear. No, the Mississippi doesn't freeze, not down here. You'll feel better after the operation." She sat and patted the settee cushion. "I brought tea with sprigs of mint. Maybe it's too cool for ice tea, but sweet tea makes everything better. Especially with mint." Clarice explored her husband's face. "Isn't that what I always say about tea with mint? Things will be better." A Polyphemus moth found a tear in the porch screen. It crawled in and circled relentlessly around the overhead light.

He stepped closer to the door. "What's that I hear?"

"Only the wind in the kudzu." Standing up, she brought him his drink. He heard the ice clinking against the glass and stepped away from her, wild-eyed.

"The ice is breaking up on the lake. But, how can that be? It's summer." Cracking the storm door open he said, "Canons. The gunboat's firing."

"It's that old alligator. It goes boom all night long. It thinks it's singing."

"I hear thrashing in the water. The soldiers, the soldiers have fallen through the ice."

"That old alligator caught something. You know it thrashes when it pulls things underwater." Tears trickled through the creases on her cheeks. "It's just an old old alligator." She wanted to calm him, but her words came out shrill. "It can't hurt you. It's down there by the river. We're up high where nothing can get us."

"They are coming...across the Delta, across the frozen lake to cut our throats."

"Nobody's coming. We're up high on Crowley's Ridge. It's just kudzu and an old gator you hear. Wind in the kudzu and an old..."

"The Chinese...the Confederates, the...Ninth North Korean Army. I see their feet. I hear the boys calling, 'The Union Forever!'"

"It's the damn kudzu you hear." She shoved herself up from the settee.

Roy flung open the door. Clarice grabbed his arm. He shook her off and headed down the terminus of Crowley's Ridge. "The Union forever!" he shouted. He'd run only four or five feet before the kudzu caught his ankle, cartwheeling him over and down the hill. The vines snatched at his arms and legs tumbling him until he landed on the twisting highway hugging the ridge. A car skidded to a stop and a man jumped out.

Clarice ran down their driveway as fast as ninety-year-old legs could go. All the way down she thought the kudzu must be blooming. The air smelled like grape popsicles. What an odd thing to think, she thought, when your husband is dying. She came upon Roy, bloody but breathing. He spasmed. With a gush of lymph, a piece of sharp metal slid out of his torn trousers. Then all was quiet except for the thrashing of the gator.

"What the hell was he doing?" The man from the car said as he tapped 911 into his cell phone.

"Preserving the Union," Clarice said. "over and again, and again and again and forever."

The window was open a crack. Trish hammered some nails into the frame so the window couldn't be raised any higher. She and Travis lived on the wrong side of the levee, up on stilts so their rat shack wouldn't go under water when the Mississippi flooded. It stunk all the time because the big catfish, the ones the size of men, wash up with the floods and stranded themselves when the water slunk back to the Big Muddy. Alligators relish those giant air-drowned fish, but it sure put a right putrid scent in the air. Gators kind of let things lay around and rot. It makes it easier for them to chew. They could eat little things like pigeons or those ratty nutria right away, but a big thing had to soak 'til it fell apart. Swept away in the gray greasy water would be the best thing that could happen to the house, but beggars can't be choosers so here she stayed, stink and all. She nailed every window most of the way shut so Travis couldn't get back in.

Dealers kept pit bulls for the most part, but Travis dug out a kind of moat and put a fourteen-foot alligator in. He called it Pitbull just to be funny. If the river was about to flood, he'd pull Pitbull by the tail to a piling and tie it there with just enough slack to let it swim up and not drown. It was not easy to tie up a gator. That's why you stayed back hanging on by the tail. Tails were the best part to eat, too, but not while the gator is alive and not if it's your watchdog. Believe you me, nobody ever came around looking for revenge after a bad deal when you had Pitbull guarding the house. Too afraid of it to even shoot the thing. Travis fed it chickens. Trish hated that, raising little yellow chicks just to watch them grow up and be eaten. And damn, when it flooded, she had to bring all those chickens in the house. Talk about stink. She thought about nailing the door shut, thought better of that, and opted for pulling the rickety wooden stairs up onto the porch.

The bellowing kept her up half the night. She kind of liked the old alligator, though. There was a fish market down on Cherry Street. She'd find big catfish heads and the snouts of sturgeon and even the feet of alligators in the dumpster. Pitbull didn't mind being a cannibal. She'd tie a string on the parts, hang them over the porch and make Pitbull jump for them. Most people don't know that alligators can jump but they can, and they jump high. She swung the fish heads way out, so Pitbull wouldn't tangle in the kudzu growing up the pilings. An alligator caught in kudzu would be a difficult thing to cut loose.

Pitbull was going ba-ba-boom all night but got quiet. She could hear a barge drifting by and saw a fog light sweep back and forth across the base of the Helena Bridge so the pilot wouldn't crash. Down in Greenville the bridge had been hit forty times. Trish thought that might be a sight and looked forward to the day a barge hit the Helena Bridge. After the passing of the barge, she heard the gentle splash of someone paddling a canoe. Damn, she forgot to tie it up to the house, letting it drift back across the moat.

Travis' voice came up soft and sing-songy. "Trish, you know you can't keep me out by pulling up the steps. I can climb this here kudzu that's growing all up and down the house. It's a-growing right up to the window."

She waited while he tied up the boat. "Trish," he sing-songed. "Don't you want to see your lover-boy after I've been locked up for so long?" The kudzu rattled when he began his ascent. By his cursing she could tell he was all tangled up. He wrestled himself loose and said, "I see your shadow by the window." All sing-songy like.

Trish stepped away from the glass. "It's nailed shut. You can't get in."

"Oh, I can get in. I can get in anywhere I want."

She scurried in her fuzzy slippers to their mildewy, moaning refrigerator. It smelled fishy in there, too, but damn, everything smelled like fish around there. The refrigerator groaned louder when she squeaked the door open. Sometimes, the way it complained, she thought even the fridge couldn't stand things anymore. Trish removed something slimy and gray and as big as a man's head.

"Trishy, I can hear you open the fridge. Are you bringing me a beer, like a good girl?"

"Better than that," she yelled to him. "Something cold and delicious."

She opened the junk drawer and pulled out a hammer and twine, taking a few seconds to fiddle around, wrapping and tying.

"You're right, Travis. You can get in anywhere so there's no point in making you break the glass. Glass costs money which we ain't got. I'm gonna pull the nails outta the frame." She put the hammer claw around each nail. They squealed when pried loose, squealed like nutria when Pitbull pulled them out of the kudzu.

Travis' head popped above the windowsill. "Hi babe. Miss me? I brought you flowers." He held up crushed kudzu racemes he'd picked on the way up. "They smell like grape popsicles."

"You're just in time for dinner." Something tied to a string flashed by his head. "Catfish tonight."

"What the hell was that?" he said. The catfish head bounced against his jeans, rolled around his ankle, and came to rest against his foot. A frantic bounding through the air, a snap on the ankles, followed by a drag down the kudzu toward the greasy gray water of the moat. Travis said, "Damn, Trish. How'd he jump so high? You must a been training him for ages." He held on tight and, tenacious as it usually was, the kudzu instead gave way, seemingly glad to be rid of him. "Babe, you cut the damn kudzu, too. Didn't you?" he said just before he went under.

"Nah," she said. "It just doesn't like you."

He struggled to get his head above water and said, "Pitbull? I thought we was buddies. Be a good alligator." Before going under again, he squealed like a nutria. There was swishing of a tail, boiling of the water, a sudden whirlpool, and the night was quiet except for some commotion up on Crowley's Ridge.

"I guess me and the gator was better buddies," Trish said to the swirling water below.

Trish pried out the rest of the nails, so she could open the windows enough to let in the cool night air. Nobody would look for a missing drug dealer, not if his departure was never called in. Cons have a way of just disappearing. She refused to feel suffocated anymore and opened the window wider. Another broad fog light swept back and forth, lighting up the path down the river. The sound of Pitbull's bellows would comfort her in her sleep.

The window was open a crack. The police chief of Helena, Arkansas dozed in bed. Helena was a high crime town, but he hoped nothing would disturb his sleep tonight. The phone rang. He prayed it wasn't going to be that kind of night and cursed because he knew it was. When he rolled over to answer, he saw that a vine had crept through the window he'd opened only minutes before. We've got to do something about that damned kudzu, he thought, before someone gets hurt. Picking up the cellphone, he said, "If you're gonna get me out of bed, this better be good." He listened. "What do you mean there's been kudzu incidents tonight? You been smoking the stuff?" He listened some more. "Two expired men tangled up in kudzu on Crowley's Ridge?" Too many damn drunks in this town, he thought. Drunks and alligators "Usually bad news comes in threes so we lucked out with only two. I'll be right in."

Maybe he ought to check out why that gator was so damn loud tonight. But no, he thought, the night was already weird. Leave the old thing alone to bellow. It was probably as worn out as he was. Refraining from smashing his phone in frustration, he slammed the window shut instead. The action severed a little piece of kudzu. It fell to the floor under the bed, landing in a thick pile of dust that stayed damp all the time because the police chief spilled his coffee in bed every morning. A node on the cutting sent out feelers. The feelers grew roots that sank into the dust bunny and sipped the coffee. A tendril sprouted. It felt around for the slats under the mattress and for the bedsprings and headboard, too.

# DEAD LETTERS
## - Christopher Barzak -

Dear Sarah,

I have heard of your great misfortune to have gone and died so suddenly. Now I find myself writing after so many years have passed between us in the hopes that perhaps this news is not true. For a long time I believed I was dead too. Then one day someone called my name ("Alice. Do you remember her? Alice Likely. How she loved that girl.") and I opened my eyes in a dark place, like a fairy tale princess trapped in a coffin. Light appeared suddenly, a flash so sharp and blinding, it pricked my eyes and made them water. Anyone passing by might have thought I was crying. I must have looked so sad.

And someone did stop beside me. I was still trapped in that dark place, my body bagged in a sack of unbeing, but the flash of light had ripped a hole in the darkness. Through that opening, two hands reached in and gripped both sides of the fissure. The hands pulled the gap wider and wider until daylight surrounded me, and trees sprang up, row after row of them. Birds called out. Their notes pierced my eardrums like needles. I heard water, and then there it was too—a stone fountain next to the bench I lay upon, and the birds perched upon the fountain's ledge staring at me, their eyes black and serious.

Whoever freed me disappeared before I could pull myself together. A newspaper lay open across my chest, and another on my legs. I sat up and the paper on my legs slid to the ground, rattling. I held on to the section covering my chest and looked at it for a moment, only to see your name glaring up at me, as if your name had a life of its own, had your eyes and the looks you could give with them, and so your name glared at me in such a way that I could not help but notice it. It said you were dead. Twenty-eight years old. A promising local artist. Survived by her mother and father. Their names were listed as well, but it hurt to look at them. Particularly your mother's. She never liked me and I still don't know why. What did I ever do to her?

I am writing in the hopes that there may still be a chance for us to reconcile, to come together, to answer some of the questions that have burned inside me since you said goodbye. Why did you betray me? Whatever happened to our promise? And where have I been for so long, asleep and waiting for someone to wake me? Why didn't you do that? I don't even recognize my own body. My legs are long, and my feet are large. When I peered into the fountain water, a face looked back that belonged to a stranger. Then the fountain turned on again, displacing the water, and the face broke apart into ripples.

Now I am writing this to you. Will you please talk to me? Can we forgive one another?

Love,

Alice

I am writing in a notebook stolen from Rexall's drugstore, the sort of book Sarah and I used in school years ago, for doodling and note-taking. The cover of it looks like the black and white static on a dead television channel. "Snow," Sarah's father used to call that. "Nothing but snow here," he'd say, flipping the channel until something lively and entertaining appeared. He favored shows about policemen and vigilantes who saved the lives of people who could not save themselves from danger. He instructed the vigilantes and policemen on how to go about all of this saving-of-lives business, spouting advice from his reclining chair, waving the remote control like a scepter.

Sometimes the vigilantes listened to him, sometimes they didn't. But they always saved the helpless victims in the end.

The pharmacist and his wife didn't recognize me. But I didn't recognize them at first either. They are old and gray now. Mrs. Hopkinsey's face sags. Her teeth are not her teeth any longer. I know this because I remember they were yellow and crooked and now they are white and bright and not so narrow; they line up in her mouth like good soldiers. She smiled at me. "Can I help you, dear?"

Such a nice woman, just as I remember. I told her I was browsing, and she nodded and turned back to shuffling cigarette packs into the storage bin over the checkout counter.

I walked the aisles slowly, touching candy bars, tubes of lipstick, barrettes in the shape of butterflies. I spun the comic book rack and paged through magazines, but the women inside were strange and alien, their faces harsh, skin like plastic or velvet. Too smooth. Their outlines blurred into the backgrounds. I found a familiar feeling, though, and felt a stab of pity for the cover girl's blurry faces.

The greeting cards stood on the same shelves that they always had; I picked through them. One said, "I feel so lonely with you not here." On the cover was a picture of a little girl looking up at the moon, holding a doll at her side. Inside it read, "But we'll always be friends, no matter what the distance." I found myself crying, and stuffed the card under the waistband of my pants, covering it up with my sweater. I looked to see if anyone had seen me take it, but Mrs. Hopkinsey still restocked cigarettes and Mr. Hopkinsey stood behind the medicine counter, measuring out pills for a customer.

If Sarah had been there, she would have been the one to take the card. I would have been the lookout. Those had been our positions when we were children. I felt a little guilty changing places with her, like borrowing a friend's sweater and not returning it, even though you know how they love it so.

I found the notebook in the next aisle over. I hadn't known I was going to take it either. I needed things without knowing what I needed, so I let my hands think for me. They reached out and took things: the greeting card, several envelopes, the notebook, pens, a bar of chocolate, a ten-dollar bill crumpled up on the black and white checkered floor. I used the money to buy a soda and a bag of potato chips, so as not to be suspicious. Mrs. Hopkinsey rang me up with her new smile still flashing, and when she handed me my change, I thought, *I am home.*

Dear Sarah,

I refuse to believe you are dead. I myself am not dead, so it goes to figure that you are alive and well. The obituary I read must have been mistaken. Or else another Sarah Hartford exists and it is this other Sarah Hartford who has died. Not you.

I have seen the Hopkinsey's, those dear old people, and they have changed enormously. Do you remember how we'd steal candy and perfume samplers from them when we were girls? We were ridiculous, weren't we? And the Hopkinsey's are such good people, I feel ashamed to have stolen from them. Why didn't we ever shoplift at the Hoffman's grocery store instead? The Hoffman's were snobs. Missy Hoffman always thinking she was better than everyone because her DADDY owned the only grocery store in Kinsman, so she had "the whole town's money." How I wanted to punch that girl. Luckily, I had you to restrain me, to whisper, "Calm down, Alice, just ignore her. She'll get hers someday." You were the one with your head about you, calm and collected, shoelaces tied, hair in place. No one could ruffle you. Not even Missy.

But what happened to change you? In the newspaper I read that you were murdered by your boyfriend. Tom or Don or Ron. Someone with a name like a mantra. Is this a true description? Did his name repeat in your head, again and again, like Chinese water torture? *Don, Don, Don. Tom, Tom, Tom. Ron, Ron, Ron.* What an awful rhythm to be ruled by.

You were obsessed with Ron, I'm guessing, because you were always obsessive, with your paintings and sketches, with your neatness, the constant smoothing-over of your clothes with the flats of your hands, erasing imaginary wrinkles. The way the part in your hair had to be perfect. The way you avoided cracks in sidewalks because of that nursery rhyme about mothers. I figure you became obsessed with this man in a similar manner.

Don abused you, the papers reported. In the past you had called the police on him. The two of you were noted for dramatic gestures. Did I read this correctly? You burned Tom on the neck with a curling iron? Or was it Tom that burned you? You hit him over the head with a Mason jar that you filled with brushes? Or did Don do that to you? Someone had to have fifteen stitches. Someone called 911 to report an intruder. By the time the police arrived, though, said intruder had vanished into thin air. In the end you and Tom reconciled. You smoothed out the wrinkles. Then he killed you six months later and smashed up all of your paintings. All the frames broken, the canvases torn with a hunting knife. Such a violent imagination. It is evidence like this that proves to me that the dead Sarah Hartford in the newspaper is not the same Sarah Hartford I once knew. She must be your double.

I am glad to know you continued painting. You had vision, I remember, even as a child. But even so, with all that vision, how could you have not seen this coming? To me it sounds as though you stood in the middle of a railroad crossing, not moving when the yellow eye of the train appeared in the night, nor when it whistled a warning. I don't mean to say you allowed Tom or Ron or Don to kill you. I mean to say, how could you allow yourself to be with such a person after the first time it happened?

If I'd been around, I would have been the one with my head about me, with my shoelaces tied and my hair in place. I would have led you by your ear out of Ron's reach, even if you struggled against me. This is a testament of my loyalty to our friendship. This is the reason why we need one another. For times like this, when we're not reasoning correctly.

Love,

Alice

P.S. You are NOT dead.

"Promise," Sarah told me. "Promise, Alice." And so I did.

"We'll always be best friends, and here is proof of it." I touched my fingertip to Sarah's. They were both bloody from pricking the skin with a needle a minute earlier. We rubbed our blood together until it mingled and Sarah sighed, satisfied that the act was completed.

"Now no one will ever separate us," she said. "It's final."

A thrill sped up the length of my spine when Sarah said that. She was the only friend I can remember having. When we pledged our undying love for one another, I believed it in every part of my being. "I'm so happy you're my friend, Alice Likely," she said, smiling. I beamed.

But her mother came in a moment later. "What are you doing now?" she complained. Her voice sounded like knitting needles, clicking over and over. I didn't say anything. Sarah had warned me not to speak back to her mother. I was to keep my mouth closed, or else we'd never be allowed to see one another.

"I was just playing, Mom," Sarah answered.

"In the middle of your room? What's that, then? Give me your hand. You're bleeding, Sarah! How did you manage that?"

Sarah's mother led her into the bathroom to clean up her finger, all the while chastising. "What's wrong with you, Sarah? What am I going to do with you? You must go out. You must make friends. You're going to be thirteen next month. A big girl!"

"I do have friends," Sarah protested.

"Other friends," Mrs. Hartford muttered. "You mustn't hide yourself away only for the benefit of your dear Alice."

"I'm not hiding, Mother." Sarah's voice, harsher now, rising.

"Well, you certainly aren't making yourself much of a presence. Now help me hang the laundry. Make yourself useful."

*Useful.* One of Mrs. Hartford's favorite words. "What does it do?" she was always asking. "What use is it?" When the neighbor boy, Jimmy, started college as a Philosophy major, Sarah's mother asked, "And what will you do with that?"

Jimmy had stared at her for a moment, then shrugged and changed the subject to the weather. What a storm that was the other night, he told her. "Yes, a whopper," Sarah's mother agreed, without pressing him any further about the Philosophy major. "I expect it will help the corn, though," she said.

The weather. An awful part of my current circumstances. Though it is summer, it rained last night, and I was forced to seek shelter. My park bench provided no protection from the raindrops, warm as they were and welcome, as I've started to stink without a proper place to bathe. I finally stumbled into one of the baseball field dugouts, the home team side, and fell asleep on the cold concrete bench in there, with the sound of the rain pattering above me, and the smell of dirt from the baseball diamond turning into a thick, rich mud.

I dreamed of Sarah. She stepped down into the baseball dugout, kneeled beside me, and placed her cheek upon my stomach. I stroked her hair. How soft it was beneath my fingers. I almost believed I was awake and Sarah had finally come to me. When the sun broke through the night, though, and morning woke me, I felt a wave of sadness. I shivered, rubbing tears out of my eyes, for I had lost her again. Like the fog that hangs over the fields of the park, she had dissipated.

Dear Sarah,

I am very angry. Why will you not speak to me? Do you believe yourself above me for some reason? I'm not certain if you even read my letters. What should I do? Stop writing you? I will stop writing if only you would say so. Why don't you say so?

When I stroll through Kinsman, I often stop stock still in my tracks for strange reasons. Here I see you everywhere. In the school yard, the grocery store, or at the Rexall's. Leaning over a water fountain, pulling your hair from your face. Running through town square, to the park, where you left me that horrible day, so long ago. Yes, I remember. Did you think I would forget the pain you caused me, or how it was inflicted? I was attempting to be the bigger person, but now I see you have changed indeed, and I no longer know you. The Sarah-Hartford-who-was-my-best-friend would never have answered my letters with silence.

I suppose your mother finally got to you. When I say your mother, I mean this town. When I say this town, I mean this town with its one miserable Main Street and its overabundance of churches. No more than three thousand people live here and yet there are fifteen churches that come to mind readily. What I mean to say is this town has you believing in its one screen drive-in movie theater, its Dairy Oasis, its Wildwood Café with the admittedly fantastic coffee, its park that consists of a water fountain, trees, a baseball diamond, and cemeteries. Granted, the cemeteries are well-groomed, and in autumn the trees light up with brilliant colors. But this town is not where you imagined yourself forever.

What happened to New York City? What happened to San Francisco? What about Europe? You said you'd die if you never made it to Paris. Now that I'm back, I discover that the only time you ever left this place was for a year and a half of college in Columbus. You never even left Ohio. Then Tom asked you to move in and you went to him. You went to him blindly, your arms outstretched, eyelids lowering. A sleepwalker.

That day in the park, it must have been fifteen years ago, you said you had something to tell me. You asked me to sit beside you on the bench near the water fountain. There were birds perched on the ledge of the fountain, dipping into the water for a drink, turning to stare at us, heads cocked at quizzical angles. Robins, I think, though I saw at least one blue jay among them, arguing. You said you loved me, but there was something you had to tell me. You said—

You said—

Damn you. Now I am crying. I can't even finish this letter. My hands are shaking so badly I want to hurt you. To hell with you, Sarah Hartford. Who needs you anyway? You are cruel, mean-spirited. Also thankless.

Signed,

Alice Likely (Or have you erased this name from memory?)

I've taken a job and found a bed to sleep in. I sell corn by the roadside. For every bag I sell, I can keep a dollar. I pick the corn every morning, while Mr. and Mrs. Carroll feed their livestock, fill up the water trough, milk the cows who have calves that won't suck, and attend to the children. They are a busy family, the Carrolls, too busy to check references, although I provided them. I am passing through on my way to California, where friends await me. Or so I have told them. How strange and liberating, this easiness in making up an identity. The Carrolls see me as a free spirit, a gypsy, someone from the

1960s, "new-agey," according to Mrs. Carroll, who has a friend who reads tarot cards and burns incense, and knows about these things.

"How long do you need work?" asked Mrs. Carroll when I came into her yard. She was beating a rug on her porch steps. Dust spun in the air around her like tiny galaxies. She smacked the throw rug, then looked back at me for an answer.

"A few weeks," I said. "I just need to make some money and have a place to sleep for a while."

"Do you have references?" She lifted her chin a little, assessing. I said that I did, and handed her a list of names, phone numbers, addresses in New York City. I made up the zip codes and phone numbers. What does a New York City zip code look like? I am no better than Sarah.

Now I have meals with the Carrolls at noon and six o'clock in the evening. They have three children: Betsy, Peter Jr., and Bennie. Betsy is seventeen and last year's Corn Queen. Peter Jr. is fifteen and a 4-H member. Bennie, ten, continually asks me what it's like to be a girl. He's curious and Betsy will not tell him.

It is a strange dynamic, this being with other people. When Sarah and I were friends, we had no desire for contact with anyone but each other. Now I speak to twenty or thirty strangers each day, by the roadside, while I bag up a dozen ears of corn. They say hello, thank you, do I know you, how have things been going, that top is very flattering, how are the Carrolls treating you? The men call me blue eyes, sweetie pie, honeyface, miss, little miss, blondie. The women call me dear, dearie, sugar, they do not refer to my body.

I saw Sarah's mother two days ago, in Hoffman's grocery store, picking through the green peppers. I was shopping for the Carrolls, but as soon as I saw Mrs. Hartford I dashed into the soup aisle. I watched her shop for an hour, following behind so she wouldn't see me, ignoring my own shopping, so that I had to go back and finish after she'd gone. I couldn't bear to face her. How that woman hated me, though at first, she'd thought me sweet and cute, would ask if I wanted anything, a cup of tea, some Kool-Aid. Then she went cold. I still don't know what I did to deserve such treatment. Sarah used to say it's because I didn't come from a good family. I said, "What? How could she think that? My mother—"

I stopped talking. I didn't know what to say, only that I wanted to defend myself. Sarah patted my shoulder to comfort me.

"Your mother is a sweet lady," said Sarah. She looked up at the ceiling, and her eyes rolled up as if she were thinking deeply. Finally she said, "She works at the factory, like my father. She loves you but is not home very often. My mother believes a woman should be at home with her children. Also, your father left when you were just a baby. He was a drinker. But I think you're better off without him."

"I *am* better off without him," I shouted. "And my mother works her fingers to the bones! Who does your mother think she is? Not everyone has the luxury to stay at home with her children."

"I know, Alice," Sarah said. She leaned in and hugged me. "I know. She doesn't matter. It's just you and me, ok?"

I've mailed Sarah the card I stole at Rexall's. I realized I'd never mentioned where she could find me. Did I feel stupid? Yes, indeed, I did. So I sent the card and wrote for her to meet me in the park in two days. I will give her another chance, and if she still chooses to not see me, then maybe I *will* set out for California. Somewhere in the West, the Southwest even, where there is more space. Space enough to make a life out of nothing. I will be a pioneer of space, living off my wits and my good fortune. I will sit by the roadside and sell beaded necklaces while my skin turns tan and leathery. I will read people's fortunes in the palms of their hands for twenty dollars. People believe in things that aren't particularly believable. They wait all their lives for strangeness, for miracles.

I eagerly await our reunion.

Sarah,

I hope this card finds you well. Saw it and thought of you immediately. I have been hopelessly sending you letters, asking you to reply, and yet I never provided an address. I am red with embarrassment. Please meet me in the park, by the fountain, you remember, at noon tomorrow. I miss you dearly.

Always,

Alice

No word from Sarah. Neither did she show up at the park yesterday. Although I did see two police officers, strolling in the general area. I nodded and smiled when they looked at me, then sat on the park bench and took out a book that Betsy lent me.

The policemen approached. They took off their caps and asked what I was doing. Reading, I told them. They nodded. "Are you waiting for anyone?" they asked. I said that I was indeed waiting for someone. "Who would that be?" asked the taller officer. I was immediately suspicious, so I told them I was waiting for Betsy, that I worked for her family. They said, "In that case, we'll need you to wait for her outside the park, Miss."

"What do you mean?"

"Nothing to concern yourself with. But you'd be doing us a favor if you read your book elsewhere." They put their hats back on and smiled. They waited for a while, badges glinting. Finally I stood to leave.

Why did she not meet me? My face is burning. I am so angry that I screamed at Bennie to leave me alone when I arrived back at the Carroll farm and he began pelting me with questions. I'll apologize later. For now I can only sit on my bed and cry. I wish my mother were still alive. Where is our house though? I can't even remember what road we lived on. Was our front door blue or green?

Dear Sarah,

You said, "Alice, I have something to tell you." Do you remember? Does it hurt to be reminded? "You are not real, Alice," you said. "You are not real. Do you hear me? I made you up, Alice. You are not a real person."

I hate you, Sarah Hartford. How could you be so filled with cruelty? But don't worry. I've given up on you. You won't hear from me again. I wish you only the best for the future. Give Ron my regards.

Sincerely,

Alice Likely

I write this hastily, as I'm preparing to leave this town for good. It is home to me no longer. But now I wonder if it ever was. It was Sarah who I came home to in the morning, in the evening, and in the night. Now I know that she is in fact not receiving my letters. They have come between us in a way in which I never would have imagined them capable.

Yesterday, after the incident in the park with the police officers, I was lying in bed, crying, because I couldn't think of anything else more appropriate, when I became angry enough to write Sarah a hateful letter, a last letter. I was ready to give up, but only if I had a chance to give her a piece of my mind. This time I decided to do things differently. I planned on delivering my letter in person, and walked across town to the Hartford house on my own. I was through with dodging her mother, through with waiting. I had waited for so long in the darkness before someone called out my name, before the light came and freed me. Uncountable days, miserable, curled up in a fetal position. A fairy tale princess, like the ones in the stories Sarah used to read me. Waiting for someone to free them, their hands pressed against the lid of a glass coffin, struggling. Not again, I decided, and opened the front gate of the Hartford house and climbed the front porch steps and knocked on the door. Three sharp raps, and it opened.

It was her that answered. Mrs. Hartford. She stood there in a floral print housecoat with an apron tied around her waist. How small she was. I looked down on her. Looked down on her gray hair, stringy and unbound, spreading over her shoulders. Gray sacs of flesh sagged under her eyes. She wore no makeup. She wore no pearls. She looked up at me, not smiling, and said, "Can I help you?"

"I'm h-here—" I said, stuttering. As small as she was, she still frightened me. Her panty hose had rolled halfway down her legs, just below her kneecaps. I wanted to bend down, pull them up for her. Brush her hair into something respectable.

She chuckled. "You certainly are," said Mrs. Hartford. "What do you need, dear?"

"I'm here for her," I said. "I've come for Sarah. Where is she? Sarah!" I shouted beyond Mrs. Hartford's head, hoping she'd hear. "Sarah, where are you?"

"*You*," Mrs. Hartford whispered. Her mouth twitched wordlessly. "*You*," she said again, and then Mr. Hartford was behind her, his face a map of wrinkles, his hair salt and pepper. What had happened to that vigilante? The man who would save others who could not save themselves? Where was he now? He could not save anyone, could not save Sarah.

"What's going on here?" asked Mr. Hartford, his blue eyes moving back and forth between us, piercing. Mrs. Hartford reached up and slapped me. My cheek burned and then she was hitting me on my shoulders, my arms, my chest, her hands lashing out randomly. I pushed out, away from her, and she followed me down the porch steps.

Mr. Hartford grabbed hold of her shoulders and turned her around to face him. She buried her face in his chest, sobbing. Her chest heaved. He looked over her shoulder at me and shook his head as if I was his own child. As if I was his own, disappointing child. Is this how he sometimes looked at Sarah? Is this how they made her feel when she said she wanted to leave her husband?

"Please leave," said Mr. Hartford. "Or I'll call the police, Miss, and have you arrested. Don't come back, and stop writing those horrible letters. Go on, get out." He nodded towards the front gate.

I stepped backwards slowly. Before I turned to go, I looked up at Sarah's old bedroom window. The lace curtains blew in the breeze. And behind them, I saw a face, the idea of a face, looking down at me.

I closed the gate behind me and ran away from the house, away from the sobbing.

Now I am writing this. It's early morning. I've gathered my clothes and some food from Mrs. Carroll. Before I left the kitchen she paid me for picking and selling the corn. She slipped me two fifty-dollar bills along with what she owed, and told me to be safe. Her hands closed around mine and they felt scratchy and worn. I kissed her cheek.

I am off now, to space, to somewhere where there is more room for me. Somewhere in the West, or the Southwest even. I will sit in the desert below the blue bowl of sky until I become a part of that landscape. But not forever. I will move on, I will go further. I will do the things for which she never had the courage to leave.

Dear Sarah,

I realize now that my words will not reach you. This is a dead letter. You will never receive it.

Still, I cannot help but write in the hopes that somewhere my words are finding you. And maybe wherever you are, you are writing me too. Long letters, beautiful letters. Letters that one day I will find and read with great pleasure. Perhaps you are having adventures elsewhere, now that you're not here. Perhaps you've moved on to a place that I will only understand as being better at some later juncture in this life, this life you gave me. But still, at some intersection, my hope is for our words to cross each other, so that we will feel, if only for a moment, infinitely loved and happy. It is the least anyone deserves.

Love,

Alice

# THE DARKER SIDE OF GRIEF

## - *Naching T. Kassa* -

The shadow passed over George Stormer like a dark spirit in search of a tomb. He glanced up into the pale blue sky and caught sight of a hawk's wings. The bird soared above the field beside the dirt road and hovered, wings flapping, above the grass. George squinted at it through his sore and puffy left eye.

"Hey, can you hear me?" Rory Franks said.

George tore his gaze away from the bird. "No. Sorry."

"What is with you these days? It's like you live in a dreamworld or something."

"I haven't slept much lately. What did you say?"

Rory readjusted his grip on the thick math book under his arm. His face grew white beneath the freckles. "You do not want Carla Runningdeer as a babysitter."

"Why not?"

"She beats people up. Did you hear what she did at the dance last Friday?"

George shook his head.

"Paul Graham asked her to dance and she threw him through a window."

"How do you know that? You weren't there. You're only eleven."

"My cousin was there. He saw it. She did other things too."

George turned back to the hawk. It dived into the tall grass and vanished among the green. Seconds later, it reappeared with a small, writhing creature in its talons. The snake struck as the bird's wings lifted them both into the air.

"What things?"

"Last summer, she stabbed a guy."

"Who told you that? Your cousin?"

"No, I overheard my sister tell one of her friends. He walked by Carla while she was lying on the sand and she stabbed him in the leg."

"Who was the guy?"

"I don't know. My sister didn't know him."

"Did your sister see it happen?"

"No. Maggie told Jennifer and Jennifer told her."

"Did the cops arrest Carla?"

"No. But, I know it happened. She's dangerous. You should tell your dad you don't want her as a babysitter."

A small, blue ranch-style house rose up on the left as they walked down the dirt road. George stopped in the mouth of its driveway while Rory opened the black mailbox on the other side.

"I don't think she'll hurt me," George said.

"What makes you so special?"

"This," he pointed to his eye.

"Your shiner? Somehow, I don't think it'll matter."

A woman stepped out on the front porch, then. When her eyes fell on George, she re-entered the house.

"I'd let you in but my mom wouldn't like it," the freckled boy said, pulling white envelopes from the box. "Mom says she doesn't know what to say to you since your mom croak—"

Rory covered his mouth with one hand. His face grew as red as his hair.

"Sorry."

"It's ok," George said.

"Please, don't be mad."

"I'm not."

"You sure?"

"I have to get home. I'll see you...tomorrow."

"See ya."

Rory turned toward the house.

"Rory?"

"Yeah?"

"It's nothing. Bye."

"Bye."

George hurried away. When he glanced back, Rory had disappeared.

He slowed to a shuffle. The sun hung bright above him, hours from descent. He checked his watch. Dad would head to work soon. Mindy would be waking from her nap.

The road stretched before him, leading him away from the fields and into the trees. He entered the shade cast by tall pines, their branches thick with emerald needles. The sun played hide-and-seek between them as he walked. A hush grew as he travelled on and though he wanted to quicken his pace, he did not.

Something moved behind him and the leaves whispered in its wake. He didn't turn.

"George," a soft, melodic voice said.

A chill prickled his skin and climbed over his scalp. A patch of sunlight lay ahead, piercing the gloom which surrounded him. He made for the spot.

"I want to talk," the voice continued. "I won't hurt you. I would never hurt you."

He stepped into the sunlight and bathed his skin in the heat. From the corner of his eye, he saw a shadow flit among the trees. He halted.

"I can't do it," he said, lowering his eyes. "I can't let you in."

"Don't you love me anymore?"

His vision blurred and his heart ached, but he didn't answer.

"You're just like your little sister. You've shut me out."

"No! I—"

The shadow had crept close to the edge of the road. He could almost make out her face.

An engine sounded behind him, breaking the spell the shade had cast. George blinked and the woman melted into the forest. He moved to the side of the road and looked over his shoulder.

A Mustang, trailed by dust, sped toward him.

George's heart pounded in his chest. He could still feel the shade's eyes upon him.

The car slowed as it neared him and rolled to a stop.

A girl of sixteen sat behind the wheel. Black hair framed her unpainted face and small diamond studs glimmered in her earlobes. Dark glasses hid her eyes and reflected his face.

The passenger side window hummed as it opened. The girl raised a hand in greeting, revealing the illustrated snake which wound about her arm, its tail disappearing into the sleeve of her pink T-shirt. A small, pink dreamcatcher hung from her rear-view mirror. The white feathers stirred in the breeze.

"Hello," she said. Her voice was high and feminine. Nothing like he'd imagined it would be.

"Hi."

"You're George Morrison."

He raised an eyebrow. "You know me?"

"I have a bunch of brothers and sisters. One of them is in the class after you."

"What's his name?"

"Alex."

"I know him. He's small but smart. People pick on him."

"He says you're brave, but you bite off more than you can chew. Nice of you to stick up for him."

George shrugged.

"How's your eye?"

"Ok. It doesn't hurt anymore."

"Good." She lowered the sunglasses. Dark eyes stared into his.

"I guess I should introduce myself. I'm—"

"Carla."

A smile curved her lips.

"Would you like a ride?"

"I'm not far from home."

"And, I'm not the type who picks up young men."

Across the road, the leaves of a wild rose bush swayed. George glimpsed a pale face with a gash for a mouth.

"What is it?" Carla asked. She followed his gaze.

"I'll ride with you," George said, pulling her focus back to his face. He opened the door and climbed inside. Vanilla wafted over him as he closed the door.

"Buckle up," the girl said. She wore denim shorts. George glanced at her long legs and quickly looked away. Carla didn't seem to notice. She repositioned her sunglasses, shifted into drive, and stepped on the gas. The car surged forward.

"My house is past these trees. The driveway is on the right," George said.

"Mmm-hmm," the girl replied.

She leaned forward and turned a knob on the dash. The rich wail of an electric guitar filled the air and Jon Bon Jovi's voice joined it.

"Blaze of Glory."

"What?" Carla turned the music down. "What did you say?"

"Just repeating the song."

"Oh."

"It's the way he wants to die. He wants to go down fighting."

"How old are you again?"

"Ten."

"You're awful serious."

"I have to be."

Carla pulled into the driveway and parked next to the Ford pickup which stood outside the garage. George opened the door and stepped out.

The one-story home, once a cheery yellow, had suddenly become drab. Paint peeled off the shutters and weeds grew tangled over the lawn. A cracked window faced the drive. George sighed.

The screen door creaked open. His father, Harley, stepped out.

He'd been tall once. George remembered him as a broad-shouldered man with a hearty laugh. The last three months had robbed him of these things. He'd become a living denizen of the grave.

Carla removed her glasses and tossed them into her seat. As Harley approached, she held out her hand.

"Hello, Mr. Morrison. Sorry, I'm late."

Harley took the offered hand, held it loose, and released it.

"You got here just in time, Carla. I'm about to leave."

"But, you don't have to be at work until four," George said. "It's three-thirty."

"They called me in early," Harley replied. He rubbed his unshaven chin with one hand, his eyes on the truck. "There are TV dinners in the freezer, Carla. I may be late getting back from my shift, but I'll pay you when I get home."

"Alright, Mr. Morrison."

"George will show you around. He can tell you what you need to do." Harley's haunted eyes turned to the drive. "I have to go."

He brushed by George on the way to his pick-up. Within seconds, he'd brought the engine to life. He pulled out of the driveway and down the road.

"Bye, Dad," George said. He turned to Carla and found her staring at him. He lowered his eyes and steeled himself for a question which didn't come.

"Your sister is Mindy, right?" Carla said.

"Yes."

"Can I meet her?"

He shrugged. "I suppose so. She won't say much though."

He led Carla to the screen door.

When they entered, they found four-year-old Mindy seated on the floor in front of the TV. A cartoon cat chased a mouse across the screen. He caught it, and shoved it in his mouth.

Clothes lay scattered across the furniture and the floor, along with several beer cans. Everything seemed tattered and filthy. George's face grew hot.

He called his sister, but the little girl didn't look up when they entered.

Carla knelt beside her. "Hello, Mindy. I'm Carla."

The four-year-old yawned, her eyes on the screen.

"All she does is watch TV now," George said. "She doesn't talk much."

"We'll see," Carla said. She rose to her feet. "Do you have homework?"

"No."

"Where's the kitchen?"

George led her through a door on the right. Something scampered across the floor when he switched the light on.

Dirty dishes filled the sink, covered the counter, and the table. Flies buzzed around the garbage can which was full of TV dinner packaging. A mélange of mold and rotten meat also wafted from the can.

"Help me clean up," Carla said. "Then, we'll have dinner."

They set to work.

It took over three hours to clean the kitchen and living room. By the time they finished, darkness had fallen.

Somehow Carla had coaxed Mindy into the kitchen. She sat with her brother at the table as the sixteen-year-old served them. Chicken nuggets, French fries, and corn lay upon their plastic plates.

"Are you going to eat?" George asked.

"No," Carla said. She peered out the window into the black and then, closed the blinds. "You need it more than I do."

He took a bite of chicken and set it on his plate.

"How long has your mom been gone?" Carla asked, facing him.

The question stole his tongue. No one ever asked.

"June," he said at last.

"Three months?"

He nodded.

"My grandmother passed on last fall. Almost a year ago. It's alright to be sad. Don't let anyone tell you different."

George stared at her. No one had ever said that before.

Carla came to the table and sat across from him. "If you want to cry, do it. If you're angry, show it. Don't keep it inside."

"Is...is that what you do?"

"It's what I try to do."

"Is that why you threw the guy through the window?"

An odd expression passed over her face, almost as though she were laughing on the inside.

"That may have been part of the reason," she replied. "The other part had to do with his hands. He put them where they don't belong."

George's eyes widened. "I thought it was a story. I didn't know you really did it."

"My dad was in the army. He taught me judo."

"Did he teach you how to use a knife too?"

This time, the grin broke over her face.

"No. I've never stabbed anyone. Not even on a beach."

"Oh," George said. His face grew prickly and hot.

"You sound disappointed."

"No. I...no."

"I suppose you've heard a lot about me."

"Some. Everybody has."

"I'm surprised your dad allowed me to sit for you."

"He doesn't care."

"Has he always been like that?"

"No. Not until mom got sick."

"How do you feel about your mom?"

George swallowed. The word leaped to his mind and flashed before his eyes, but he wouldn't allow himself to speak it. A second later, someone said it for him.

"I'm scared," Mindy said. They both turned to look at her.

The little girl looked up at Carla, eyes shining. She slipped out of her chair and walked around the table, then climbed into her lap.

Carla wrapped her arms about her. "I won't let anything hurt you."

Mindy nestled against her. Within seconds, she had fallen asleep.

"That's a first," George said.

"What?"

"She usually sleeps in front of the TV."

"Do you sleep?"

He shook his head.

"I thought so. Tonight, you both will."

George took another bite of chicken. The nugget had lost all flavor.

After dinner, he led Carla to Mindy's room. She set the little girl on the bed and covered her with the comforter.

"You're good with her," George said.

"Like I said. Lots of brothers and sisters."

"Do you protect them?"

"Sometimes."

She ushered him from the room. They crossed the hall and entered his bedroom.

Posters of various action stars adorned the walls. Clothes and toys littered the floor. It looked as though a tornado had touched down at the center of the room. George snatched up a pair of underwear and stuffed them into the hamper near his desk.

Carla didn't comment on the state of the room. She avoided the obstacles on the floor and made her way toward the cracked window near the small, twin bed. She drew the curtains, then turned her attention to the floor. George joined her. Within minutes, they had created a path through the room.

"Could you stay?" George asked as Carla picked a baseball bat up off the floor. She leaned it against the wall near the doorjamb, and then looked up.

"I have to lock the door. I'll be back soon."

When she left the room, George struggled into his pajamas and hurried to the bathroom to brush his teeth. When he returned, he found her seated on the end of the bed. She rose when he entered.

"Get into bed," she said. He obeyed and she tucked the comforter up to his chin.

"Are you afraid to die?" he asked. He didn't know where the question had come from.

"Yes," she replied.

"You don't act scared."

"I hide it well. Are you scared?"

"I can't be scared."

"Who told you that?"

"Nobody. If I were scared, I couldn't help Mindy. I couldn't do...the things I need to do."

Outside, a night bird screeched. Carla rose and crossed to the window. Lifting the curtain, she peered through it.

"My brother was right about you," she said. "You do bite off more than you can chew."

George lay in the darkness of his room, his shallow breathing accompanied by the swift beat of his heart. Carla had gone an hour previous. The TV no longer blared cartoons.

The walls of the house seemed paper thin this night. Crickets chirped, frogs croaked, and the night bird screamed. They all grew silent when the muffled sound of footsteps approached.

His heartbeat increased. A thin sheen of sweat broke over his skin.

The footsteps vanished as the grass hushed them. He started when the voice spoke.

"Don't you love me? Can't you let me in?"

He didn't reply.

"I'm cold. Cold and so hungry. And, I miss you. I want to hold you in my arms. I love you so much, my son."

He rose from the bed and stepped onto the floor. Pulling back the drape, he looked out.

Dim light from the naked bulb above the porch spilled across the lawn. It illuminated the features of the shade outside and revealed flaking skin, crimson-crusted lips, tangled hair, and eyes filled with animal shine.

"Please, just a little to eat. You've both kept me out for so long. Please, George. Do as Mama says. Open the window."

The creature looked up and caught his eye. He released the curtain and stepped back.

"Please."

"I can't let you in," he replied.

"You little shit," his mother hissed. "Open the goddamn window."

George clenched his teeth as a torrent of obscenity filled the air. At one point, he could take no more and covered his ears with both hands.

At last, the sound died away. Soft weeping reached him.

"Mama's sorry," she wailed. "Mama loves you. She'd never hurt you."

He pulled the drape aside. His mother sat huddled on the lawn, her emaciated body wrapped in the rags of what had been her favorite floral print. Pale, thin hands covered her face.

The song Carla had shared with him, filled his head. "Blaze of Glory."

"Mom," he said.

She continued to weep.

He pulled back the curtain, unlocked the window, and pushed up the sash. "Mom?"

She looked up at him, tears glittered in the dim light.

"Oh, my baby."

"Make me one promise."

"Anything, my little love."

"After I feed you...you can't come here anymore. You have to leave Dad and Mindy alone."

The creature scrambled to her feet. She didn't resemble his mother the way he remembered her. His inner eye, however, had always seen her this way.

"Of course, my dear." A row of sharp, white teeth gleamed. She grasped hold of the window ledge and pulled herself up.

George took a step back.

"I love you," the creature said, though her expression said otherwise.

Someone moved behind George, quicker than he'd thought possible.

Carla's eyes blazed as the bat filled both of her hands. She pushed him aside with her hip, and stepped forward, swinging. The wood connected with the shade's chin. Bone crunched and the thing shrieked.

Carla struck out again, and the blow glanced off its shoulder as it fell to the ground. The creature screamed again.

Carla started through the window, hair flying, face red. George watched as she leaped to the ground and raced across the lawn in pursuit of the shade.

Minutes ticked by.

He wanted to go after her, but Mindy, sleeping in her room, held him back. He couldn't leave her.

Twenty minutes later, a figure strode toward him from the darkness. George took a step back as the baseball bat flew through the window and fell on the carpet. Carla climbed in and closed the window behind her.

"I couldn't catch her," she said, out of breath. She bent and picked up the bat. "She'll be back."

George sat on the edge of the bed. A tear tracked down his cheek, followed by another. Carla sat down beside him until they stopped.

He fell back on the pillow and she covered him with the comforter.

"I know you don't need me to do it," she began. "And I know you're not afraid, but I am. Can I sit here with you for a while?"

George nodded. A smile, long absent, touched his lips.

"I can't believe you went after her," he said. "Why did you do that?"

Carla settled at the end of the bed, the bat across her knees. "I had to," she replied. "Now, go to sleep."

# WELCOME TO AUTUMN

## *- Daniel Crow -*

*To my late father*

P lease come in," Varvara says, opening the door. "Oh, it's pouring outside, isn't it, miss? I never knew it could rain so hard here in the South. Let me take your umbrella, I'll put it somewhere it can dry."

"Thank you so much. I would like to offer my sincere con—"

She disappears before I even finish my short, but well-prepared speech; a moment ago, she was here, faking a welcoming smile, but now off she is, gone with my soaking wet umbrella.

The entryway looks nice and cozy. Soft brownish colors everywhere, with beige wallpapers and a huge oak wardrobe that I leave my leather coat in, and a big mirror in a carved wooden frame next to it. No paintings, though. There will be a couple in the corridor, as far as I can remember, but not in the entryway.

I take off my black shoes and put on the slippers, hearing Varvara's footsteps in the hallway. She must be in no rush to see me again: she's walking slowly, like a child that's about to get some broccoli or an adult on the way to the gallows.

"I left your umbrella in the kitchen, it should... Oh God!"

She stares at me with fright and disgust; must have noticed the bandages on my face.

"Sorry for this." I say humbly. "I've had a skin disorder for years. It's dermatitis, and it's got quite ugly recently. I can leave if it makes you uncomfortable."

She blushes, visibly embarrassed.

"No-no," she says hurriedly. "No problem at all. And the gloves..."

"Yeah, I'd like them to stay on as well, if you don't mind."

"Sure, of course. No worries at all."

"Thank you. And thank you so much for accepting our interview request. Again, on behalf of the editorial staff, I'd like to offer our most sincere condolences."

There is still suspicion in her eyes, but at this point I also notice a glimpse of gratitude. Just a glimpse, nothing more... But that's enough for a start.

"I still haven't heard anything from the *polizia*," she says, her voice slightly trembling. She's clearly struggling to keep it together, that's for sure. "They're looking for him, but I don't think they have any idea where he is. Or how he was taken. Or who took him. I don't even know if he's still... You know... They just seem so completely stuck, that's all."

"I'm sorry. I'm so sorry, really. I mean, he was such a good artist..."

"Was!" she exclaims with a sob. For a moment it looks like she's about to cry, but then she manages to choke back her tears. "Don't say that. He *is* a great artist."

"Oh, I'm so sorry," I mumble. "I really didn't mean to make it sound like that."

She gives me a disgusted look, but says nothing. I can feel that she's wishing she could show me the door right now, without any interviews. But she lives in a big, luxury apartment in a good neighborhood, and that makes for a bill she can't pay on her tiny wages. That's why we offered her so much, and that's why there's no way she can get rid of me so easily.

"*Bozhe*, where are my manners?" she tries her hardest to look ashamed. "Let's go to the living room, I'll make us some tea."

Yeah, I was right—some of the paintings are in the hallway, their frames made of some whitish wood, which fits nicely with soft cream and gold wallpaper. Most of them are simple landscapes, nothing too deep and personal about them. A golden forest beneath a clear sky, a river carrying dried leaves away, another forest, this time in red…

He loved to paint autumn—not the one that I knew, the murky season of rains drawn in a gray palette, but a radiant autumn, brimming with life and bright shades. It looked almost blasphemous, like a short sequin dress at a funeral.

She keeps mumbling something about tea, and the horrible, horrible weather outside, her voice so monotonous that all this talk almost sounds like some sort of a mantra for her ailing mind. I'm not really paying attention, though. The paintings do enthrall me, I must admit, although I'm not too keen on such art. Or, at least, I'm not too keen on artists who prefer bold colors.

There are also a few paintings in the living room, again, nothing too complicated in terms of composition or technique. I like the still-life best of all, it is so simple and yet perfectly complete: two ripe red apples on a small plate, some flowers in a vase, and, of course, another vase full of fiery-red maple leaves.

But thankfully, there is nothing as audacious about the table Varvara has set for us. Biscuits, *baranki*, marmalade and other sweets, two teacups, and not a single hint at her husband's vision of my rainy mistress. No bright leaves in vases, no painted acorns or other decorations people come up with on this season. Nothing of the kind. All of a sudden, I imagine her reordering all these plates and saucers again and again, trying to fend off the grim autumn's thoughts as she waited for me…

"To be honest, I don't really know what you're expecting to hear from me," she says, reaching for her teacup. "I mean, he's been gone for just a couple days, and, well, there's still hope."

"Of course there's still hope," I try my hardest to speak comfortingly, and this time she rewards me with a grateful semi-smile. "But how do the *polizia* know so little? From what I know, the kidnappers made quite a ruckus."

"Well, you see…" she sighs. She's clearly unwilling to tell me anything, but at the same time she's so desperate to share her pain with someone, with anyone who can listen and maybe say a couple warm words. I'm not too good with those, but well, you've got to do what you've got to do.

"You don't have to tell me, if you don't want to."

Ah, an illusion of choice, the good old trick that has never failed me. It has kind of lost some of its charm these days, because you see it way too often, but she seems to have fallen for it.

She will tell me everything, I can tell by her eyes. She doesn't trust the weirdo with bandages on her face, but it makes her feel embarrassed, because, after all, she has a kind heart and understands that it isn't my fault I have a skin disease. And this kind heart of hers—it is still haunted by the memories of the night she came back home and saw their flat in a complete mess. Front door kicked open, dirty stains everywhere, all wardrobes and drawers emptied right onto the floor... And husband gone, nowhere to be found. She will tell me all about it, she will spill it all out in a desperate hope that this way these scary memories would stop haunting her.

And besides, this is her first time giving an interview herself. She has never been in the spotlight, this gray little mouse of a woman. Her husband was a brilliant artist, and she was always by his side, silent and unacknowledged, her voice lost in all the *shumikha*. But now, I am here to let her tell her story, and the very fact of my disgusting presence flatters her, makes her feel more important. People like her are like moths—give them just a tiny bit of attention, and there they are, spreading their wings to fly into the light.

"They found nothing, that's true. I have no idea why. Are they trying to say it's possible just to break into someone's house like that and not get caught? Kidnap someone right from their home? My neighbors, they said these guys made so much noise. They even saw them, said they looked like big black blots... All dressed in black, and so dirty, all of them. They left so much mud in here, it's unbelievable! They called the *polizia* at once, the officers were here quickly... But he was gone. And the bad guys were gone. I have no idea why they would want to take him, or what they were looking for."

"Maybe, money?"

"Money," she sighs sadly. "They did find the money. But they didn't take it. I don't know why. They took only him. And... there's something else."

She interrupts herself and shakes her head. There is more to all this, she knows that, but she doesn't want to tell me.

"This is so strange. Pure insanity," I say and hit the nail on its head. Insanity is the key; that is the word she just had on her tongue, and hearing someone else say it makes her want to keep talking.

"You're right, you're so right! It's absolutely insane. You know, it might seem funny, but I was most scared of the dirt they left. This muddy, slimy, rotting goo, with rotten leaves, mud, even a couple worms. So disgusting! And so weird, it's like they were, I don't know, ghouls or something."

"Yeah, that is strange. But why did it scare you so much? I mean, it's natural for leaves to rot in autumn."

She looks at me with confusion, and I rush to add: "Don't get me wrong, I never meant any offence. But that's just such a weird trace to leave for a criminal."

She squints at me with suspicion, but then her eyes turn sad again, and she lowers her head.

"I must sound like I'm all out of my mind." she speaks slowly, very slowly; we must have been on to something personal, something kept secret. "But he once told me... Well. He said he was out in the park, painting, as usual, and he felt like some guy was watching him, so he turned back and saw that person. He was a bit like a spy from the old movies, you know, with a long leather overcoat and a black hat. But my Andrei, he said the guy looked more like a blot to him, an ugly dark stain on the autumn's canvas. The next day there were two of them. And then, there were more and more. When they came, the sky turned gray, and it started to rain, and the leaves, red and golden...they started to wither. He said they were killing the autumn. You know, his autumn, neat and colorful, the one he loved. They wanted it to die and rot. They wanted all bright colors to die, because their own souls were bleak and rotten, and they couldn't stand anything beautiful. He said they had dried mud for flesh and pus and rot for blood. He would call them the rain people. They came to kill his autumn, but he turned them away with his brush. But then, there were too many. He said they were all around the place looking for him, he was afraid they will find our home and come for him.

That's why we moved here, to the South. He said they would never find us here, and he could finish…"

She interrupts herself again, and I struggle to hold back my anger. Why now, why at the most interesting part?

"So he was working on something new, wasn't he?"

Suspicion and mistrust, here we go again! Come on, that's exactly what a journo would ask. You can't write an article about nothing, right?

Fortunately, it seems she doesn't think so either.

"Yes, he was. The door into autumn, that's what he called it. He was always making these jokes that should the rain people come for him, he would just open the door and lock it behind him."

"That's so exciting. May I have a look?"

I hope I said it with just the right kind of curiosity, one that would fit a girl whose task is to write a good story about the missing master's last painting and then never come back to it again. She wants to see the door, she might ever be eager to peek into the keyhole, but no more than that.

"My boss wanted something exclusive, you see. And that makes for a great story."

"Yeah, but you're not going to mention all this, are you? I mean the rain people and all?"

"Of course I'm not. I'll write about the painting, about what it is and what it, well, could have been. It's unfinished, right?"

"Right." she gives me a blank, melancholic look. "This is all so personal to me. This picture, it…it reminds me of him. I…sometimes I even feel that he's somehow in there. Trying to reach out to me."

"I understand. And I'll try my hardest to give all our readers a glimpse of this sense of tragedy and nostalgia without crossing any boundaries, I promise."

She hesitates for a bit, mumbling something about sweet memories and privacy, but then stands up and invites me to their room. It looks more like an art gallery, and the paintings hanging there are more than just pretty pictures and landscapes. They make you feel the passion, thoughts and emotions he had put into every stroke of the brush to forge them in a scorching hurricane of images and colors that could burn you alive and turn you into ashes.

One painting, with the name "Elena" carved on the frame, almost makes me break down and fall apart right there, in front of Varvara. It shows a park drowning in my autumn, one that was dark, and cold, and murky. Skeletal trees lining up along the road in a ghastly cohort, their bark bluish-pale, like a dead man's skin. Through their leafless branches, raised in a grim salute, you can see the onyx sky, a dark abyss molded of countless deformed figures in long black overcoats.

But in the front, right at the center, shines a lonely *beryoza*, birch tree, its leaves ablaze with defiant golden flame. The undead soldiers reach for its throat with their crooked knotty hands, and yet it doesn't bow to the night and the wailing wind. No, it stands strong and proud, its roots burrowing into the soil, for it knows: a single candle is enough to see your way through the dark, and a single glimmering soul is enough to light dozens of worlds.

And that's just one out of the dozen paintings on the wall...perhaps, the grimmest and the most touching one, the rest are not as good. They don't have the same fiery feel to them, one that is set to leave a brand on my haggard eyes. But there is more to come: Varvara unlocks one of the drawers and takes out a small rectangle covered in cloth.

"That's his latest," she says. "A miniature. You wanted to have a look, right?"

"Oh yes, please, if you don't mind."

She hands the painting to me, and I take the cloth off. Yeah, definitely a miniature, perhaps three by five inches. Far from finished, half-sketched, in fact, and the composition is fairly simple: a wall, a small cabinet...and a door.

A door into his autumn.

I can't tell why I thought so; there are no signs on it, of course. But I can catch a glimpse of a golden and red palette through the tiny keyhole, and there is even a small red leaf on the floor—a glimmering guest from the other side lying right next to a pair of rain boots. The boots look dusty, as if no one had worn them for years; and that is probably true, since it never rains in the painted autumn. It has never seen death, it has never drunk rot, and has nothing to cry for.

But here's the best part: someone is knocking on that door, from the other side. I have no idea how he has managed to draw the sound, and yet it is there, I can almost hear it—with my eyes, not ears. He fled into his autumn, and the lock clicked shut behind him, leaving his pursuers clueless about his hideaway. But there was something the unfortunate master had forgotten...

The key. There it is—on the cabinet, drafted with a couple hurried strokes, a shadow of what it was supposed to be. I have no idea whether the key was even meant to exist in the first place. Maybe, the door was initially to be open for anyone to behold what was inside, but then, as he saw more and more black silhouettes shadowing him all around, he re-drew it with a lock on the door to his little temple of autumn. And when they finally came for him, he escaped into this sacred refuge, but with the key unfinished, there was no way he could go back.

"I have a confession to make," I say slowly, my eyes locked onto the painting. "I'm not exactly a journalist, you see."

She gasps and steps back: her eyes widen with fear.

"I am more of a...connoisseur, if you please. I collect rare paintings, it's an old passion of mine. And I would be most happy to buy this one."

"No!" she screams. "It's not for sale!"

"Please don't rush to reject my offer. I am more than willing to pay you thousands, and, you know, there's no such thing as too much money. Especially given the circumstances. With all due respect, I would advise you to consider, well, different options."

She takes a deep breath, ready to curse my lot and me for ages and ages to come, but says nothing. Instead, she turns away to look at the maple tree. Two worlds, one of light and bright colors and the other of twilight and rain, clash inside her soul, and I swear, I swear even I can hear the sound of their collision.

"This will be rational, more than rational on your part. You'll make profit and make me happy, and your husband will paint something else when he's back. He'll draw many more doors, and landscapes, and everything, don't you believe that?"

Now she is looking me in the eyes again. There is still some flame left in her, but it is slowly fading—that is a fire of a red leaf about to get carried away by the current in the sewers.

"Well, I mean, I don't, I'm not really comfortable with this," she mumbles as the cold waters carry the leaf to a place where every flame dies.

Just a few more moments—and there it goes, floating into my autumn.

"To be honest, neither am I. But this one, there's something magical about it, something captivating, and I can't, I really can't resist the urge..." I reach for my wallet. She watches as I take out banknotes, one after another, all rustling with temptation, like in a magic trick of some sort.

"Please, please, just tell me the price. I'd give anything for this masterpiece."

"That would be enough, I'm sure," she says, putting the money into her pocket. "This is more than enough, thank you. God, is your wallet bottomless or something? It didn't look, you know, too fat. Sorry, I shouldn't have said that."

"No worries at all, my dear."

"It sounded really, really awful."

"What's money?" I say as my wallet returns back where it belongs. Yep, I probably dished out too much. "Money's like mud, really: some people can't stand it, others bathe in it. And if you save it up until the day you die, it will just rot in the ground by your side. So, do we have a deal?"

She nods and hands me the painting, with obvious sadness and despise for herself. Where are you now, my fallen leaf, a tiny reflection of a distant blaze? You are no more—you drowned in the lake of two bleak eyes, and a shameful fake smile was your gravestone.

"Oh damn!" One of the nails in the picture frame sticks out a bit, and I cut my hand against it.

"Are you alright?"

"No worries, it's just a small cut. No worries, no worries at all. Well, thank you so much for your hospitality and for the painting. I have no words to describe my gratitude."

"Thank you, too." she doesn't sound too sincere when she says that, and even less so when she asks if I want another cup of tea.

"No-no, thank you kindly. I'm in a bit of a hurry, got a lot of work left for today."

Putting my shoes back on, I put my hand on the wardrobe—my left hand, the one I just cut. Stupid, stupid, stupid! Funny enough, I kept telling myself not to do that all the way to the entry, but well, shit happens. Luckily, she can't wait for me to go away, and does not really pay attention to details.

"I think you forgot something," she says suddenly. I give her a confused look. "Your umbrella. It's still in the kitchen, I'll go get it for you."

And there she goes, rushing to fetch me my umbrella, that is still probably soaking with water. I won't wait for her, of course. I just leave, close the door behind me, doing my best to make as little noise as possible, run down the stairs and rush past the concierge's window straight into the rain and mud, leaving only a stain of pus on the wardrobe where I touched it and a cold pile of rotten leaves in Varvara's pocket.

It feels so good to be back in the right autumn—cold, even freezing, gray and faceless, shapeless, like a huge dark swamp where pure souls rot and tainted ones feel at home. Many years ago it welcomed us, nursed us on its cold breasts, it breathed life into us with its ice-cold winds and caressed us with its wet hands...and we shall pay what's due. We will gather in the park this night, we'll bring crowbars, lockpicks and rams. We will break through the painted door and make a sacrifice for our mother, our queen, our goddess.

It feels so good to be back in my autumn...and dealing with the imposter will feel even better, I'm sure.

# STILL LIFE
## - Kelli Owen -

The body was found, as dead as the dried section of riverbed it had settled into, along the portion of River Road where the gravel looks like chips of gleaming bone. The young couple who found it were out past curfew. Because the girl's parents had repeatedly told her *not* to see this particular boy, it was almost two weeks before they told the police what the moon had revealed, what had caused them to cut their dalliance short and scurry back to their homes. And before the police had typed the first word of the report, news had spread through the quiet little town—details blossoming like blood from a wound, based on nothing more than guesses and gossip.

The county's strategically placed dam, meant to reroute nature, had exposed more than rocks and roots as the waters ran dry. It had revealed a human carcass, which nature hadn't had enough time to strip to the bone. Bits of waterlogged flesh and torn cloth hung from the bones camouflaged among the roots. Nature's scavengers and carrion lovers picked and pulled at the remains, doing a fair bit of damage to the scene and almost cleaning the corpse of meat before the police arrived.

With the officials came the curious, and the road along the dried riverbank changed. No longer a casual lane time-shared by morning joggers, evening lovers, and occasional fishermen, it became a popular stretch to drive through—gawking, pointing, and feeding the rumor mill.

The dark-haired girl looked up from her sketchbook and took in the landscape. She'd once drawn the same area at night, the moon low in the sky as it hung close to the now-drained water. The orb had been represented on her page as a void of charcoal—a hole among the smudges and smears, the lines and edges. She wished she'd been there when the body had first been discovered. To draw the fleshy bits still clinging to bones and witness the wildlife pick what it could from the remains. She always seemed to find her subjects *after* death had claimed and cleaned the scene, once life was still.

Her eyes darted across the area while she decided which parts to draw. What should be highlighted in sharp charcoal lines, and which parts should be blurred? The young death artist had been choosing darker subjects for several years, much to the disapproval of her mother. Her drawings usually included abandoned houses, aged statues, or the various areas and angles of the town's two cemeteries. But occasionally something provided new fodder, and being different than the *norm*, seemed somehow darker—like the dead rabbit she'd found stuck to the barbed wire fencing just outside of town. It had looked placed, *on purpose*, and therefore out of place. When she'd finished that day, her fingers were dark with smudged charcoal and the only clean lines on the entire page had been those of the barbed wire itself.

Charcoal in hand, poised and waiting for direction, she focused on the road in front of her. What had once been secluded and serene had become overrun with officials and onlookers alike with the discovery of the missing girl. But in the year since the body had been found, the case had grown cold, and the traffic on the road had changed yet again. Given new life by the morbid curiosity of death, River Road was now a makeshift park of sorts.

Further down, beyond the skinny dried-up patch in front of her, the river continued, being fed only by the wider east branch now. In response to the displacement, it had swelled and broadened, pushing its banks back and becoming something one could be convinced was a small lake, but which narrowed again into a recognizable river several miles down. Gravity and the compass permanently kept the water away from the riverbed husk on the west side near the road. Only winter's melt and heavy rains ever made their way back up into the dried portion now, even with the dredging and digging the riverbed had suffered under the direction of investigators.

The water and activity surrounding it were subsequently moved further down the road, to the swell of the makeshift lake. Children too young to know what had been in the water would splash and chase minnows under the supervision of those staring at their cellphones rather than stepping into the water themselves. And though the parking area near the water's edge was clearly visible down the road, it was currently deserted.

Flanking the road opposite the river was a steep hill covered in wildflowers, brush, brambles, and occasionally berries. A train track topped the hill, changing the foliage to chipped gravel laced with wood beams and strips of steel, like stark industrial frosting atop the cupcake of hillside. Older kids tended to wander that direction, away from the water itself. They were prone to lay pennies on the tracks to be flattened by passing trains or dare each other to place an ear on the rail to feel for the vibration of danger. Every couple miles or so, a rickety plank staircase made its way from the road to the railway—a forgotten access system for engineers, now used by penny-toting teens and the dog walkers choosing to avoid the road. The weathered wooden steps were almost hidden among the foliage of the hillside, and the girl knew if you sat still, or under cover of night, you could go unnoticed by most.

She was perched halfway up one such staircase. The staircase directly across the road from where the body had been found.

With no human activity down at the river's parking area, the world was quiet, yet screaming in the silence. She listened with a smile. The rustling noises of small creatures came from the dried grasses around her. While the river had been rerouted, and the area had been a veritable circus of mud and men for weeks after the body was found, it was nice to hear the animals had retuned. Nature had reclaimed what was hers, and life continued along the dried riverbank where death had been discovered.

A squirrel burst from the grasses of the hillside and froze in front of her. The nervous flick of its tail was the only movement for several heartbeats as it studied her. She studied back, wondering if it saw her as a threat or simply an intrusion. It suddenly lowered and slipped down into an opening between the steps, its tail giving one last twitch before it went back to being part of the steady cacophony of small movements around her. Returning her focus to her sketch pad, the noises around her began to fade as she concentrated, her hearing as tunneled as her vision.

Roughly a third of the pages in the notebook were flipped to the back with the cover, previously used, as evidenced by the smears at their edges. If she had looked through them, she would have found the houses and graveyards. She would have relived the day she stumbled upon the rabbit. She may have wondered why she chose to blur the foreground rather than the background the day she captured the police activity out at the old abandoned drive-in. Instead, she had gone directly to the next clean page and sat down, ready to record what had become of the roadside memorial.

Her charcoal pencil hovered over where the road and riverbed met on paper. Her fingertips were already blackened from her smudging of the dried mud and several large tree trunks. She recalled how fresh flowers had once been routinely laid at the base of the makeshift cross next to the biggest tree. Now, fake flowers were stuck into the ground and poked through the thick twists of the tree's exposed roots. Plastic and silk, bunches and single buds, they were meant to keep the area colorful, but the sun had begun to leech the vibrancy of convenience. Stuck to the tree, above the flowers and cross, was one of the posters which had littered the town after the body was found. The bold plea for help clearly legible, even from a distance: IF YOU HAVE ANY INFORMATION...

No one did. And like the flowers, the posters faded. Torn and clinging to the tree by the now-rusted staples, the ripped edges of the paper flapped gently in the breeze—ghostly butterfly wings against the bark. Here, the poster had been left as an obituary of sorts, while elsewhere in town they'd been stealthily removed like forgotten yard sale signs.

She lowered her hand and began lightly making the rough outlines of the cross and poster against the smudged embodiment of the tree. She added several quick swirls meant to represent the flowers. She darkened the line where the grassy edge of the road dropped into what was once water. Where it was now only a shadow of the depths beyond, rather than the flowing stream with a reflection that hid the bottom.

Gravel crunched above her again and she raised an eyebrow. Pre-teens slinking along the tracks with pennies? No, kids usually made noise with *more* than their feet. A stray dog, or perhaps a fox? She hoped it would come down the hill and cross the road, she could add its blur and change the focus of the sketch in an instant. *Much like the town had changed its focus.*

She shrugged off the animal and flicked the charcoal across the page while considering the truth someone in town was living with. No one talked about her anymore—the girl found in the riverbed. No one looked for her killer. Missing for several months before the dam revealed her rotting form, she'd originally been presumed a runaway. What had been perceived as a youth's horrible decision and a topic of shame, quickly became a tragedy of unanswered questions. Somewhere in town were parents who had to accept their daughter's death with no one to blame. No one to punish. The town had moved on to a new death, a new mystery— that of a strangled girl left in broad daylight at the side of the road several towns over. The dark-haired girl imagined there were posters hanging there now: IF YOU HAVE ANY INFORMATION...

A bird hopped down from a branch and pulled a piece of faded ribbon from one of the silk flower bunches. It didn't know it was stealing from a memorial, a supposed holy spot. It held no reverence for the relics fading in the sunlight there. It only knew there were shiny bits and loose material for its nest. The girl smiled as she imagined the squirrel nests in the area with dirge blossoms poking out from among the dried twigs and leaves.

She moved the charcoal to the edge of the riverbed in the sketch, and began filling in the details of grass and rocks, as they would have been *before* the authorities ripped up the land with their boots and equipment. She streaked the grass taller and added tufts of the late summer buds that would have been present the night the girl had originally gone missing. Dragging two fingers from the road toward the river, she smeared the charcoal to make it look like imperfections in the crisp details. The two streaks marred the clarity, skid marks across the page.

The girl stood and set the sketch pad down, laying the charcoal pencil across it carefully so it wouldn't roll into the crevasse between the steps and be lost to the squirrels. She made her way down the steps and across the road.

As she approached the tree, she looked past it and the poster, beyond the little cross and faded flowers.

Instead she followed the roots of the ancient tree as they crawled down the side of the riverbank and stretched out toward the middle in a tangled mess. Branches from other trees were still visibly snagged in them. An old forgotten shoe someone had lost while swimming was wedged between the roots and half buried in what had once been soft silt. She cocked her head and considered the roots for the strainer they had become.

The girl had not expected the body to get stuck in roots the night she pushed it into the water. She had expected it to float downstream, taking all the attention of its death and discovery to the next town.

She wasn't a murderer, not really. She had been startled that night, and swung defensively toward the voice in the darkness, her pencil suddenly a weapon outstretched in her hand. She wasn't a *killer*, so she hadn't taken a trophy. She had panicked. Reacted. And fled. But now she could sketch the area and no one would single it out among her other pages. No one would see it for what it was. They would see only memorial, not memory.

She looked at the smears of charcoal on her fingers and wondered if, when the small fish ate the soft tissue of the body's eyes, did they clean out the charcoal trapped in there? She'd pulled the pencil back out that night, only noticing *later* the tip had broken off. She knew where she'd left the tiny bit of sharpened charcoal, and wondered if anyone else had found it.

The gravel crunched behind her again, as the animal made its way from the tracks to the hillside. Moving forward cautiously, it paused briefly to consider the drawing the girl had left on the steps. Once to the bottom, it took several quick steps to greet her as she turned.

The girl looked behind her to locate the fox. Instead, she found a dirty smile and a blur of flesh moving faster than she could react. Before she could scream, fingers wrapped around her throat. The animal towered over the girl, its palm as wide as her face.

The sudden violent movements disturbed the bits of nature, which had been ignoring her presence. She saw several squirrels scamper away behind him, exploding from their hiding spots in the dry grass of the hillside. She heard the birds above her in the trees, as they burst from their branches to flee the scene.

He squeezed and watched her, like the smaller animals had watched her. His eyes danced across hers, studying her expression, as she had studied the memorial.

Her small hands came up to claw at his, streaking black charcoal across his flesh, much like she had pulled it across the page. Beating at her attacker, the smears and smudges transferred from her fingers to his face and neck. The saturation of color lessened with each frantic clawing, the fading charcoal dust mirroring the weakening of her flailing actions. Prying at the fingers that held her, her nails scraped at immovable flesh. Her eyes teared. Her bladder released.

She stopped struggling.

She felt heavy, and he stared into her vacant face. As the moisture in her eyes began to dry, so too did his desire. She was no longer dancing in his grip. No longer playing. She was still. She was nothing more than litter now, an empty wrapper. He released his grip with a slight push, causing her body to tumble past the memorial. Her feet dragged through the loose gravel at the side of the road, creating two streaks marring the landscape. She fell over the edge of the roadway and landed among the twisted roots in the dried riverbed.

The man sighed and turned back to the stairs leading to the train track. He took them two at a time, pausing long enough to smile at the sketch and pick up the charcoal pencil. He retrieved his weathered backpack from the brittle grasses at the edge of the railway. The chipped gravel crunched again as he continued along the track, following the iron roadway to the next stop.

He scrubbed the charcoal across the pads of his fingers, and then wiped them against his jeans. The dust faded from his fingers as it smeared across fabric. He smiled. He repeated the process, having already forgotten where he'd gotten the strange black pencil.

# THREE MASKS
## - Armand Rosamilia -

I
f you wear a mask for too long you start to forget who the real you is. Unlike the lie your mother used to tell you as a kid, *stop frowning or your face will permanently stay that way*, masks become your true face.

Tonight Lenny was wearing an actual mask, not a metaphorical one, as he stood near the bar, one hand resting on the worn surface. He'd been at the Lakeside Manor for an hour and had yet to make eye contact with anyone. That really wasn't his thing, truth be told.

Lenny was more an observer. He liked to watch, whether it was sitting on a bench inside Wal-Mart and killing time while crowds came and went, or spending his money on live webcam girls who did whatever you asked them to do as long as you gave them your credit card number and asked nicely.

His mask was a store-bought superhero one covering his eyes and nose with pointy dark ears. Lenny wasn't much for movies and especially not comic book films, and he'd already forgotten what the name of the character was.

Lenny had no idea why he'd come to this mixer tonight. It was themed and he hated themes at parties. He hated parties, period.

It wasn't like he'd been invited by anyone from work or a friend.

On a whim he'd shown up in his mask. He didn't know why. He'd driven past Lakeside Manor a hundred times on his way to work. The marquee didn't announce a costume party, yet here he was.

He saw her flitting around the room, his antithesis: she was outgoing. Smiling. Attentive and fun to be around. Lenny wanted to hate her but he couldn't. He had a strange feeling...he liked her.

Lenny loved her even though they hadn't said a word to one another. She hadn't even looked in his direction yet. This was nothing more than a fantasy. He'd go home and think about her, beating off until he was done so he could sleep. She'd be in his sex dreams for the next few days until he saw someone else, even though he knew the next one wouldn't be nearly as pretty.

He blinked and she was in front of him. Invading his private space. Closer than a woman had ever been to Lenny.

Lenny didn't mind. In fact he welcomed it, leaning slightly closer to this beautiful and strange woman. She was bold and smelled like a fresh rain.

"Hi," she said with a drunken smile. She leaned in and kissed Lenny on the lips with a grin. "I'm Sammie."

A real man makes hard decisions. It isn't about what's right or wrong. It only has to do with whether it was a hard decision or not. Your father told you from an early age, *you only got ahead with hard work*. It was the only way to make an honest living and get ahead in this world.

There was no such thing as an honest living. Only getting by.

Leonard noticed the woman staring at him in the supermarket. At first he thought she was simply moving the same pattern as he did: far right aisle, with your vegetables and fruit and various juice and moving to the last aisle on the left: milk, cheese, yogurt and beer.

It became obvious when he moved into the pet food aisle. He had no pets to speak of, but he wanted to see what she did.

She followed, staying at the other end of the aisle but clearly watching him.

Maybe she was store security. No teenagers trying to steal beer so she was shadowing him. Wasting time until she got to punch out and go home to her miserable life.

Leonard had a rich, full life. Work kept him busy. Friends and barbeques on the weekends. Dating a myriad of women and hiking in the parks.

Tomorrow he was thinking of taking the day off and getting the kayak ready. He'd drive up through the city and put the kayak and a sealed lunch in the river and paddle out to the island where the remnants of the fireworks castle used to be. Have a quiet island lunch and listen to the birds and the water.

In the next aisle Leonard squeezed several loaves of wheat bread until he found the perfect one for his picnic sandwiches. He'd need to go to the deli and get salami and ham and turkey, all thinly sliced. Maybe sliced Swiss, too.

She was in the aisle again, watching him while looking at potato chip bags, as if it was hard to find the one you liked. Everyone knew their favorite brand and flavor.

Leonard went to the end of the aisle and made like he was going to the next one but doubled back. She had also moved so he ran as fast as he could down the length of the bread aisle, past the snacks and the potato chips and the bagels.

She was in the next aisle, balancing back and forth on her feet. Looking confused.

When Leonard nearly bowled her over she gasped.

For some reason the sound made Leonard chuckle. She was very pretty up close.

"Would you like to go on a picnic with me someday?" Leonard held up the loaf of bread. "I'll bring the sandwiches."

They shared a laugh and a few pleasantries as they shopped down each aisle together before getting in line and paying for their items.

The woman wrote her name and number on the back of Leonard's receipt. He waited until she walked away before looking at it.

Her name was Samantha.

You must eat all of your vegetables. It helps to build strong bones. A better diet means a better person. Besides, as your grandmother was wont to say, *there are starving children in Africa who haven't eaten in weeks and you're*

*going to waste good broccoli?* If you answered with common sense about packaging up the broccoli and mailing it to the starving children in Africa, you got cuffed in the ear.

Len enjoyed a good action movie, although his secret love was romantic comedies. Anything with Jennifer Aniston. He wished she went back to making more of them like she used to. If he had to pick one actress to bend over a table, it would be her.

Instead of Jennifer Aniston he was watching the latest comedy from Will Ferrell, although his films had become increasingly juvenile. Even for him.

He was supposed to be out with friends at dinner but he'd blown them off. It was something he'd done more and more lately. The guys at work didn't understand him. His pals he'd grown up with would judge him.

They'd tell him what a hot wife he had, and that his kids were amazing. His life was amazing. Everything in Len's life was fucking amazing.

Only he wasn't happy. He was bored to tears. He needed a release.

Some nights it was legitimately working late. Other times it was a hooker picked up on Ridgewood and taken roughly in the backseat. He'd begun meeting women by swiping right.

On this night he was watching a movie. Alone. Without his wife talking and asking idiot questions. Without the kids fighting and ruining it or asking for more popcorn or needing Len to miss half the movie because they couldn't hold in a piss for another hour.

He'd purchased three different boxes of overpriced chocolate, a large popcorn and soda, and he was going to eat as much or as little as he wanted. It didn't matter because it was all his.

The theater was nearly empty. It was a late showing on a Tuesday night, which was the best time to see a movie. Especially one that had been out for a few weeks. At times Len had the movie theater to himself and dreamed of being single again with money and the movie was being shown in his private home theatre in his mansion.

As the credits began to roll someone walked in and stopped at the end of his aisle. He was seated in the cherry spot: eighth row up in the center.

He tried to ignore the person but they were still standing, casting a shadow. Bothering Len.

The credits began but he couldn't enjoy them because of this annoying person.

Len finally gave in and looked. It was a beautiful woman and she was smiling at him.

As if his glance had broken the spell, she walked to him and pointed at the seat next to Len.

He nodded and she sat.

They didn't say a word. Len didn't even look at her although he felt himself getting hard. He could smell her perfume and it was delightful.

As the actual movie began the lights went dark and he felt her hand on his crotch.

When she was done giving Len the unexpected but amazing hand job in the theater, she kissed his cheek. "I'll meet you back here tomorrow. Same time. I'm Sam."

Lenny saw the mask and smiled. It was similar to the one he'd worn the first night he'd met Sammie, the start of their whirlwind romance.

They'd been to several other parties since they'd begun dating, although never another masked ball. Lenny missed the excitement of being someone else. Creating a story inside his head. Acting like he was someone else. Anyone else.

Sammie had been in a mood the last couple of days. As they moved from row to row in the flea market she barely registered, even when he pointed out the mask.

She'd shrugged and pulled him along, as if they were in a race and needed to get to the finish line.

Lenny wanted to browse. See what new old paperback books were for sale for pennies on the dollar. He loved the smell of dog-eared copies of books. He wondered if Sammie read. He imagined she knew how to read, but did she enjoy reading books for pleasure?

He'd need to ask her when she wasn't so dark.

When he tried to stop her, setting his feet to pull her back to where he'd seen the dusty records, Sammie let go and kept going.

Lenny wasn't going to let his day be ruined. Instead of chasing her past the knickknacks and tchotchkes he took his time perusing. He stopped to purchase two hot dogs and sodas in small paper cups. Maybe Sammie needed food. At times she forgot to eat.

Despite his goal to not let her sour mood destroy his outing, nothing he saw interested him now. He didn't want to put the food and drink down and study the movie posters or go through comic book boxes. Look at antiques and make pretend he knew their real value.

He gave up after ten minutes. Head down, he headed for the exit, ignoring the smiling faces and families.

Lenny found her standing next to his vehicle covered in sweat but shivering.

The hot dogs and drink forgotten, he unlocked her door and helped her to the passenger seat. He had a passing thought to kiss her cheek and tell her it was all going to be alright.

Lenny didn't.

He got in and remembered the food and drink, but he had no idea where the items had gone.

Sometimes he misplaced small things.

He wondered where the mask he'd worn on their first date was now.

Sammie was crying. "Lenny, it's not you…it's me. I don't want this anymore."

Leonard saw the mask and frowned.

It reminded him of…he couldn't place where and it annoyed him. Lately everything was annoying. Especially Samantha.

He turned off the computer and stopped looking at auctions online. He didn't want to buy her anything for Christmas.

She'd been clingy the last few days, wanting to hang out more. Even when he brought his work home and had to stare at numbers on his computer screen, she was nearby. Curled up on his couch with one of his books, one eye on him.

When he moved or turned in her direction she'd beam. Smiling. Happy. Content.

Leonard was anything but happy in this situation. He was too busy. Work was kicking his ass but instead of being understanding she kept smothering him with her presence.

They were at his company holiday party. He'd introduced Samantha simply by her name but she'd jumped in with a smile and laugh, adding *girlfriend*.

Leonard mentally considered her his wife, and that wasn't a good thing. His parents had been married. When his mother died at age ninety-seven his father had smiled for the first time in years. He'd closed his eyes and put up a hand, asking Leonard if he heard that. Heard what? Silence. She was finally going to shut up.

Samantha had been nice enough to be the designated driver tonight, which suited Leonard's purposes for getting shitfaced and hitting on the new secretary.

He wasn't only cute and buff but he'd been sending vibes to Leonard for weeks with flirtatious emails and grins in the office.

Five drinks later, while Samantha was squawking with the other girlfriends, Leonard made his move. He cornered the hunk coming out of the bathroom and smiled.

After a few quick words and the hunk trying to get back to the party, Leonard made his move. He moved in for a kiss but was rebuffed, the man frowning. An explanation he was engaged to another man, who was at the party. He wasn't interested. Leonard had his wife with him, too.

*She's not my wife. She's barely my girlfriend. I'm breaking up with her. After the party. After this is all over. I want you. I want to be with you.*

Now Leonard was angry at Samantha for handcuffing him. Chaining his life to hers. She'd hinted at moving in together because they lived too far apart. She was getting tired of staying the night but having to go back and forth. His apartment was much closer to her job.

Her new life was with Leonard. She said it like a damn mantra.

Samantha was grinning when Leonard took her by the elbow with a laugh, as if he was going to tell her a private joke or finally propose to her in front of all these people.

Instead he took her to the same spot he'd talked to the hunk, placing her in the same exact spot. If he was in a play she'd be standing on the proper x on the floor.

Life was about hard decisions.

It was over. Leonard was done with her. He wanted her to leave. Go home. He'd mail her things tomorrow. He needed space. He didn't bother with the *it's not you, it's me* speech.

Not because he wanted to save her from the hurt but because he'd checked out. He didn't care anymore. She meant nothing to him.

Samantha was crying. "You can't break up with me, Leonard. I'm pregnant."

Len saw the mask and shuddered. They were giving them away as an incentive for those who'd purchased advanced tickets to the premiere.

He didn't even want to watch the movie but knew Sam would be here, hiding in the crowd. She had a way of sneaking up right before the movie began and getting frisky.

Not every encounter had been sex. They'd seen a Disney film and held hands. Watched the new Bruce Willis movie and she'd fallen asleep on his shoulder. They'd had sex in his mini-van afterward and then fast food dinner.

If his wife suspected anything she didn't let on. She was too busy with the kids and the bills and the day to day bullshit Len hated to deal with.

He wanted to stop the affair. He owed it to her. Didn't he? While he was running around behind her back and spending money they really didn't have, lying about being at work or out with the boys, she was the perfect wife.

She cleaned. She cooked. Raised the children to be better than their father would ever be. She dealt with his insecurities. His problems at work became her problems. His stress was massaged away. She'd listen to his stories, even when he knew they didn't make sense and he rambled at the injustices he faced daily.

Len thanked her by having an affair with a woman he knew nothing about. She'd told him after their third 'date' she was also married and had no plans to leave her husband. She just wanted something exciting to do a couple nights a week.

She'd made it clear, if Len wasn't available on the specific nights, she was still going out.

On this particular night he'd seen her walk in right before the previews were over.

He'd taken off his underwear before leaving the house and wore loose sweatpants. She'd complained how hard it was to take care of him when he wore tight pants. In return she'd worn short skirts with no panties for easy access.

The movie began and Len looked around. Where was she? Did she not see him? It had never happened before.

He saw her...actually the back of her head. With another man. Three rows down and to the right.

Len watched the movie with tears in his eyes. Even though he'd wanted to break off the affair, it felt wrong to end it this way.

In the lobby he'd lingered, acting like he was trying to decide which candy to buy, when Sam appeared. Alone, which was a good thing.

"We need to talk," Len said.

Sam was dismissive. "Len, I'm over you. You're boring. Leave me alone or I tell your wife."

On a whim he'd purchased the mask when he saw it in the thrift store. This far after Halloween he had a pick of quite a few. It was the closest to the one he'd worn the first time he'd met Sammie.

He thought she'd get a kick out of it. Maybe it would remind her of the good times. The best times they'd shared in the weeks they'd been together.

There had to be a way to make her realize what a mistake this temporary breakup was.

Sammie had slapped him with a restraining order. Lenny was dumbfounded. What had he done to deserve that? He'd been nice. Pleasant. He'd shown up at her work a few times and left messages every night, but he'd never threatened her. He'd never been violent and never raised his voice.

All he wanted was an answer.

If she was going to hide behind a piece of paper and change her phone number and the locks on her door, Lenny would not be deterred.

He let himself in through the back window. Once they'd kissed and made up he'd replace it. Maybe buy her an alarm system. There were creeps in this world.

It wasn't supposed to be this way. They should be happy and together. Raising a family.

Lenny was sitting on the edge of her bed when she came home.

Wearing the mask because it would make her smile.

She looked stunning as usual. Like the day they'd met.

Her scream annoyed him. If she didn't stop she'd confuse the neighbors. They'd think she was in trouble.

Lenny stood and began to explain to Sammie it was all a mistake. A big misunderstanding.

Sammie didn't want to hear it.

He thought maybe leaving and coming back in the morning would be better for both of them. For their relationship.

As he went to push past her in the small hallway Lenny heard the explosion.

Confused, he looked down and touched the burning, gaping wound in his chest. "No. I love you," Lenny said.

Sammie shot him again.

"How about this?" Leonard held up a kitten mask. "It could be perfect."

Samantha groaned. "You never put a stupid mask on a newborn." She patted her sizable stomach. "Sometimes I wonder about you."

*Sometimes I wonder about why I'm still with you,* Leonard thought and studied her movements.

Samantha was as big as a Volkswagen. Everyone always said pregnant women were glowing. Beautiful. Leonard didn't see it.

He felt trapped. He'd had to sell some of his collectibles and clear out the second bedroom for a baby. Moving Samantha into his apartment meant no privacy and no fun. She was cranky. She puked every morning and craved weird foods at midnight.

Leonard played along and went to buy her bacon double cheeseburgers or a strawberry milkshake, using the drive to crank his music and scream about how unfair life was.

Until he couldn't live this life anymore. He could run. Try to start over in a new city. Find a way to get a fake ID and hide.

Samantha would tell the police. Hire a private detective. Track him down and get him to pay child support on a baby he wanted nothing to do with.

He'd broken into the tallest building he could find.

Leonard felt the wind pushing at his back and he welcomed it. None of this was supposed to have happened. Especially this way. He didn't want to be a father. He couldn't afford it monetarily or mentally.

He needed an escape, and the life insurance for Samantha was perfect. It would give her the financial freedom he'd never be able to give her.

As their daughter (son?) grew up Samantha could lie and tell their child wonderful things about their biological father. When she remarried and another man raised the child as his own, Leonard would finally be happy.

Someone else would deal with the burden of being with Samantha and dealing with a child.

He closed his eyes and felt as light as a feather as he stepped off the rooftop, careful to keep his mask in place.

Len wore a mask, sitting in his rental car across from the movie theater. He didn't want anyone walking past to notice his real face, even though he imagined alarms might go off in someone's head if they saw one of the former Presidents in the driver's seat.

He knew Sam would be here with her date of the week. After the affair he'd tried his damndest to let it go. Move on with his life. Understand he'd been lucky and his wife would never find out.

Except...he couldn't forget Sam.

She was all he thought about.

Sam showed up to the theater right on schedule. Alone.

He ran across the street and hooked her arm in front of a dozen people, all the while laughing so it seemed like this was a game.

Sam was confused and didn't fight at first, being led half a block before she stopped and dug her nails into his arm.

"Stop. I only want to talk," Len said.

"There's nothing to talk about," Sam said with venom, spitting the words out. "You're yesterday's blowjob. I'm telling your wife."

Sam turned. To leave and go back to the theater? To her car to go home? To drive to Len's house and tell his wife everything?

He was enraged. He grabbed her by the hair and spun her around. Len wasn't going to hurt her. He wanted to talk. Set this straight before she ruined his life.

Sam screamed for help.

He slammed her into the wall and looked around. Even though it was a main street and the crowds in front of the theater were within earshot, no one seemed to be paying attention.

"We need to talk," Len said. "I'm sorry. We should go see a movie."

She didn't respond and he felt her go limp in his arms.

Len stared at her lifeless body and frowned. It wasn't supposed to happen this way. She was going to realize her mistake and stop cheating on him...even though he had a wife. A family.

It was all going to go away.

Len placed the mask on Sam's face because he didn't want to see her accusing eyes anymore.

He took a deep breath and decided to head to a movie.

"You're wasting your time. The male won't even blink unless the female is in the same room. They need to touch hands, in fact. It's the craziest thing. The heart rate spikes back up to normal levels. The eyes will open on L7. He might even crack a smile. I've seen him get an erection."

He's a hundred and fifty years old.

"The old man is still excited when she touches him. You'll see. Bring in S14 and put their hands together. You'll get some amazing readings. If you break protocol and let them sit next to one another touching for a few hours they'll both actually sleep. REM, even. They dream. The boss says they're dreaming together."

You believe it?

"We're dealing with the two oldest people in the world. Still alive. Still able to breathe. Shit, I believe anything is possible."

Were they married?

"Hell no. Both of them were on death row. Commuted to life without parole. Now we wait to see how long they last, although it seems when they get to be together it gives them energy to live longer. Damndest thing."

Then why not keep them apart and let them die?

"Not my call. Not your call, either. I'll call for S14. You gotta see this. It's really cool."

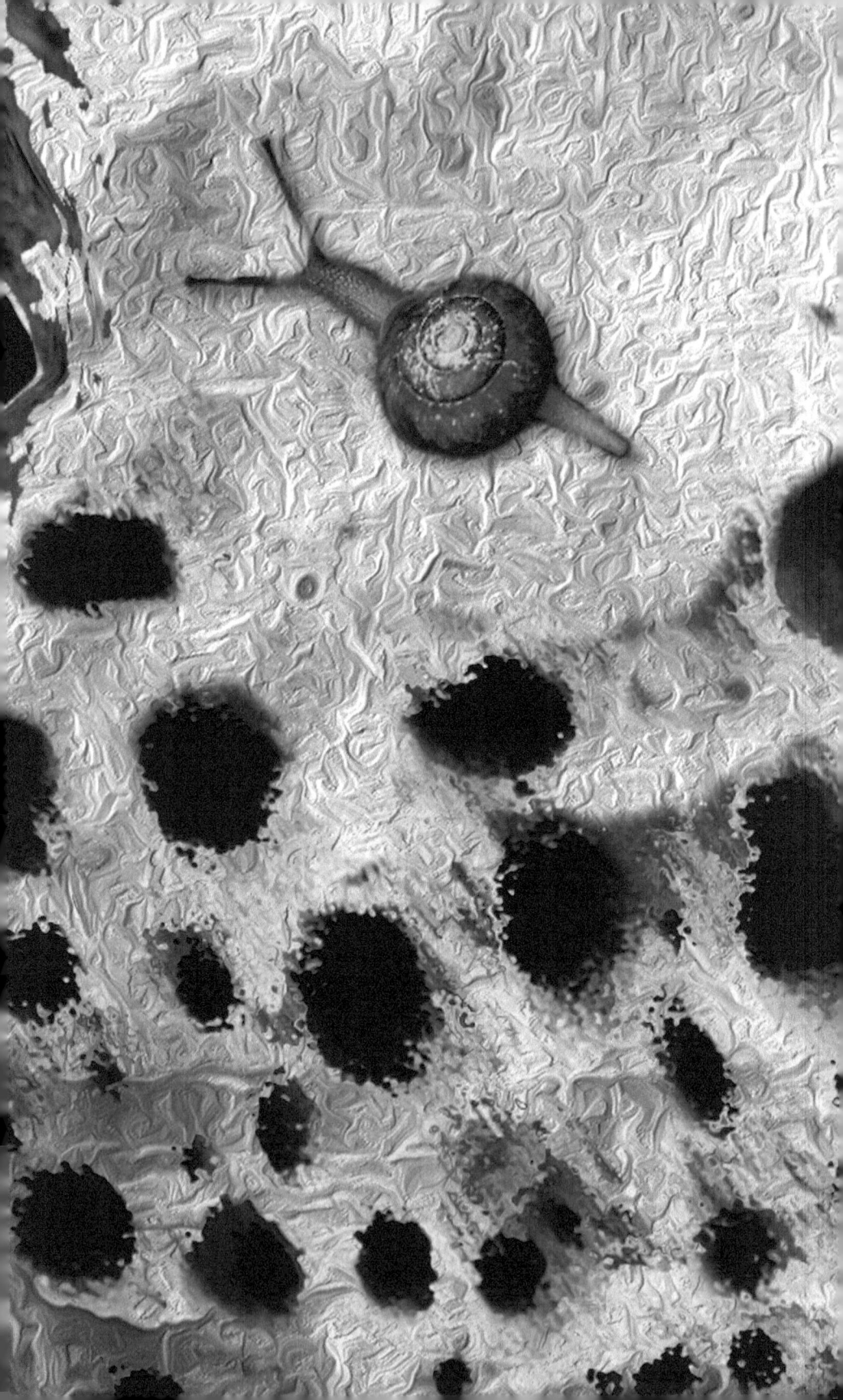

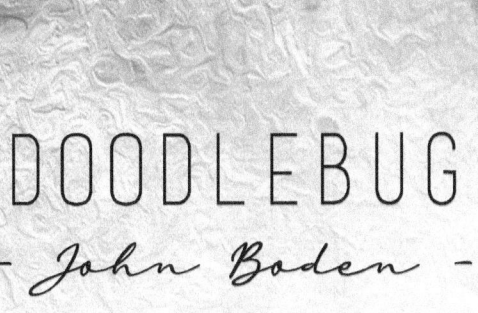

# DOODLEBUG
## *- John Boden -*

### 1.

That girl over there pouting by the shed again?" Mrs. Amber spoke in her succinct manner, almost biting words in half. Not as haughty as her voice would misdirect you to think. Just the way she came across.

"Probably." Her mother had replied, pausing to swallow smoke and spew it into the drab air around them. "If misery were water and woe was liquid dinosaur, our little Marta'd be the best dowser around." Her mother had said, so matter-of-factly that it was akin to a mild sweep of the hand to shoo a gnat. Marta kept her back to the women, their words bouncing off of her slightly stooped spine like falling acorns.

### 2.

That recollection echoes in Marta's mind, like the honking of autumn geese making their escape before that first snow. She stares at the house as it bleeds orange fists of flame, disgorges thick coils of smoke into the early morning sky. The smells of water and ash, of rendered wood and scalded metal and that underlying tang of cooked meat-all of them congregating and ushering her into a sermon of destruction and death. She stays back behind the rest of the crowd, behind the yellow tape that flutters in the air, barely craning her neck to watch the firemen carrying out the three stretchers.

Stretchers bearing cargo less than half their length. She notes the plastic playhouse in the side yard near the burning structure, warping from the heat. The men's faces are bright red and slicked with sweat or tears, not much difference is there? Salt water is salt water. Marta looks at her feet. Her white sneakers speckled with ashen mud. She hears one of the firemen bellow for more water and she bites her lip. She bites hard enough to feel the edge of a tooth break skin, taunt blood and swallow it. Her skin is dancing. She looks at what is left of the house-a charred skull devoid of flesh-and beholds it as the castle of her dreams. A smile threatens to bubble up but she bites her lip even harder and that stops it. There is a tremendous sound as the back portion of the roof caves in, she imagines it being under the weight of the fist of God. She deeply inhales another lungful of the smells and turns to walk away.

She keeps walking and in her mind she walks backwards over years as cracked as the sidewalk.

### 3.

"Where's that girl now?" Pa's voice was tilted and stumbling over his tongue. He was drunk again. She heard him stomping through the trailer. Frankenstein foot thumps on plywood covered with thin carpet remnants.

"She's out burning the trash." Her mother answered.

"What, is she gonna crawl in that barrel herself?" The man sneered and laughed that bloody kicked thing he called a laugh. Then there was no sound from inside the home. A place where silence had a tendency to grow fists and hit hard and where quiet almost always gave birth to tears and bruises.

Marta stood out in the far corner of the yard, beside the leaning garage and peered into the depths of the burn barrel. The flames down there devoured everything she tossed in, they were as starved dogs in a pit-snapping and chewing up whatever was thrown to them. The newspapers and old catalogs. The cardboard trays the beer came in. The flames ate it all and were never full. She felt the warmth on her face as she watched the fire whirl and dance. She held her hands just above the rim of the barrel, the heat from the metal lightly pushing against her palms like a kitten's paws. She closed her eyes and listened to the crackle and hiss of it. It whispered to her a poem of devotion and devastation. Her heart beat faster and sweat coated her pale skin. She stood there and prayed with the burning and in her self-imposed darkness she saw shadows scuttle and scurry behind shrouds of smoke and pillars of angry orange. They rose high into the sky before a castle of flame. Windows bowed and melted and from behind them faces screamed. She smelled hot metal and charred paper and with her eyes still closed and her mind still dreaming, she smiled. The saliva that coated her teeth dried in the heat that caressed her face. She had witnessed Heaven and it was beautifully burning.

Inside the trailer, there was a loud crack and something made of glass broke. Whimpering followed.

### 4.

Marta awoke from dreams filled with smoke and bright orange kisses. Faces of people she once loved or never loved all reduced to cinderous visages that crumbled and blew away. She rubbed an arm across her drooling mouth and smelled the thick sweat that sheened her. It was like she was slick and fresh from the womb. She nearly smiled. She looked at the clock on the box that served as a nightstand. The zeroes blinked and blinked. She sighed through her teeth and sat up, allowing the stinking sheet to slide from her chest. She looked down at her pallid breasts and the freckles that lived there. She felt the corners of her mouth droop, a divining rod that's found water. She stood and stomped into the bathroom. Sitting on the toilet, she lit six matches as she stared at herself in the mirror over the sink. She gazed at her plain face through the flame of each match and let them burn until they hissed out against calloused fingertips. She ate every one and to everyone she assigned a name. More than one was called Papa. She looked at herself and turned away, she was always prettier through heat waves. She began brushing her teeth and did not stop until the foam she spat was berry red.

### 5.

In pictures she is char and bone. Black crackle and tooth. A handful of diamonds scattered on fresh tar. Of all the fire's she's started...the ones behind her eyes burn with the most ferocity. Memories are inexhaustible fuel.

She watches as the corner of the picture starts to curl, as the wisps of black smoke start their serpentine crawling in the air. She looks at the girl in the photograph. The girl looking just like her only younger and smaller and rounder of face. The gingham shirt. The stringy hair. Marta frowned and waited for the girl to burn. She'd spent all these years waiting for that girl to burn. She held it until her fingertips grew hot and then she let it drop from them. It fluttered like a wounded dove until it landed on the pile of papers on the porch. Marta waited for the consummation of flame and newsprint. The ferocious copulation that would explode and climax with full-blown fire and fury. Marta stepped back around the truck that was parked there and peered around the rusted bumper. She watched the window of the house. The curtains did not flutter. The Oxygen In Use sign in the window. She watched as the flames began to devour the porch and lick the door. She imagined she heard a voice from inside. A raspy plea for help. In her head it was her mother and so she paid it little mind. She watched as the trailer twisted in on itself like a diseased spine, bleeding smoke into the overcast sky. Marta started back home and kept her head down as the fire trucks sped by.

## 6.

"What do you want out of life?" The man with the notepad asked teenage Marta. She sat on the couch and fiddled with the small hole in the leg of her jeans. Feeding it her fingers so it could grow.

He stared at her, patiently. His eyes were warm and he had a sad smile on his face. "Marta?" he paused and leaned forward, elbows on his knees. "What would you like more than anything in the world?"

"To burn." She muttered and never took her focus off of the hole that was enlarging with the help of her probing fingers.

"That's what got you here. You burned down a school building and a shed."

"Not to burn as verb. To burn as destiny." She looked at the man and he did not look away.

"Why is that?" He asked.

"I've been doing it since the day I was born. I always burn inside."

The man closed his notepad and stood up from his chair. He went to the desk and gave her a fraudulent smile as he picked up the phone and pushed some buttons. Marta worked at making the hole even bigger, while in the background the man spoke in the hushed tone of spies.

## 7.

Marta sits at her desk and lets the phone ring. She has her earpiece plugged into the jack so the droning ring is unheard by the others in the office. She stares at the computer screen and allows the electronic trilling to invade her head. She flares her nostrils and thinks she smells smoke. A quick glance as the snobby girl from the adjacent cube walks by, fresh from a cigarette break. Marta closes her eyes and inhales deeply. She recalls wishing she were the ash of a cigarette, to be flicked to the wind and ride it to everywhere. She remembers being envious of the Pompeiians. She sniffs again and fantasizes she is the smoke squirming through the woman's lung tissue. Exchanging breath for cancer like bleak currency. Marta feels her mouth flood with saliva. She swallows it and it tastes of sulfur. The phone has stopped ringing but her ears have not.

## 8.

She was released from the juvenile center a few days before her eighteenth birthday. She was already approaching eighty in her mind. Wrinkles in time and short-circuits of thought had been a constant for years. She was old when she slid from that rancid womb, she thought as she ascended the small porch and opened the door. The sticking stink of too-many cigarettes in too small a space greeted her like an anxious dog. She stepped over the shoes and boots strewn inside the doorway and into the living room. She sat on the sunken thing that was once a couch and looked at the ancient coffee table before it. Scoured with cigarette burns and marked with so many cup rings it looked like the underside of a tentacle. She saw a newspaper and picked it up.

She saw the pipe and the empty baggies underneath it, wishing they'd scurry from sight like pill bugs. She looked around the room. The house she'd lived her entire life in-a long aluminum box on flat tires. Filled with sweat and anger and more misery than the Old Testament. She held her breath and heard the ragged snoring from the back bedroom. She looked at the clock on the wall and saw that it marked the time as 2:35 just as it had for the last decade or so.

Marta rolled the newsprint in her hands and walked back the length of the trailer's hall. The worn carpet whispering secrets to the bottoms of her shoes. She peeked into the bedroom and saw the piles of stinking laundry. Saw the sheet covered forms on the sagging bed. Saw the hairy forearm of her father hanging over the side. That awful jailhouse tattoo of a tiger looking more like an ink sketch on a napkin that got wet. Marta bit her lip and pulled the door closed. She tied the pantyhose around the knob and stretched them to the bathroom door where she did the same. Pulling it as tight as possible. She reached into her jacket pocket and pulled out the Bic. She bought it at the Qwik Mart down the street once she was out of sight of the state bus that dropped her off. It was blue and had a fish painted on it, leaping gape-mouthed at a dragonfly. She flicked the wheel and the flame appeared. She touched it to the newspaper in her other hand and held it a second or two until they were well acquainted. She laid it down on the carpeting and put a few pieces of laundry nearby for it to eat. She went back to the front of the trailer.

## 9.

As the sun sank and the trailer burned. Long after the muted screaming stopped, Marta still stood at the edge of the field and watched. This was the only time she could recall being appreciative of her father's insistence at living out in the sticks. She watched the ashes dance in the glow. They were memories. That big one dancing over by the fallen down shed-might have been the time he broke her collarbone. The small one that landed on her lapel was the time her mother told her to just be quiet and things will be easier. "Silence is golden for a reason, pumpkin." She had slurred before she dropped the bottle in her claw.

Marta closed her eyes and stepped forward with her mouth opened as wide as she could.

## 10.

The breeze that slithered through the screen was humid and thick. It undulated rather than blew across the room. Marta lay on top of her bedding.

Bathed in silver and shadow. Her pale skin was downright alabaster in the darkness. She stared at the ceiling and watched the shadows flex and whisper there. She interpreted their secrets and filed their promises. She remembered the first moment she realized she was a myth. A walking talking anecdote that was easily ignored and sharply forgotten at will. She was always the stain on the carpet in the corner of the room. The stain on her parents in the corner of their lives. She was just always. She sniffed back the tears that were running down her face and smiled a little lopsided thing. On the dawdling air was the scent of charcoal and flame. That flammable lullaby sang her to sleep.

### 11.

The day after she turned twenty-four: The man sits in the chair. He hardly ever holds the notepad anymore. The pen stays in the stupid pocket of his stupid pressed shirt. He tents his fingers and touches the tip of his nose and spits out his questions like darts.

"How are we doing with the memories?" The question is drab beige paint on drywall.

"I eat them and never seem full," she replies.

"They aren't very filling, are they?" A small chuckle goes ignored.

"I'll spell it out for you. You take a memory. Pull it out slow. Dip it in that cloudy cup of nostalgia and lay it on the table before you. See if that helps. Usually doesn't for long. They aren't always pretty. Often they twist and squirm like that fat ol' worm when you lift the rock it lives under. Happier to be in the dark and wriggling in the mud and pitch black. Happier isn't always in the vocabulary though. Sometimes happiness is just nine letters someone scrawled on the shithouse wall when they were out of paper."

The man reaches out for his tablet, lets his forefinger touch the corner but does not pick it up.

"What are we after here, exactly?" The eyebrow above his left eye is the top point of a triangle.

"I'm not sure. The court made me come here, remember?"

"I do. But I feel as though we're not mining any new ore."

"Sorry to be boring you."

"You know that isn't what I meant."

"Do I?"

"You do."

"Ask another of your questions."

"When your parents died...after all of the abuse you suffered at their hands, did that feel freeing? It's completely normal to answer yes."

"It felt earned." Marta paused and felt out the words eager to leap from her tongue for betrayal. "My papa was a beast and my ma his shadow. When I got the call they'd been killed, I was sad but it was more a reflex than an actual feeling. The indifference felt like a new pair of shoes, a size too small."

The man slowly nodded and touched the pen in his pocket but did not remove it. "Do you miss them?"

"Only as a person who's lost a limb might miss it after the stump has healed. It's gone but they still feel it. My parents were phantom limbs well before they were dead."

He looked at the clock. "2:35. Session is over. You know you never answered me when I asked why you wanted your hour to end at 2:35 every time."

"Because that's when the time ends. It's been as such for years." Marta slipped out the door with no further banter. The man put his pad and pen in his desk and loosened his tie. He could smell the sweat that soaked his undershirt.

## 12.

She sat on the back steps of her building. The cigarette nestled between her fingers emitting curls of smoke. She put it to her lips and brought them into her lungs. She felt them swirl and swim like tadpoles. She held the cigarette upright and touched the glowing tip to the string dangling from the cuff of her sleeve. She waited for the fabric to darken and flare a little. The flame sniffing for purchase before growing. She held her arm still and waited for it to blossom. Small petals of fire dancing on denim. She saw the police car approach from the opposite side of the intersection so she blew out the infant flame like a birthday cake candle. She would add it to her growing list of almosts. She often felt like that's all she was.

### 13.

"You're very pretty," the boy with the hair in his eyes said, his eyes darting like little fish when she tried to catch them.

"Thank you," she heard herself reply. Had she ever said those words before? They sounded nonsensical.

"I see you sitting out here all the time. I live in the apartment above you." So awkward, he was. She smiled and nodded. She looked over the edge of the steps at the collection of debris and trash deposited there by a myriad of storms. Paper cups and plastic wrappers and a population of cigarette butts. She flared her nostrils and smelled their wet ashen reek. She felt him still there, still looking at her but he'd turn his face away slightly when she caught him looking at her. "I hear you up there sometimes, you try and walk softly." She raised the corners of her mouth a bit.

He smiled and nodded. "I try to." She just looked at him and he, at her. The night stretched like shadow taffy. The silence was pregnant but would need a cesarean section. Taking the hint, the boy nodded again and held out his slender hand.

"My name is Roy. I guess I'll catch you around."

"I'm Marta," she whispered. It sounded like blasphemy. She took his hand in her much smaller one. She felt the scar that lived on the back of his, raised and smooth, a burn. She smiled and looked him in the eye. "I'm pleased to meet you." He freed his hand and went up the steps and in through the door. If he had done it any faster he would have been running. Marta stood and touched her face with the hand that had grasped his. She felt her freckled skin. It was flushed and warm. She heard sirens in the distance and the sounds of a television wafting above her. She went inside and into her apartment. And dreamed of burning in the arms of a boy named Roy.

### 14.

"You know this is our last session?"

"I don't need you anymore. I'm normal." Her smile is an uneasy thing.

"No one is saying that, I don't believe a normal person exists." He smiles as well, his fits better.

"What are you going to do?"

119

"Keep on keepin' on as they say. I have dreams like everyone else. I'll try and live them."

"That's a good strategy to start with. Marta, you have my number, I'm always around if you need me."

"I know."

"Let's chat a bit before we say our fond farewells...what's this week dealt you?"

"I smell ashes and mud and it makes me homesick."

The man nods and does the little circular thing with his hand that tells her she's to continue.

"I met a boy and he was kind to me. Smiled at me. Said I was pretty."

"That's great."

"He lives above me in my building."

The man nods again and taps his upper lip with his index finger. "Do you think anything will come of it?"

She shrugs and her shirt rides up from her midriff. He sees her navel and the scar that neighbors it. He looks away quickly. He stands and leans over her, both hands on her shoulders.

"I've greatly enjoyed the time we've had all these years, what is it? Four? I've seen you make a lot of peace within yourself. I think you're ready for the world and with any luck, it will be ready for you." He steps back and she rises like heat and smoke and floats right out the door.

### 15.

Roy hunches over his desk and draws the monster. It towers protectively over the frail girl with the freckles and the wayfaring smile. Her eyes are sad. He mutters to himself as he renders her. He looks at the clock and sees it is after two in the morning. There is a knock at his door, timid and small.

"Who is it?" He calls and it sounds weak and uneasy.

"Marta," she replies and he opens it and invites her in with a sweep of his arm. The hallway is hazy.

He wrinkles his nose. "There a fire somewhere?"

"There always is."

"I mean, did you walk by one. I smell smoke and it's strong."

"I don't know."

"I need to finish this artwork, you can watch and talk to me while I work on it if you want."

She nods and he sits and picks up the pen. She watches the shine of his scarred hand fence with the light of his lamp. She lets it dance in her eyes and smiles. He looks at her and his hand stops moving. She lays her hand on top of his and he does not pull away.

"How?" She asks.

"Fire."

"When?"

"Forever."

"That's the way."

Outside the sound of sirens grows louder, closer. The flashing red lights paint the walls and windows in strobing rubies.

"What's going on?" Roy asks but he does not rise or take his hand from under hers, his eyes from hers.

"We are," she whispers. Smoke curls a finger under the door and then another.

At 2:35, they begin to smolder.

# HAPPY PILLS
## - Todd Keisling -

Marcus Taylor had a name for the nothingness inside. There were other words for it—melancholia, ennui, depression—but "Absence" described exactly what it was to him: a paradoxical emptiness embodying the essence of himself. A black hole tugging at every moment of his life, forcing his personality inside out. And after thirty-plus years of fighting against the pull of its gravity, Marcus was starting to lose his footing.

"It's not that I've given up," he said to his psychiatrist, "it's that I just don't care if I succeed or fail. There's nothing there to make me feel a sense of pride or responsibility, no sense of urgency or repercussion. Like, I've resigned myself to my fate, if that makes sense." He shrugged. "Whatever happens, happens."

Dr. Wilson looked down at her notes, scribbled something in Marcus's file. "Like a leaf in the wind."

Marcus nodded. "Something like that."

"I suppose this *laissez-faire* attitude hasn't gone over well with your manager?"

"It hasn't. That's why I asked to move up my appointment to today."

"Did something happen today at work?"

"Yes...no. I mean, sort of."

She clasped her hands together, placed them on her lap, and smiled. "Do you want to talk about it?"

*No*, Marcus wanted to say, *I really don't*. Instead, he recounted the meeting that morning, flushing with embarrassment all over again.

"How did that make you feel?"

"On the surface? Like garbage. When my manager said I made the rest of the department uncomfortable, I wanted to scream. He questioned my reliability, brought up Cathy and our separation, said he needed someone who could be happy, who could smile. Said he was putting me on notice. And I sat there and took it..."

He trailed off, replaying his manager's words in his mind. *You come into the office late. When you do show up, you're a mess, like you haven't showered or slept in days. You're irritable with your coworkers. When I try to talk to you about it, you look right through me—like you're doing now.* His manager's words faded into the background, lost among a tumult of white noise and a constant barrage of dark thoughts. *Loser. Failure. No one wants you. You can't do anything right.*

"And below the surface?"

Marcus returned to the present and sighed. "Aside from the usual feeling of worthlessness and failure? Nothing at all. Less than nothing. Frustrated and stuck. It's hard to explain to someone that you're incapable of feeling happiness or anger or anything else for that matter. How do you explain to someone that the act of smiling is like lifting the heaviest weight on the planet? I just can't."

"How did it make you feel when he brought up your wife?"

"I wanted to feel angry. I wanted to respond with indignation like anyone else would, even if he was right. But I didn't. I didn't say anything. No feelings, no words. Empty inside."

"The Absence."

Marcus nodded. "Yeah. The Absence. You'd think all that nothing inside would add up to something..." He looked away, chewing idly on his thumbnail. "Is there maybe another medication I can try? It's been a month since the dosage increase, and I just don't feel any different. Like, no different at all."

Dr. Wilson frowned. She spun her chair around, tapped a few keys on her laptop. "You've made progress, Marcus—don't think you haven't—but we've tried every SSRI and NDRI available. We've maxed out the dosage on each one, including your current prescription." She turned back and offered him an apologetic smile.

"Okay, so, what's that mean? I'm a lost cause? That this is as good as it gets?"

"No, it means we try a different combination of medications. What works for one doesn't always work for another, and it can require some experimentation to see what's most effective. There's no magic bullet..." She paused, considering her words before speaking, and closed her mouth. Instead, she returned to her laptop and opened her email client. "Actually, I might have something for you."

Marcus chewed his lip while drumming his fingers. His fingernails were chewed down to the quick, the soft flesh swollen and caked in dried blood. How long had he suffered from these nervous tics? He couldn't remember. Maybe his whole life. Every second of every day raced through his mind at light speed, every possibility and scenario crashing headfirst into one another on repeat, over and over and over again.

Dr. Wilson's face fell when she looked away from her laptop. "Are you okay?"

"Yeah," he said, wiping sweat from his forehead. "I'm fine." The lie was out of his mouth before he could stop it. "Do you have something for me to try?"

She reached for a sheet of paper on her printer tray, glanced over the contents on the page. "I might," she said. "How would you feel about participating in a clinical trial?"

A week later, Marcus checked in at a doctor's office across town. The act of going somewhere different, seeing someone entirely new and being honest about his ailments shifted Marcus's anxiety into overdrive, but he didn't have a choice. Dr. Patel was the only doctor in the region administering the clinical trial. If he wanted a shot at this, this was it. He waited half an hour before they called him back to an exam room. A few minutes later, a short man with glasses and a lab coat entered the room. He held a thick folder in one hand. The words "ZZ INITIATIVE—CONFIDENTIAL" were printed on the back.

"Mr. Taylor, good afternoon. I'm Dr. Patel. You're here for the Endoximine trial, yes?"

"Endoximine?"

Dr. Patel flipped through his chart, noted Marcus's name, and smiled. "Yes, Endoximine Xytocyclene-44. There isn't a sexy marketable name for it yet. But just between you and me..." He took a seat and swiped his badge at the computer terminal. "I hear they're thinking of calling it Euphoria, but you didn't hear that from me." Marcus feigned interest with a nod. Smiling was out of the question, too much effort. "Anyway, I just need to record some vitals first. Do you have any questions for me before we jump into the trial?"

Marcus tore off a bit of his thumbnail and chewed on it. "How many of these trials have you administered?"

"This will be my third. Endoximine-35 and -39, previously. Hold out your arm for me, please. Going to take your blood pressure."

"And...I mean, how effective were they? Did they help?"

Dr. Patel smiled, pumping air into the sleeve around Marcus's arm. "I'm afraid I'm bound by a non-disclosure agreement and can't reveal details of prior trials."

Marcus nodded, rolling that response around in his head while the doctor tended to his pulse and temperature. *Non-disclosure agreement? Maybe he meant doctor-patient confidentiality?*

"Right, everything looks acceptable." The doctor retrieved the plump folder and extracted a series of documents. "You'll need to sign these before I can formally release the prescription to you."

Consent forms, mostly, authorizing the release of his medical records to the pharmaceutical company conducting the trials. A non-disclosure agreement concerning the trial itself. He looked up at the doctor and tried to smile.

"They're big on privacy, aren't they?"

"Oh yes," Dr. Patel said, "it's all proprietary chemistry, and they're particular about how it's conducted. When the trial is over, they'll want everything back, too. The orientation pamphlets, the pill bottle, residue samples, everything."

"Residue?"

Dr. Patel smiled impatiently. "I'll explain in just a moment, Mr. Taylor."

Marcus returned to the documents, scribbling his name on each form and fighting off the slow-motion panic building within. He'd broken a sweat by the time he was done. Dr. Patel looked them over, initialing and dating where required, and set them aside. "I'll have my staff provide you with copies of these on your way out. Now, for the fun stuff..."

The doctor spent the next fifteen minutes speaking in jargon, explaining the chemical composition and how it was expected to interact with Marcus's brain chemistry. Marcus understood some of the terminology—serotonin and norepinephrine-dopamine reuptake inhibitors—but the rest was lost on him, and he found himself nodding every time the doctor paused to move the conversation forward. *Just want the pill, doc. Don't care how it works, so long as it works.*

But would it work? That question wedged itself into his brain like a splinter and would not come out. He told himself to hope for the best, but the anxiety whispered the same question repeatedly, feeding the Absence inside him. *Would it work? Probably not. And if it doesn't? Oh well, it doesn't matter—just like you.*

"—what sets this medication apart from the other SSRIs and NDRIs on the market is that it works fast."

Marcus returned to the conversation, his mouth dry, his forehead dotted in sweat. "How fast?"

"You should see a difference in less than twelve hours from the time you take your dose."

"Twelve hours? Holy shit."

Dr. Patel grinned. "Uh huh. It's powerful stuff."

"There have to be some serious side effects, though. I mean, something that strong..."

"Well, Mr. Taylor, that's the purpose of this trial: to determine any major side effects. Considering the chemistry involved, I'd say you can expect for it to make you feel a little weird at first. Drowsiness, maybe some abnormal mood swings, and so on. And like any other similar medication, should you begin to experience suicidal thoughts, you're to call me immediately, night or day. My number is in your packet."

"Understood. Would you say it's a good idea to take this before I sleep?"

"Absolutely. It's a requirement of the study." Dr. Patel paused, glanced at Marcus's wedding band. "You may want to consider isolating yourself from any loved ones. The process can be somewhat...*unpleasant* to witness."

"Unpleasant how?"

"I'm afraid I can't disclose—"

"Right," Marcus sighed, "the non-disclosure agreement. Got it. My wife and I are separated, so..." He trailed off as the familiar heat of embarrassment choked his words. *Please don't say anything. Please don't make me lie to you.*

"Good," Dr. Patel said, forcing a smile. "Very good." He clapped his hands, startling Marcus from an anxious stupor, and climbed to his feet. "I think that covers everything. Good luck to you, Mr. Taylor. I think you'll be pleasantly surprised when you wake up tomorrow."

When they finished, Marcus collected his packet of orientation materials at the front desk. Among them was a pamphlet labeled "Endoximine Xytocyclene Trial #44: Read Before Dosage" and the holy grail itself, a clear prescription bottle containing a single black pill.

The receptionist smiled and handed him his appointment card. "We will call you in the morning to check on you, Mr. Taylor."

"Thanks," he said, and gathered his things. He tried to smile again, but the weight was still there and all he managed was a sneer. He hurried out of the office before his embarrassment got the better of him. When he reached his car, Marcus looked back at the office complex, puzzled. *Residue samples,* he thought. *He never explained that.*

Marcus considered returning to ask, but the anxiety crashing against his resolve decided otherwise.

He lay on his sofa, rolling the plastic bottle in his hands and watching the black capsule tumble end over end. The pill looked like a licorice jellybean, with a faint purple hue when the light caught it just right. *Better living through chemicals,* he thought, and set the bottle on his coffee table.

Marcus pulled his phone from his pocket and googled "Endoximine." A list of results appeared, most related to older trials, but what caught his eye was a medical forum discussion between what he assumed were former trial participants. The comments ranged from the effectiveness of the drug and side-effects to more conspiratorial topics. One user suggested the trials were being conducted by the military. Several referenced the "ZZ Initiative."

*Keep it up and you're just going to stress yourself out over nothing but ghosts.*

He eyed the bottle while fending off the doubts creeping out from the shadows. What if this didn't work? What would he do about a job? Maybe he could fake it?

*No, you tried that already, and it didn't work. You can only force a smile for so long before it starts to weigh on you. Sooner or later, those cracks will show, and they'll know you were lying to them. Besides, Cathy would know you're faking. She always did.*

Marcus frowned, recalling the start of this whole mess. The Absence was with him his whole life, but it truly made itself known in the few years after he started working in the office. It crept in slowly, inching itself deeper into his gut, widening and growing like a cancer until there was nothing left but a husk. His demeanor changed, his relationships disintegrated, and that's when things went south with Cathy.

*I can manage it myself,* he'd told her. *I'll try harder.* He did try for about five years until the mask he wore grew too heavy. And then came the cracks, splintering outward, shattering the façade he'd built around himself. Defeated, he'd made an appointment with his doctor, who referred him to Dr. Wilson.

"It's too late," Cathy told him, and Marcus knew she was right even if he was afraid to admit it. The gap between them started growing the moment he began isolating himself from everyone, retreating into himself to fight a battle he would never win. Even with therapy and a gamut of medications, the effigy of Marcus Taylor was crumbling, and everyone saw it except him.

Cathy Taylor was the first to notice and the last to hang on, and the lack of her presence in their apartment was a constant reminder of his failure as a husband. The color and light had bled out of his little world when she left, and now Marcus struggled to even find where the lines were drawn, where they met, where he ceased and the Absence began.

"Stop."

His voice echoed in the emptiness of his living room. A frail and desperate sound, like what a scarecrow might sound like if given voice. Marcus took a breath, in through his nose and out through his mouth, willing his heart to slow. He wiped the sweat from his forehead, and when his heart ceased its pounding, he picked up the pamphlet and began to read:

- Do not take with alcohol.
- Do not combine with other SSRIs or NDRIs.
- Do not take on a full stomach.
- Hallucinations are common.
- Some discomfort may be experienced in the abdominal area.
- Patient MUST take dosage prior to sleep. Expect to sleep for at least twelve hours.
- Avoid premature waking—turn off all alarms, phones, and other electronic devices which may interrupt slumber.
- Relax. You're one night away from a completely new you.

Marcus paused at the last bullet point, wondering what the hell people were supposed to do if they had small children or if they were light sleepers by nature. *They'd make arrangements,* he thought, *if they're desperate enough. Like me.*

He looked at his phone and turned off the ringer but considered the gravity of what he was about to do. Instead, he selected his contacts and called Cathy's number, imagining her across town in her own apartment, maybe making a late dinner, maybe on a date with someone. He ran his thumb along the rim of his wedding ring while he waited for her to pick up. *She's not going to answer. She can see it's you. You think she hasn't filed for a divorce because she wants to be with you? You think she's waiting for you to get yourself together? No way. She's waiting for you to do what everyone else is waiting for. Just do it and get it over with already.*

The phone beeped, followed by Cathy's soft voice instructing him to leave a message. Another beep, and Marcus was confronted with the sound of dead air. He cleared his throat.

"Uh…hey, Cath, it's me. I—well, it's been a while, so I thought I'd check in and see how you're doing. I'm, uh, I'm doing all right. Started a clinical trial for a new kind of medication. Hoping it'll work, and that we…well, you know. I miss you, hon. I'll have my phone turned off tonight, but give me a call in the morning, okay? Love you."

Marcus hung up and hesitated, considered calling her back to say more, but decided against it. Instead, he forced himself off the sofa and plucked the prescription bottle from the coffee table. He took a few minutes to prepare for bed, brushing his teeth and relieving himself one last time. When he was ready, Marcus moved to his bedroom and set the pamphlet on his nightstand.

He opened the bottle and cupped the pill in his hand. To his surprise, the gelatin-coated surface was warm, sticky. It clung to his skin like Velcro, eliciting a faint ripping sound as he rolled it in his palm. He grimaced at the odd sensation before popping the pill into his mouth and chasing it with a gulp of water. The warmth flowed down his throat and into his gut.

*God, I hope this works. For me. For Cathy.* Wouldn't that be something? No more constant worries, no more panic attacks, no more worst-case scenarios. Actual feelings and emotions. The ability to smile again. Something to fill the Absence inside him. Something—

*Relax.*

Lights out.

There were dreams, and there were nightmares. Marcus only remembered the latter.

In the gray wasteland of his mind, he walked alone through a funhouse filled with mirrors. There were other versions of himself, some short, some tall, some wide and thin and distorted. Waiting at the end of a long hall was a mirror that didn't look like a mirror at all, and when he reached it, he discovered his observation was correct. It was no mirror, but a doorway, and standing on the other side was another version of himself.

Marcus Taylor 2.0. Nude, smiling, seemingly happy. The doppelganger was the same in appearance except for his coal-black eyes. Cathy approached from beyond the opening. She stood beside the double, draping her arm over his chest as she kissed his chin. When she looked back at the real Marcus, he saw her eyes were scratched out like a damaged Polaroid. She smiled.

"You're more agreeable when you're like this," she said, her voice layered over itself, creating a harmonic dissonance within the empty hallway. "We can be together again, if you will submit."

The doppelganger grinned. Dark tears trickled down his cheeks. Bloated, purple tendrils spilled from his mouth and slapped wetly against his chin and chest. They sought the air, sensing Marcus's presence before them, and reached in his direction like a thick clump of sentient yarn.

"Submit. Without us," they hissed, "you are only you."

One of the tendrils flopped against Cathy's neck. She took the swollen thing in her hand and gave it a kiss. A moment later, it shoved itself into her mouth and down her throat. Dark residue secreted from its flesh and spilled over her face, melting the skin like wax.

Marcus opened his mouth to scream—

—and launched himself out of bed, retching. His guts twisted and churned, burning with a cold fire that resonated to every corner of his body. He fumbled his way through the dark apartment to the bathroom, where he could no longer hold back the gurgling chaos climbing up his throat. Marcus collapsed and vomited into the toilet. When he was finished emptying his guts, he fell backward on the floor and stared at the ceiling.

Except the ceiling wasn't there. Marcus strained to make sense of what he was seeing. The plaster was gone, replaced by the starry expanse of the cosmos. Gas giants spun lazily in the infinite, their atmospheres a mass of swirling chaos, while galaxies collided light years away, and Marcus cried out in terror when he realized they weren't gas giants at all. They were eyes, their pupils swirling and dilating, dividing from one another like cells—and they all turned to focus on him. The universe stared him down. Marcus blinked.

*Not real,* he thought. *It's the medication. This isn't real. It's—*

A quick stabbing pain shot through his gut and up his chest so suddenly he lost his breath, his vision, his thoughts. The world of his apartment ceased to exist. There was only Marcus Taylor and the singular pain occupying every inch of his body, defining him in these fractured moments of mental static while the universe watched with cold indifference.

Voices spoke in a chorus, rising from the tumult of his agony, filling the room with their booming command.

*Submit. Submit. Submit.*

Marcus gathered his wits and tried to steady himself, fighting back the urge to vomit once more. Something stirred in his stomach, a violent churning that forced a cry from his throat. His skin was on fire, burning at a thousand degrees, a fever so hot he feared he would melt into the floor. Pressure swelled upward from his belly and crawled into his chest, a pair of heavy hands pressing against his insides.

Mind racing, struggling to keep his sanity in the face of such horrible pain, Marcus crawled toward the doorway in a fit of stops and starts. He managed only a few feet before his fingernails cracked and split apart. Thick strings of black goo dribbled from the bloody fissures in his fingertips and seeped across the tile floor. The dark ooze joined together before him in a singular mass, ripping, pulsing in time with his racing heart.

Features sprouted in the puddle. A small mound became a nose, cheek bones, eye sockets, the smooth plate of a forehead.

Marcus watched, stupefied, while a voice in the back of his mind assured him it's a hallucination, this is just a side effect, he woke up too soon—

The dripping shape expelled a choked, guttural sound like words spoken underwater: *"Glory be to the Many."*

*133*

Marcus recoiled from the oily puddle, scrambling backward until he met the bathroom vanity. Above, the eyes of the universe watched with rapt attention, the swirling storms of their pupils colliding, dividing, destroying and birthing one another for all eternity. From beyond the void of impossible space slithered dark appendages, slipping along the wall until they found the congealing mass on the floor. Once there, they inserted themselves into the empty eye sockets of the shape and began to retract, wrenching the dark figure into being.

*"Submit,"* the shape said, *"it is the will of the Many. Kneel and be one with us."*

A head became a torso, arms formed at the sides, followed by hips, legs, feet. A living shadow in the shape of a man, and to Marcus's horror, the longer he stared the more he realized it looked just like him. The void within given life. The Absence made manifest, pulled into reality by the indifferent universe above.

Marcus tried to scream, but no sound came. His voice was lost to the glacial terror coursing through his body and the agonizing heat swelling in his chest. Every muscle in his body spasmed in unison, forcing the air from his lungs in a pained gasp. Something was pushing against him from the inside. Something that wanted out.

*What the fuck was in that pill? What did I swallow? Warm, sticky—yes, it was warm. Alive. God, was it alive?*

The tendrils recoiled from their dark marionette, slithering back up the walls and over the threshold into the vacuum of space. The living shadow took a step toward him. Black goo crawled and rippled across the surface of its body.

*"I will fill the emptiness in you and together we will serve the Many. You and me. One."*

Marcus raised his hands in defense as the doppelganger closed in, but his gesture was in vain. The force welling up inside finally broke through his chest, tearing through sinew and meat and the fabric of his T-shirt. Flowers of pain blossomed before his eyes, and before he lost his mind to the sweet relief of unconsciousness, he glimpsed the source of his agony: small hands extended outward from his chest cavity, reaching for the dark shape standing before him.

Their fingers entwined and pulled themselves together. A perfect union. One.

A phone rang from somewhere else in his apartment. Marcus Taylor opened his eyes and found himself staring at the bathroom ceiling. Sunlight slipped through the curtains in vibrant sheets, and he watched dust motes float lazily in the air. A dark, viscous puddle surrounded his body, and it rippled with life when it sensed movement.

He climbed to his feet and walked into the bedroom to answer his phone. He nearly fumbled the device and struggled to move his fingers across the screen. The sensation was new, weird. Electrical impulses commanding tissue to pull and contract. Such an odd vessel.

"Mr. Taylor?"

"Yes."

"This is Veronica at Dr. Patel's office. I'm calling to follow up on your clinical trial. I just need you to answer a few short questions." She waited a beat, took his silence as affirmation, and went on. "Did you ingest the dosage of Endoximine Xytocycline-44 yesterday evening?"

"Yes."

"How do you feel?"

"Whole."

"Did you commune with the Many?"

"Yes."

"Wonderful. Welcome to the ZZ Initiative, Mr. Taylor. Glory be to the Many. Enjoy your new vessel of flesh. Be sure to collect any residue for processing."

"Glory be to the Many," he said, canceling the call. He took the empty prescription bottle and returned to the bathroom. The black puddle on the floor shuddered in his presence, seeking his vessel of flesh. He collected the sample, fascinated by its darkly purple hue, and watched as it shaped itself into an oval.

Satisfied, he stood in front of the mirror. The sunlight warmed his skin, burning away the excess residue coating the contours of his chest. Thin trails of black smoke rose from his body, but he did not perspire. Those days were beyond him.

Marcus Taylor 2.0 stared at his reflection and traced fingers along the lines of his face, testing the rigidity of his skin, the resistance of the muscles there. He pulled down one of his eyelids and examined the gelatinous globe sitting firmly in its socket. Dark veins squirmed along the rim like tadpoles, vanishing just beyond the horizon of flesh. He reminded himself to blink from time to time. *They have to blink on occasion.*

He took the phone and dialed Cathy's number. She answered on the third ring.

"Marcus?"

"Hello, darling. Would you meet me for coffee? I've experienced a breakthrough."

*And smile, too. They're more pliable when met with a smile.*

"A breakthrough? What do you mean? With the medication?"

"Oh yes," Marcus said. "I'm a new man."

He pulled the muscles in his face, lifting his lips, marveling at the expression staring back at him in the mirror. It took no effort at all.

# WHAT REMAINED
# OF HER

*- Jennifer Loring -*

The media never identified the women as "beloved sister" or "cherished daughter" or even "devoted mother." It was always "dead hooker" or "slain prostitute." Funny how that was the only time they defined women by their profession and not their relationship to a man.

Funny.

Jamie skateboarded through her neighborhood —*You're too old for that*, her father had said, though she'd just turned eighteen. She suspected he really meant, *Stop acting like a boy*— the myth of suburbia perpetuated with cookie-cutter houses and HOA-approved landscaped lawns. Homogenized, bourgeois happiness. It was a myth as rancid as meat left in the sun. As a body dumped on a desolate stretch of highway. Wherever the nightmare ended, if it ever did, it began here.

Her middle-aged neighbor knelt in his front yard with a hacksaw, attacking fallen branches from a recent storm. He was proficient, focused, and she wondered what else that saw had cut through. Whose basement was hiding the secret. The rumors had sprung up like weeds as soon as the case broke—sex rings, orgies, corruption in the highest echelons of county law enforcement and government. But not here. Here, the community repelled those rumors by spraying the media with one sentence: "It's not a local."

It was never a local, until it was. And those same residents would gaze into cameras with tearful eyes and hands over their hearts and bleat, "I had no idea. How could this happen here?" As though "here" were some fairytale plane of existence immune to the ravages of a national heroin epidemic, a far-right economy, and an explosion of racial and class tensions. "Here" was an illusion painted white and protected with six-foot privacy fences, where women insisted behind glassy-eyed Xanax smiles that they were content to be housewives and soccer moms because that's what God intended.

In the city, no one wanted to get to know you at all, but it wasn't "here," and that had been enough for Jamie's sister. Morgan had run from the lurking darkness, toward the lights. There was money to be made. A life to be lived. The irony being that she was more famous missing—presumed dead—than she was ever likely to be alive.

Jamie's neighbors returned her glances but without sympathy. They'd never say it aloud, that Morgan got what she deserved. They just wanted the story, the blight upon their community, to go away.

Her skateboard wheels rumbled along the asphalt as twilight spread across the sky in a purple stain. Her parents had warned her not to stay out after dark; everyone's parents had. Especially after "Morgan" had appeared on her phone's screen two weeks ago, when Morgan was still a missing hooker and not a presumably dead one. A relief too good to be true flooded through Jamie even as the voice on the other end began speaking. A voice that did not belong on Morgan's phone.

"Is this Jamie?" Oddly, she could not distinguish whether it was male or female. That the voice seemed so far away, so distorted, as if it were speaking to her on a frequency she wasn't meant to hear, raised chills down her spine.

"Yes. Who is this?"

Jamie's mother scuttled into the dining room with her phone and dialed the police. Jamie heard her murmuring about pinging Morgan's cell.

"Your sister is with us," the caller whispered. "Are you like her?"

"What the hell are you talking about?" *Just keep them on the line long enough for a trace...*

138

But they were too smart for that. The line went dead after sixty, maybe ninety seconds. Every time—and there were several. When the cops finally did ping the cell towers, they pinpointed the calls as originating in mid-city during rush hour. It could have been literally anyone.

The final call, a week to the day Morgan's clothes were discovered.

"Please," Jamie said, struggling to maintain any semblance of composure. The psycho wouldn't keep calling if not to feed on her emotions. "Just tell me where she is."

"Are you like her?" The same question every time. "I know where you live, Jamie. I know what you look like. But you don't yet understand."

A gasp slipped out. She sealed her lips together.

Dead air.

Another week had passed since the unearthing of the clothes. Maybe they—he?—were waiting for a moment like this, when she was alone and distracted. And part of her didn't care, because she owed it to Morgan to look into that man's eyes and understand the horror her sister had experienced in her final moments.

Jamie remembered watching her from the kitchen window that last night, the darkness folding in around Morgan as though it had been waiting for her. She had a job, and Jamie's voiced sense of foreboding did not dissuade her; he was paying a thousand dollars. Her job had been their little secret, until she went missing. Jamie had fled the house and her parents' wrath and stayed with friends for three days.

"I'll be fine, just like always." Morgan hugged her. "I'm already gone," she whispered.

Jamie's voice caught in her throat. Ice crystallized down her back.

Morgan had vanished into the suburban night, into a car whose plate Jamie could have read if she'd followed as instinct had begged her to. Her failure was the kind of torment in which hindsight specialized.

After another awkward dinner with her parents, who had nothing left to say to her or to each other, Jamie retreated to her room. She spent her nights searching for clues in Morgan's online profiles, chasing leads down the internet's darkest alleys where the cops fear to tread, at least the ones who weren't perverts.

"21 & ready 4 fun!!! w4m" screamed the headline of Morgan's last ad. Beneath it, she posed bent slightly forward. Black lace panties revealed her ass cheeks to the camera. This was what men learned of Morgan: that she was a thing. A collection of body parts used for their pleasure. She was desperate for something, so desperate that she was no longer afraid of the dark. "Will do almost anything," the ad boasted, and Jamie wept. Her sister, who would have done almost anything, could have done almost anything. Not all dead hookers came from broken homes or lacked an education.

Morgan's room had been untouched, a museum exhibit on lost daughters, except by Jamie. She tried on Morgan's favorite lipstick, "Marilyn," a deep red that gave her lips a lustrous wet look. She flicked through hangers of clothing in her closet, pieces Morgan had ordered online or picked up from sex shops in the city. The clerks must have known they were selling mostly to strippers and prostitutes, not housewives looking to spice up their marriages. Did they ever wonder what became of those girls, especially the ones who suddenly stopped coming in?

Jamie stuffed a few outfits—her own and Morgan's, shoes, and the lipstick into Morgan's overnight bag. Morgan had stashed her money on the top shelf in the back of the closet, in a makeup box. Jamie emptied it into her purse. She spied Morgan's journal on the nightstand, felt under the mattress for the key, and stuffed both into the bag.

Her mother was locked in the master suite, crying again. She didn't know where her father had gone.

There was approximately one serial killer for every six million people. One grain of sand on a vast beach. One drop in an endless ocean. The cops wouldn't risk one of their own to lure him out, not for missing hookers.

But it was summer, and Jamie had had all day every day to educate herself. He wouldn't stop until he was in prison or dead.

Neither would she.

Not a local. Right. Only a local knew there were almost no lights out here and night was like the bottom of the ocean. Until the missing girls, only locals knew this place existed at all.

Jamie had called her mother but didn't tell her where she was. No way to explain what she was doing without breaking her heart.

The cops didn't make connections, because they didn't care. Call them when it wasn't a prostitute. They insisted that similar murders all along the coast weren't related. They'd never do simple research into the sites where women listed their services and with dawning horror realize that nearly two dozen had abruptly stopped advertising. Even if they did, they'd rationalize it away. The girls must have cleaned up and gone home. All right, maybe they *had* been murdered, but most likely by a pimp or a john. The cops wouldn't confess that they had intentionally failed.

Even though serial killers' favorite targets were and always had been prostitutes.

Jamie sat in her car. Occasional headlights flared in her rearview; taillights faded like red eyes closing. Countless other clues lay in the reeds the police claimed they'd scoured, except that clothes—only clothes—kept turning up. All along a stretch of highway hundreds of miles long.

*Unrelated.*

*I could wait for him,* she thought, gazing out at the waves where moonlight danced like ghosts that died again when they struck the shore. A stupid thought. Too much ground to cover.

Jamie drove on and pulled into a diner parking lot. Recent rains had left the city slick and glistening as if newly born, awash in neon that reflected in windows and puddles. The greasy perfume of grilling meat, frying onions, and hot oil enticed her into a booth at the back with a chipped Formica table. Her shoes stuck to the checkered floor and a caramel stain that suggested spilled soda. She eyed the dessert display in a glass case up front, then turned her attention to the smudged menu, sweeping away granules of salt or sugar left by the previous customer. At the next booth, the wet-fart squish of a ketchup bottle cut through the din of clanking silverware and small talk.

Jamie ordered a cup of strong, burnt coffee and a cheeseburger. When she pulled a napkin from the metal dispenser, it shredded in half. She laid her phone on the table and waited for her food.

Jamie glanced around the diner. She didn't make eye contact; she was already afraid of what she saw in other people. The effortless capacity for evil.

Her skin crawled. She'd lost her appetite, but she wasn't ready to leave. She was safe here. The bright lights, the chatter, the sizzle of the flattop all grounded her in the world she thought she'd been prepared to abandon for her sister's sake. But she couldn't stay forever.

Jamie paid her bill, her untouched food cooling on the table, and dashed to her car. The city was an orchestra of sirens, hydraulics, shoes clicking on concrete. Dense with people and yet she was utterly alone, as if drifting through space.

Nothing stood between the city and the suburb where Jamie and her sister had been born and raised except that long, barren, lightless tract of highway. In the summer, the beach drew anglers and the occasional swimmer, but that was not what the county had envisioned. The development intended to exploit tourist traffic fell through year after year, as though already haunted by its future. The voices of the dead whispered through the reeds, through the surf breaking on the shore.

Sometimes Jamie dreamed that she was Morgan on the night she'd made her fateful decision to get in that car. Now she stood on the shoulder of the outbound lane, facing the marsh where flourishing vegetation had consumed memorials to the presumed-dead girls, but she didn't think of Morgan. She thought instead of the catalyst that drove one to view other human beings not as peers but as prey. The itch so maddening that only the taking of life could satisfy it.

It was in everyone, she believed, lying dormant. Most would never encounter their trigger. But for that tiny percentage of the population...

Jamie waded into the reeds. The toothy plants along the estuary bit at her arms and face, opened her skin in offering. In sacrifice. She owed the girls that much for still being alive.

Jamie checked into a Holiday Inn Express on the outskirts of the city, where she lay in bed and dreamed without sleeping. Morgan was staring into her mirror, her eyes wide but empty as she stroked the air over her body.

*There's nothing here,* she murmured. *It's all gone. Do you see it?*

*I'm already gone.*

The key to tracking down Morgan's killer lay in those words; Jamie was sure of it. Something beyond their work in the sex trade tying all the girls together. Something she'd missed.

Jamie sat up and opened her laptop. She kept a folder full of documents and photos regarding the case, but newspapers and magazines cannibalized interviews with the victims' families and friends from each other and offered no new insights. Just the usual speculation of drugs or mental illness that might drive a young woman into dangerous sex work.

Her stomach growled. She ordered a pizza and soda online and returned to the gigabytes of documents that, no matter how she scoured them, revealed nothing. Jamie groaned and slammed the lid as someone knocked on the door. She dug a twenty out of her purse, then peered through the peephole at a guy in his mid-thirties holding a pizza box and a twenty-ounce Coke.

She opened the door. He remained oddly silent as she accepted the food, and scanned her head to toe as though he'd seen her before and was trying to place where.

"Thank you." Jamie held out the cash pinched between her thumb and forefinger so she didn't have to touch him. "Keep the change."

A shadow passed over his face, his eyes. Did he recognize her from TV? The media loved a serial killer story, and she'd been on every newsmagazine and crime show there was.

"Have a nice night." He stuffed the bill into his pocket but kept looking back at her as he walked away, as if he wanted her to remember him.

Jamie shut the door and engaged both locks, then set her food on the desk and rooted through the overnight bag for pajamas. She remembered Morgan's journal.

*I've learned something we were never meant to know.*

*One day I was looking in the mirror, and it was like a lightbulb went off, to use a really stupid cliché.*

*It happened a few days later. Small parts at first, fingers and toes. Then whole limbs. My body. My head. My face was the last to go, and for a couple of days, there was just a skull looking back at me.*

*I met someone who said they helped people like me. I thought they meant prostitutes, but it's not like that. It's so much more.*

Jamie's blood curdled. She shoved the pizza away.

*I'm going to meet them. If anyone reads this, please don't be sad. You can let me go now. They'll understand one day, when we're all gone. They'll see what they've done. And we will haunt them for the rest of their lives.*

Jamie dropped the journal as if it were coated with poison. How had Morgan hidden it so well, that she'd lost her mind so quickly and with such devastation?

The cops had been going about it completely wrong. He wasn't hunting them. If Morgan was telling the truth, the girls had sought him out.

There were sections of the city where women were not people but body parts. They were headless mannequins in storefront windows; they were neon signs with exaggerated breasts and waving legs. They were skintight dresses and booty shorts accentuating their most important assets, and calves defined by six-inch heels. This, Jamie thought, was how it began. The depersonalization. The loss of identity. Few of the women out here even used their real names. When you were a mouth or a vagina, maybe a pair of feet if you were lucky, you didn't need a name.

The liquid shine of the glass and steel skyscrapers in the downtown core just over a mile away painted a stark contrast to the red-light district's graffiti-streaked buildings and trash-strewn streets. But this was the city's true heart, which kept beating long after those shining monuments to capitalism emptied out for the night. Sex was the heart of everything.

Jamie stopped in front of a boarded-up window. Across it, spray-painted in red: *Do you see behind the curtain?*

She didn't know what she was looking for, only that someone—some*thing*—had wanted her to see this. The people prowling about grew more sinister, more desperate as the night wore on. Drug deals were brazen and so were the johns who invited women into their cars. Jamie said a silent prayer for their safety, and her own. The more she lingered, the more cars that slowed as they passed and the more that pimps hunting for new pussy ogled her. She reached into her purse and lifted her phone just enough to check the time.

An unread text message: *Do you know what you're looking for?*

She snapped her head up and scanned the passersby, the shadowy alleys where cigarettes flared and money was exchanged, for her tormentor. She wanted to grab these women and shake the truth out of them. Prostitutes always knew something, even if they wished they didn't. They were the city's eyes and ears, but they'd only talk if it benefitted them in some way. Just a matter of survival.

*No,* she texted back, *but I need to.*

*Come find us, then.*

She received no further messages.

They were called "lot lizards," the women who roamed truck stops and offered sex to long-haul drivers. If her ultimate destination lay somewhere along this highway, both truckers and the prostitutes who serviced them would have heard of it.

*Keith Hunter Jesperson. Scott William Cox. John Robert Williams. Bruce Mendenhall.* All long-haul truckers. Even the FBI had admitted it was the ideal profession for a serial killer. Over five hundred murders near highways. Two hundred suspects.

Jamie made short trips at first. Some of the truckers were kind—family men worried about her because she reminded them of their daughters. The kind ones told her stories, urban legends about the black dog, high beams, vanishing hitchhikers, The Devil's Highway. Many others were loners, antisocial, and she couldn't tell by looking at them that they would beat her, or attempt to rape her. A blast of pepper spray had bought her several narrow escapes, and now when she arrived at truck stops, she peered in through the windows before stepping inside, scanning for the men who had already assaulted her so she could hide until they left.

She didn't fit in, and her keen awareness of it heightened her self-consciousness. She didn't smoke, when *everyone* out here smoked. Fine lines framed their mouths from the puckering of lips around a pack-a-day habit. The lot lizards clustered in twos or stood by themselves, cigarettes in hand, tight skirts or pants and tank tops revealing everything a man cared to know about them. Freckled chests and necklace lines around their throats. She was so much younger than most of them, and she could feel the resentment rippling off them like heat from sunbaked asphalt. Nipples prominent in the cooling night air beneath thin, cheap fabric, braless. An advertisement.

"You lost?"

Jamie looked up. A trucker, in a hat from beneath which spilled reddish curls matching a fluffy beard. The hat sported a picture of a bear with the caption "Grizzly." A T-shirt with faded grease stains conformed to the contours of a beer belly. "No," she said. "I'm just...looking for someone."

The trucker extracted a cigarette from his breast pocket and a lighter from his jeans. The brass Zippo was engraved with "Daddy" on the lid; she hoped it was from his kids. "Yeah? Maybe I've seen him. Or her. You with them?" He cocked his head toward a couple of women at the corner of the building.

Jamie took stock of her black jeans and blousy black top. "No...?"

The trucker chuckled. "Trust me. Out here, days and weeks on the road, doesn't matter what a woman is wearing. One of these guys will think you're for sale."

She rubbed her arms. "I need to go somewhere. I need to...know something. About the prostitutes who disappear."

He took a long drag and blew the smoke toward the sky. He said nothing.

"The highway. The stories."

"Yeah," he said after another long silence. Another long drag.

"I want to ride with you for a little while."

"How do you know I'm not one of them?"

A black eye and a constellation of bruises along her neck and collarbone told him her tale. The hookers side-eyed her and went their separate ways, one into the diner and the other into the darkness. The edges of the moon looked sharp enough to peel open the sky.

"I don't," she said.

The cab smelled of diesel, unwashed flesh, and nicotine, despite the pine air freshener's best efforts. Greasy fast food wrappers were lodged between the seats, and a Big Gulp sat in the cup holder, its contents sloshing back and forth.

"Lots of urban legends out here," the trucker who had eventually introduced himself as Steve said. Steve's handle was indeed "Grizzly," but he'd confessed that truckers rarely used handles anymore. Some companies had even banned CBs.

"There are twenty-five long-haul truckers in prison for serial murder." She'd heard the legends already and needed to steer the conversation in her desired direction. She watched the lights flicker by, studied license plates and memorized the funnier vanity plates before their cars darted into another lane and away. C4TL4DY on a KIA Soul. F3ATUR3 on a Beetle.

Steve lit up a smoke. "That right?"

"There's a story that a network of serial killers operates along I-95. Have you heard it?"

He flicked some ashes out the window. Even fresh air streaming in didn't kill the odors that had seeped into every surface. "Hear a lot of things over the radio. Most of it's bullshit."

"What about girls who..." Jamie chewed on her lip, trying to find an explanation that didn't sound crazy. Except it *was* crazy. "Who think their bodies are disappearing. It's a psychiatric condition. Cotard's delusion. I read about it."

"Nothin' psychiatric about it." Steve didn't speak again until they pulled into the next rest stop. "See these women? Not just the hookers. See the way men look at them? The way they look at *you*? The way they're always gonna look at you." He opened the cab door and climbed down.

"Where is he?"

"Not 'he.'"

Jamie slammed her fist on the dashboard. "Then who? *What?*"

Steve shook his head. "You're not ready. You still think you can change it, but men aren't smart. Only thing that'll get through to us is if you're all gone. And it knows." He shifted his gaze to a hooker climbing into the cab parked a few yards away. "You should get out."

*They'll understand one day, when we're all gone. They'll see what they've done.*

"I have to know what happened to my sister. It said it knew where I lived. What I looked like."

"Of course it does. Look, I heard about you over the radio, all right? The girl who keeps asking questions. You're not looking for a serial killer. You're not even looking for a man."

"Then what? How do you know all of this?"

"I wish it wasn't like this for you. For any of you. We should've been better." Steve slammed the door. He tugged the brim of his hat down and, hands stuffed in his jeans pockets, trudged into the service plaza.

Jamie carefully lowered herself from the cab and dropped onto the asphalt. Her phone buzzed.

*Unknown caller* glowed from the cracked screen stepped on by a would-be rapist.

The air had gone cold and still. She answered but said nothing.

"Don't worry," the voice whispered. "You're so close."

Jamie shoved the phone back into her pocket. When she withdrew her hand, she could no longer see her fingers.

They were looking at her. Leering. They were always looking, leering, and so Jamie had half-convinced herself that she did indeed still exist. They would wink at her, call her "honey" or "baby" or "sweetheart," pat or pinch her ass when she walked by to use the invariably filthy bathroom. The haggard waitresses met her with sympathetic gazes but, in the interest of self-preservation, no assistance. It was already too hard to get by in this world, and in this corner of it, the twenty-first century did not intend to arrive any time soon.

She was almost gone. She stared into the mirror where a blue-eyed skull grinned back at her as though withholding a life-changing secret. The overwhelming urge to rush outside possessed her.

It was early September, yet icy air sucked her breath away. Beyond ragged hedges and the picnic tables accompanied by rusted grills, a massive shadow coiled through the trees and along the ground. Lights twinkled within it like stars, like entire galaxies, so beautiful that it blinded her. The diner's neon and the lights in the parking lot dimmed. Even the moon itself faded, a bulb experiencing a sudden energy drain. Within the blackness, stars flared in explosive birth. The void's edges now obscured the entire world. What remained of her was dissolving into particles, molecules, forming new bonds within it. They were all there, a planetary history of women, and the rest would come in time. Watch it all collapse together. Drive men mad with memories and yearning.

It was the least they could do.

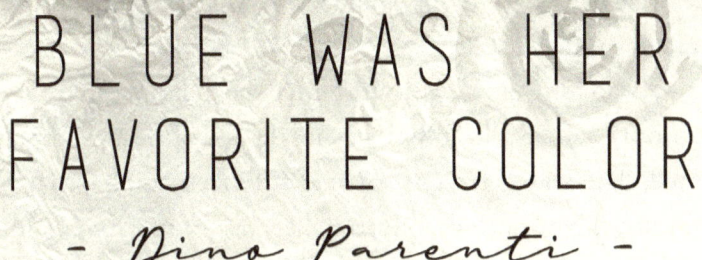

# BLUE WAS HER FAVORITE COLOR
## - Dino Parenti -

T hree Sundays in a row now, the ritual the same each time.

Abby would leave in the morning after a hasty breakfast. What had been a steady custom of piled flapjacks, two scoops of scramble, and three sausage links—a monstrous appetite for a ten-year-old—had progressively shriveled to one piece of plain toast and half-a-glass of OJ.

A quick jaunt to the florist at the corner came next, always bustling on a Sunday for a small farming community. People buying blossoms for church, for weddings, for the succor of color.

Her flowers procured with chore money, she skipped to our garage—a repurposed barn separate from the house—her blonde ponytail cropping the air behind her as if urging time to keep up.

She ducked inside, emerging minutes later with a mason jar full of water, topped with a handled cap. This she swung against her leg in time with whatever hippie ditty her mother had been fond of humming before dying with a placid smile, staring up at hospital ceiling tile.

Flowers and water secured, Abby loped across knee-deep fescue towards the gulch rifled by water not a month earlier by the storm. The storm that washed away her little brother.

The little brother who, eighteen months prior, traded his mother's life for his right to emerge into the world at the angles he best saw fit to.

The wash I couldn't bring myself to come within twenty feet of even at the height of the search, but which Abby traversed as if breaking a gateway into a realm for which I lacked all charms or sorcery for admission.

Beyond the wash, the tree line of sugar maples swallowed her as she took a southwest bearing along the borders of the Anspaugh and Frick farms.

If the ritual held to form, she would return well after lunch, tired of body but revived of spirit.

I started watching her go last week after she'd disappeared for half-the-day the prior Sunday, heaping on me levels of fear I thought well surmounted. The search for my boy had still been going strong that day, along with hope. Not of finding Justin alive, but of just *finding* him, for at only eighteen months old, survival was beyond any honest expectation.

I wasn't even aware Abby was gone until I returned from combing the northern shores of Newport River to rest and sneak a gulp of whiskey, and spotted her through the living room window emerging from the woods. The entire time I'd figured her for upstairs in her room.

When I asked her where she'd gone, she said she went to talk to Mom.

There was no anger in our exchange, no judgment. We'd both been wrung of most all emotion by then. Whatever worry I entertained was brief, knowing her mother's grave resided on her parents' farm an acre away between trusted neighbors. I chalked it up to fatherhood nerves wiggling through—the redundant panic of a man who grew up fostered and never figured to make a family of his own someday.

In the end I let it go. She had a right to cope her own way, and it seemed safe enough now that the rains were over for the year.

And now on the third Sunday after losing Justin, I watched Abby from her bedroom window leaving for her mourning errand. Her mother's book of flowers sat on her desk, opened to hydrangeas. They were Larissa's favorites, and I wondered when she told Abby this because I never did. The book had become part of her post-storm ritual, as if Justin's disappearance-death had sparked a communion dormant during her mother's life.

Watching Abby pass through the trees from her room, last month's events unspooled in my head on cue. I'd left for the airport in Durham four hours earlier to beat the storm. A work weekend in Boston. Milly, their grandmother—Larissa's mother—watching them both for me, had fallen asleep. It was what she kept apologizing for on the phone before I could pry any information from her. The facts remain muddy to this day, and I couldn't remember who saw what when, but *someone* claimed to have spotted Justin's little form, etched by lightning strike, arms out in airplane liftoff mode, waddling through rain and tall grass until suddenly he couldn't be seen anymore.

After landing in Logan I immediately booked the first flight back to Durham, which wasn't till 4AM. The whole time I was being fed details over the phone, first by Milly, then by the local police.

Harlowe Creek had swelled and crested its banks, trenching a roiling brown finger across our front yard. They surmised Justin had simply not seen it and walked straight into it.

I kept picturing Justin in his bright blue Thomas the Train overalls with the puffy, jiggly eyes on the front lapel. The right one always came undone and we were perpetually gluing it back on to little success.

A hand-me-down from Abby, who'd herself worn it to death.

Justin's screechy peals of laughter between thunder cracks. How he loved the water and being wet, even clothed. Many a time I'd have to catch him before he hopped into the half-filled bathtub upstairs while still dressed, breaking into contagious belly-laughs without fail.

By the time I got home after several flood detours, the sun was up, the storm long past, and a division of police and volunteers had besieged my property.

After hugging Milly and Abby inside the house, both of whom were still soaking wet, I was beckoned outside by the police chief and asked the standard questions—where I'd been, what time I'd left, etc. Then he broke it down: the flash flood likely swept my boy into the Newport River, its current pushing him into the channel, then through Beaufort Inlet, and finally into the Atlantic.

He promised to search every pebble of shore, every drop of water, but it didn't look good.

So for the next two weeks I searched with them, barely going to work, spending all my downtime near Abby. Always a reserved child, she was likely internalizing, surely levying blame on me for her family getting halved in under two years. And then she started taking flowers to her mother, and I kept searching. But I worried as to what else she might've been doing while gone. What thoughts caromed through her head while unburdened from home. Unburdened from me.

The following Sunday, Abby kept to her sacrament: a next-to-nothing breakfast, buying flowers, grabbing water, and plunging into the woods.

This time she returned near dark, close to suppertime.

As upset as I was, I couldn't bring myself to yell at her, though I did ask why she was so late.

"It took me longer to pot the flowers," she said.

Her chocolate eyes and mouth pitched in an undying backslash that perfectly ghosted her mother's. Faces crafted for hoarding retorts and denunciations.

I was exhausted, having spent hours up and down the southern shore of Newport River, probing the sandbars, all for naught. The search parties had dwindled in the last two weeks, as Justin had been all but officially declared dead, but I kept looking. There was simply nothing else I could do.

In the end I hugged Abby. Her arms gradually wound around my waist—the most reaction I'd gotten since before Justin disappeared—but she said nothing, retreating to her room without dinner just as Larry arrived.

Larry Anspaugh, our neighbor to the southeast, had been checking on us every day since the storm, often bringing leftover dinner his wife made. He was a kind old coot with pomaded gray hair and eyes greener than jades, a wicked chortle that time-warped me back to middle-school hijinks always at hand.

That night I told him about Abby's sojourns, and asked if he'd seen her by chance late Sunday mornings.

"Oh yeah," he said, forking half-a-yam into his mouth. "Seen her skipping along the meadow, borders mine and the Frick farm. They got this old potting shed out there."

He must've caught something shift in my expression, because he stuttered to a stop and squinted at me over his fork, tongue sliding between the seam of lips.

"Looks like I hit a nerve," he said.

Being in no state to explain myself, I shoved in a mouthful of chicken stew and waved him on, asking him to tell me more about Abby and this shed.

"Well, she's gone in it the two times I'd seen her. Doubt even the Fricks knew about it, the damn thing's practically more on my land than theirs. Far as I knew they didn't even bother to clean it out before moving two months ago."

Thomas and Pamela Frick. The trashy but affable young couple to Larry's east, now in Oregon plying their trade, riding the pot wave.

"In any case," continued Larry, "I'd hear Abby singing in there. Lord knows what a girl her age occupies herself with, but about an hour later she'd come out, a clay pot of flowers in her arms and jar of water clipped to her belt, and she'd keep on heading southeast. Never see her on the way back, so I reckon she takes a different route home. All that terrain's safe though—level and unpopulated—so I wouldn't worry much. But I promise to keep my eye out just the same."

We finished dinner, then shared a shot of Jim Beam on the porch where he mocked my embarrassing lack of pastoral acumen, and I his technical ones—how something called the *internet* allowed me to still work remotely as a financial planner—and before long he slouched back home chuckling to a crescent moon.

My thoughts rarely shifted from that shed. Whatever Abby did there, it seemed to be making her happy. And yet I still fretted.

The following Sunday, I decided to follow her.

Fog had slithered in, knuckling over the hummocks to the southeast like fig tree roots. I had half a mind to tell her to stay home, but neither did I want to interfere with whatever passed for healing, so I let her pink jeans and olive bomber jacket get a head start before peeling myself from behind the garage to follow.

Crossing the wash accused of taking my son proved the hardest, partly from a sudden need to imagine a final imprint of his small feet in the dry clay. A marker of his last earthly moment.

All that remained was a smooth channel marred by recent adult and canine tracks.

Regardless, the footing proved daunting and twice I nearly face planted on the bronze clay. By the time I scampered up the opposite end I just glimpsed the pink of Abby's pants vanishing into the tree line between nimbus bands of fog.

Entering the gauntlet of trees, it didn't take long for me to lose my bearings. Even if the fog, warping distance and time alike, hadn't been present to blot the sun, it was easy to picture myself walking in endless, panicked circles. Had I not managed but a hint of rose bobbing in my peripheral vision, I might've done just that.

I pushed on, moving in the direction of color, trusting that my ten-year-old had developed a mastery of instinct now shuttered in her middle-aged father. The fog kept congealing, extracting metal and brine from the air, as if sky and sea had joined forces to reclaim the earth, and by the time I wandered flailing and stumbling into what seemed like an opening, my heart was drum-rolling and icy sweat shivved all my folds and creases.

Down at my feet, what was dense root and a carpet of leaves had become the lumpy crabgrass of a meadow. The fog waned in enough places there for me to see an opposing tree-line, which I started for.

I'd made it partway when I heard something behind me. What began as the sputter of a distant car with bad timing quickly morphed into the looming breaths of something unmistakably four-legged and aggressive, and it jumpstarted me into a high-step for the trees.

Risking a look back, I beheld the charging mongrel as it coalesced from the pall in a time-lapsed Polaroid.

I huffed and kicked my all, and only the tapping out of its tether waking the grass behind it—a sudden jerk that put the yowl in its otherwise chomping jaws—kept it from easily chasing me down.

Hands on my knees, coughing and spitting out my shredded lungs, I glanced up at the massive bloodhound as it repeatedly yanked itself towards me before settling into a left-right pace, head low, scarlet eyes locked, saliva snarling in coils onto the grass.

"Fuck you," I said. A stupid, useless gesture, and it boomed several retort barks that pummeled my chest.

Wind gathered, I lumbered towards the trees, eyes smoldering back what I hoped translated to explanation, challenge, defiance in my canine foe's brain.

The tattered bloodhound kept stalking its ground, all the muscle and kinetic go-get-'em of ancient predators, its howl-barks echoing in French-horn peals across the glen.

Having lost Abby by then, I settled for making it out of the woods, hedging towards what I figured was the highway. Eventually I stumbled onto Harker Road. I was pretty certain south was to my left, and before long Larry Anspaugh's colonial revival peeked between the leaves.

All told, I'd wandered nearly a mile from home.

Larry sat on his porch, seeing me before I saw him and waving me over.

"What the hell are you gallivanting out in the fog for?" he asked through pipe smoke, tittering as if from a joke unearthed after years.

I shrugged. Told him that morning walks did me good. That I thought I'd emulate Abby.

That just invited more good-natured chortles and further condemnation for my country ignorance.

The bloodhound's distant baying still scoring the morning, I asked Larry if he knew anything about it.

"Oh, that," he said, switching the pipe to the other corner of his mouth. "The Fricks left her. Word is the dog went mad, though she's just plain mean. Sometimes animals, like people, they aren't born right, yeah? Never even knew the dog was there until I all but stumbled over Pamela Frick sunbathing last summer. Hot little number that woman, even with all them tattoos." He suckled on that reverie, offering it smoke and smirk. "Thank god that dog was asleep and tied up, or it would've chomped my balls off. Anyway, I've been lobbing her hotdogs from afar. Filling her trough from a hose while she eats so she won't charge. Keep meaning to call animal control. Ain't no way to leave a dog, no matter how bad a bitch she is."

He rambled some more about the Fricks's "queer" ways before slowing himself down with wistful small-talk. I said little, thankful that he never brought up Justin and the search, and left shortly thereafter.

That evening, after Abby came home and I heated up a pizza for dinner, of which she only had a slice, I asked her calmly but point-blank where she went and what she did on Sundays.

She just gazed out the window, smile floating someplace uncharted, and said, "Mom and I just talk."

The whole time she watched me through a steady sidelong, probing my thoughts and tsk-tsk-ing me for their flights and heresies.

I brought up the bloodhound. That Larry Anspaugh had told me about it, and that she should be very careful to avoid on account of its meanness.

She said that she knew. That kids in school have told her about it, and that she gives it a wide berth each time.

Then, as if changing a TV channel, delight swelled her face, and she said, "Dad, the Pollard's mouser cat had kittens, and I would love to have one if that's okay. They're *soooo* cute."

Despite her rare display of joy, I was unsure if that was a good idea. She locked again with those dark eyes of hers, knowing I was thinking precisely that. Her impish smile so like her mother's, mining my defenses, siphoning my spirit, and for the briefest, most lucid of moments, I understood odium for a child.

As private amends for my heinous thoughts, I took her to the Pollard's the next day after school, and she picked out the two sister calicos of the five-kitten litter. The whole way home they purred against her chest like idling Harleys.

I sat on the porch the following Sunday as Abby bought her flowers. Before going to the garage to fetch her water jar, she stopped by and showed them to me.

"These are lupines," she said, her voice measured, academic. "Most were purple, so I had to dig around to find the blue ones. Aren't they beautiful?"

Of course I agreed that they were, and no sooner was mason jar in hand than she was off.

I went up to her room to watch her from the window, and on impulse looked up lupines in her mother's flower book. Along with biological and regional information, each flower's mythological and symbolic properties were also listed

Their standard color, purple, had been underlined in pencil.

Purple is the color of majesty. Of good judgment and trustworthiness.

Under that, in Larissa's tight script, she'd written: *All reminders of their famine in our world.*

The undertow in the words pulled the Frick property shed into view, and a shudder mainlined through me from another realm.

That night, well after Abby had gone to bed, I decided to clean the upstairs bathroom, a chore long delayed.

Since it held the only bathtub in the house—a century-old claw-foot— it was Larissa's preferred bathroom, as well as the only place to bathe Justin. I don't remember even having set foot in it since he disappeared.

I grabbed gloves, sponges, and Ajax from the hall closet. From downstairs I could hear the kittens mewling and roughhousing in their box. It reminded me of Abby as a toddler, wreaking havoc. I went to work, starting on the toilet, then the sink, biding my time on the tub until I could no longer defer it, and just dove right in.

Some triviality Milly had shock-mumbled upon my return from Boston skipped through my brain. About the sinks not draining that night because of storm backup.

Milly, always suspicious of me. Never one-hundred-percent on board with the city boy wedding her country daughter.

No sooner had I thought that when something drew my attention. An object caught in the mesh plug. I reached in and picked it up.

One of the wobbly eyes from Justin's Thomas the Train overalls. The one that never stuck.

It sat in my palm, wavering of its own accord, as if searching my thoughts.

I put it in my pocket and walked out, leaving the tub only partially cleaned.

Outside, the Frick's abandoned bloodhound howled its grievances to a leaden sky.

Woke up the next Sunday to dreams of storms and iceboxes, and decided to head off Abby this time instead of following her to Larissa's grave.

Once more after breakfast I took my spot on the porch swing and watched her bound for the flower shop before returning with a single blue orchid.

Walking back to the garage, she said, "So many green ones, and only this one blue!" And she cocked it triumphantly in the air like a blue ribbon.

Before she even grabbed her customary water jar in the garage, I was hoofing it up the stairs and thumbing through Larissa's book for orchids.

Underlined: Green is harmony and tranquility.

Right under that in pencil, large as a theater marquee: *Green is also jealousy and fertility, but who needs those reminders?*

White-hot anger surged before I could tamp it down. I hadn't wanted a second child, but Larissa pressed it. Her payback for returning her to the life she swore never to relive. But it had gotten expensive living in the city. Plus, Abby was becoming more withdrawn. Quieter. Larissa felt she would grow out of it. I wanted her to grow up someplace safe, far from the danger and temptations of cities.

Larissa called me a quitter.

I slammed the book shut, then changed into shorts and running shoes, and jogged north on Harker Road towards Larissa's parents' farm.

Her final resting place.

By the time I got there I was on my last wind, thighs roaring and heart punching through my throat.

Making sure to skulk behind the trees so Milly or Don wouldn't spot me, I fumbled through prickly red buckeye and squatted between twin oaks about a dozen yards from Larissa's grave to wait for Abby. I didn't approach the raised plaque, still too vexed by Larissa's barbs, both from life as well as the grave.

I must've dozed off against the trunk because Abby's singing nearly prodded me to my feet, giving me away.

Turning onto my belly I watched between the fork of trunk as she approached her mother's marker, a terra-cotta pot as wide as a Frisbee embraced against her tummy. The orchid sprouted from it at an angle, as if a palm tree under serious gale.

Her process was fluid and precise, scooping out a hole near the lupines while speaking casually to her mother as if knelt right there next to her, asking how she enjoyed having Justin all to herself, especially because she never got to meet him outside her belly.

While her sincerity saddened me, it also nudged at deeper nerves. She was never that chummy with her mother in life, nor with me after her death.

After planting the orchid, Abby poured the water from the mason jars over all the flowers.

"Water from home," she said, smile flat upon her work.

I shuddered at the sight. An Andrew Wyeth come to life.

She then stirred the soil of the pot that held the orchid, and I thought I saw plastic poke through, like a grocery bag, before gathering up the pot, the jar, and starting back.

I toyed with the impulse to touch Larissa's grave after Abby was out of sight, but channeled that unrequited energy into beating my daughter home.

The subsequent Sunday was bright and clear for the first time in weeks.

Spying her from behind the oaks, I watched Abby smile into the sun, the blue hibiscus potted like a tiny piece of Hawaii captured, and she got right to work planting.

Before leaving the house, I looked them up, of course. There waited Larissa's writing under some yellow hibiscus.

*Yellow is cowardice. Yellow is milksop.*

Her task done, Abby started back.

I let her get a lead, but not enough to lose her, determined to ascertain her route from the grave to home.

For insurance, I brought binoculars.

With plenty of sunlight breaking the canopy, I had a good bead on her course, basically keeping to the Frick-Anspaugh boundary. Occasionally I'd have to mark her through the glass as she got well ahead, but through magnification, her pink jeans were easy to spot.

When I passed the clearing with the potting shed, I barely gave the slumping little shack a look. The icebox inside. How I dreaded what inferences, if any, my intrepid Abby may have determined.

I kept going.

A hundred yards later, Abby veered sharp to the west, and before I realized it we were in a meadow.

The same meadow with the bloodhound.

Which, to my horror, she walked straight towards.

The mongrel was a matted-henna lump laid out long under the sun, tied to the charred trunk of a dead hickory rising from the middle of the field. The amount of unspooled leader suggested it could cover virtually the entire perimeter of the paddock.

Too shocked at first to move, I almost hollered at Abby to run when the dog stirred.

Except that upon looking at her, it whipped its tail against the dirt and rolled onto its legs before sidling towards her in a full-body waggle.

Abby knelt before it, holding out her hands, which the dog submitted quickly to and licked.

From her pot she drew out what I could just confirm through my binoculars as a ziplock bag. Because of our angles I couldn't tell what was in it, but I assumed it to be kitten food she was feeding the mongrel.

Sated, the dog rolled onto its back and Abby rubbed its belly and even laid next to it for a hug—the beast easily longer than her—before leaving the pot and jar off to the side and heading home.

Through the binoculars, past the yawning animal, about half-a-dozen pots and mason jars stood empty in a tight flock.

The following week, Jacob's ladder for Abby.

Her face screwed in contempt, she cupped the little bushel of blue trumpeting flowers to her chest.

"Almost all of them were white! Who buys white Jacob's ladder?" she said, less to me on the porch than to the wind sighing from the north.

Into the garage she went as I stole back into the house.

The kittens were quiet in their box in the kitchen. Had been for a couple of days now. Abby finally taking the initiative to feed them early before doing anything else so they would sleep.

Upstairs to Larissa's book.

*Blue is soothing. Blue is peace.*

She'd underlined it three times.

What she'd written under that caused all the suspicions that scurried in the undergrowth of my brain for the better part of a month to leap out in unison.

I followed Abby straight to the shed this time.

She was in there for an hour. True to Larry's account, she hummed and sang the entire time, and I wanted to believe the thumping I heard was her foot in time with her music.

Jacob's ladder potted, she headed for her mother's grave where she whispered so I couldn't hear.

Her planting completed, I took a wider route back, passing her as quietly as I could, beating her to the bloodhound, keeping downwind, adjusting my angle and distance for best viewing optimization before hunching behind some boulders for cover.

By its perking ears and windmilling tail, it heard Abby from afar and threw up its snout to verify her, but never stood. How and when Abby and the mongrel made their accord, I couldn't say, this animal that would've ripped out my throat weeks back had its tether been less merciful.

Only in seeing Abby did the bloodhound finally rise.

Through the binoculars I watched her kneel before it, the animal slavering its muzzle as my daughter drew the ziplock baggie from the pot.

From my better profile vantage, I could see chunks of what looked like leathery meat she put up to the dog's nose, the animal lapping it from her palm with a puppy's tenderness.

Feeding done, Abby used the rest of the water from her jar to wash the dog's slobber from her hands before depositing it and the pot with the others—a colonnade of glass and terra-cotta.

Petting the dog a final time, she skipped back home.

With Abby out of the way, my eyes fell naturally on the dog again through the glass, and with it standing now I could see what it obscured while it was still lying down: bones of different sizes, some old and nearly black, some much fresher.

Scattered about them, matted fur, lumpy and rusted through with dried blood. But enough of the calico peeked through. Enough to know that Abby knew. What Larissa had written under *blue* left little doubt.

*He fucks that whore in that disgusting shed!!!*

Having wandered back home in a daze, my body listed towards the garage.

In one corner under a tarp, a couple of dozen mason jars filled with water. Each one I lifted and examined until I spotted the black fleck floating at the top of one. It had to be there. Neither one had been on Justin's overalls when I'd found him.

The second Thomas the Train eye.

Like the sinks, the tub wouldn't drain because of storm backup. Milly would've seen that if she'd gone upstairs, but couldn't because of her bad hip. She also would've seen Abby scooping the water out of the bathtub with mason jars. Exactly how I found her when I got home from Boston. Police were already searching for Justin in the storm, but that's just the story Abby had told them.

Because she wanted to show *me*.

Justin in the tub, face-down and stone-still. And by Abby's cocked head at seeing me—eyes full and sparkling with deed—I knew there was no accident to any of it.

The shed. The icebox.

I could no longer avoid it.

Into the clearing now, the shed loomed before me like a confession booth. I pictured Pamela Frick, her come-hither eyes beckoning me inside. We were meeting in Boston that weekend after having arranged it months in advance. Finally, after all that time—ever since learning of Larissa's pregnancy with Justin—we'd have a bed instead of hasty, sweaty, stolen minutes taking each other on and against a filthy icebox.

I told Abby not to say anything. That I'd hide Justin until the police ended their search and it was safe enough to dig a grave. That I loved her no matter what, and that she should keep draining the evidence while I secreted his little body in my luggage until I could stash him in that ice box off our property.

But as I entered the shed, evidence was exactly what I found, along with verdict. It thrived in Thomas the Train blue, balled as a heap without eyes to the side of the chopping block. Preserved in the icebox in pieces, this work I'd halfheartedly begun, and which she'd finished with conviction.

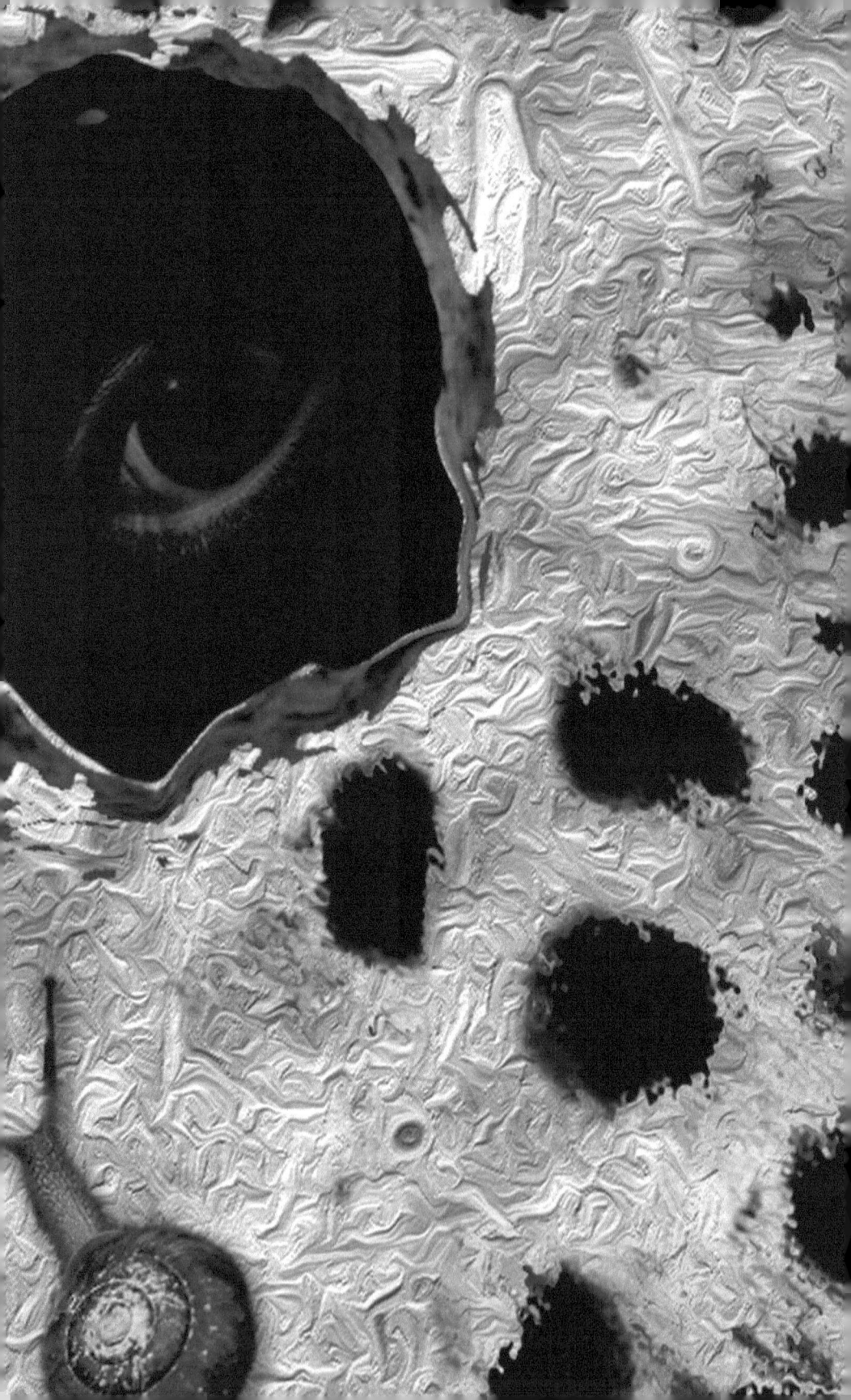

# IN THE LOOP
## - Ken Liu -

When Kyra was nine, her father turned into a monster.

It didn't happen overnight. He went to work every morning, like always, and when he came in the door in the evening, Kyra would ask him to play catch with her. That used to be her favorite time of the day. But the yesses came less frequently, and then not at all.

He'd sit at the table and stare. She'd ask him questions and he wouldn't answer. He used to always have a funny answer for everything, and she'd repeat his jokes to her friends and think he was the cleverest dad in the whole world.

She had loved those moments when he'd teach her how to swing a hammer properly, how to measure and saw and chisel. She would tell him that she wanted to be a builder when she grew up, and he'd nod and say that was a good idea. But he stopped taking her to his workshop in the shed to make things together, and there was no explanation.

Then he started going out in the evenings. At first, Mom would ask him when he'd be back. He'd look at her like she was a stranger before closing the door behind him. By the time he came home, Kyra and her brothers were already in bed, but she would hear shouts and sometimes things breaking.

Mom began to look at Dad like she was afraid of him, and Kyra tried to help with getting the boys to bed, to make her bed without being asked, to finish her dinner without complaint, to do everything perfectly, hoping that would make things better, back to the way they used to be. But Dad didn't seem to pay any attention to her or her brothers.

Then, one day, he slammed Mom into the wall. Kyra stood there in the kitchen and felt the whole house shake. She didn't know what to do. He turned around and saw Kyra, and his face scrunched up like he hated her, hated her mother, hated himself most of all. And he fled the house without saying another thing.

Mom packed a suitcase and took Kyra and her brothers to Grandma's place that evening, and they stayed there for a month. Kyra thought about calling her father but she didn't know what she would say. She tried to imagine herself asking the man on the other end of the line *what have you done with Daddy?*

A policeman came, looking for her mother. Kyra hid in the hall so she could hear what he was telling her. *We don't think it was a homicide.* That was how she found out that her father had died. She didn't cry then, and wouldn't cry until much later.

They moved back to the house, where there was a lot to do: folding up Dad's uniforms for storage, packing away his regular clothes to give away, cleaning the house so it could be sold, getting ready to move away permanently. She caressed Dad's medals and badges, shiny and neatly laid out in a box, and that was when she finally cried.

They found a piece of paper at the bottom of Dad's dresser drawer.

"What is it?" she asked Mom.

Mom read it over. "It's from your Dad's commander, at the Army." Her hands shook. "It shows how many people he had killed."

She showed Kyra the number: one thousand two-hundred and fifty-one.

The number lingered in Kyra's mind. As if that gave his life meaning. As if that defined him and them.

Kyra walked quickly, pulling her coat tight against the late fall chill.

It was her senior year in college, and on-campus recruiting was in full swing. Because Kyra's school was old and full of red brick buildings named after families that had been wealthy and important even before the founding of this republic, its students were desirable to employers.

She was on her way back to her apartment from a party hosted by a small quantitative trading company in New York that was generating good buzz on campus. Companies in management consulting, financial services, and Silicon Valley had booked hotel rooms around the school and were hosting parties for prospective interviewees every night, and Kyra, as a comp sci major, found herself in high demand. This was the night when she would need to finalize her list of ranked preferences, and she had to strategize carefully to have a shot at getting one of the interview slots for the most coveted companies in the lottery.

"Excuse me," a young man stepped in her way. "Would you sign this petition?"

She looked at the clipboard held in front of her. *Stop the War*.

Technically, America wasn't at war. There had been no declaration of war by Congress, just the President exercising his office's inherent authority. But maybe the war had never stopped. America left; America went back; America promised to leave again some time. A decade had passed; people kept on dying far away.

"I'm sorry," Kyra said, not looking the boy in the eyes. "I can't."

"Are you *for* the war?" The boy's voice was tired, the incredulity almost an act. He was there canvassing for signatures alone in the evening because no one cared. When so few Americans died, the "conflict" didn't seem real.

How could she explain to him that she did not believe in the war, did not want to have anything to do with it, and yet, signing the petition the boy held would seem to her tantamount to a betrayal of the memory of her father, would seem a declaration that what he had done was wrong?

So all she said was, "I'm not into politics."

Back in her apartment, Kyra took off her coat and flipped on the TV.

*...the largest protest so far in front of the American Embassy. Protestors are demanding that the U.S. cease the drone strikes, which so far have caused more*

*than three hundred deaths in the country this year, many of whom the protestors claim were innocent civilians. The U.S. Ambassador...*

Kyra turned off the TV. Her mood had been ruined, and she could not focus on the task of ranking her interview preferences. Agitated, she tried to clean the apartment, scrubbing the sink vigorously to drive the images in her mind away.

As she had grown older, Kyra had read and seen every interview with other drone operators who suffered from PTSD. In the faces of those men, she had searched for traces of her father.

*I sat in an air-conditioned office and controlled the drone with a joystick while watching on a monitor what the drone camera saw. If a man was suspected of being the enemy, I had to make a decision and pull the trigger and then zoom in and watch as the man's body parts flew around the screen, as the rest of him bled out, until his body cooled down and disappeared from the infrared camera.*

Kyra turned on the faucet and held her hands under the hot water, as if she could wash off the memory of her father coming home every evening: silent, sullen, gradually turning into a stranger.

*Every time, you wonder: Did I kill the right person? Was the sack on that man's back filled with bombs or just some hunks of meat? Were those three men trying to set up an ambush or were they just tired and taking a break behind those rocks by the road? You kill a hundred people, a thousand people, and sometimes you find out afterwards that you were wrong, but not always.*

"You were a hero," Kyra said. She wiped her face with her wet hands. The water was hot against her face and she could pretend it was all just water.

*No. You don't understand. It's different from shooting at someone when they're also shooting at you, trying to kill you. You don't feel brave pushing a button to kill people who are not in uniform, who look like they're going for a visit with a friend, when you're sitting thousands of miles away, watching them through a camera. It's not like a video game. And yet it also is. You don't feel like a hero.*

"I miss you. I wish I could have understood."

*Every day, after you're done with killing, you get up from your chair and walk out of the office building and go home. Along the way you hear the birds chittering overhead and see teenagers walking by, giggling or moping, self-absorbed in their safe cocoons, and then you open the door to your home. Your spouse wants to tell you about her annoying boss and your children are waiting for you to help them with their homework, and you can't tell them a thing you've done.*

*I think either you become crazy or you already were.*

She did not want him to be defined by the number on that piece of paper her mother kept hidden at the bottom of the box in the attic.

"They counted wrong, Dad," Kyra said. "They missed one death."

Kyra walked down the hall dejectedly. She was done with her last interview of the day—a hot Silicon Valley startup. She had been nervous, distracted, and flubbed the brainteaser. It had been a long day and she didn't get much sleep the night before.

She was almost at the elevator when she noticed an interview schedule posted on the door of the suite next to the elevator for a company named AWS Systems. It hadn't been completely filled. A few of the slots on the bottom were blank; that generally meant an undesirable company.

She took a closer look at the recruiting poster. They did something related to robotics. There were some shots of office buildings on a landscaped, modern campus. Bullet points listed competitive salary and benefits. Not flashy, but it seemed attractive enough. Why weren't people interested?

Then she saw it: "Candidates need to pass screening for security clearance." That would knock out many of her classmates who weren't U.S. citizens. And it likely meant government contracts. Defense, probably. She shuddered. Her family had had enough of war.

She was about to walk away when her eyes fell on the last bullet point on the poster: "Relieve the effects of PTSD on our heroes."

She wrote her name on one of the blank lines and sat down on the bench outside the door to wait.

"You have impressive credentials," the man said, "the best I've seen all day, actually. I already know we'll want to talk to you some more. Do you have any questions?"

This was what Kyra had been waiting for all along. "You're building robotic systems to replace human controlled drones, aren't you? For the war."

The recruiter smiled. "You think we're Cyberdyne Systems?"

Kyra didn't laugh. "My father was a drone operator."

The man became serious. "I can't reveal any classified information. So we have to speak only in hypotheticals. Hypothetically, there may be advantages to using autonomous robotic systems over human operated machines."

"Like what? It can't be about safety. The drone operators are perfectly safe back here. You think machines will fight better?"

"No, we're not interested in making ruthless killer robots. But we shouldn't make people do the jobs that should be done by machines."

Kyra's heart beat faster. "Tell me more."

"There are many reasons why a machine makes a better soldier than a human. A human operator has to make decisions based on very limited information: just what he can see from a video feed, sometimes alongside intelligence reports. Deciding whether to shoot when all you have to go on is the view from a shaking camera and confusing, contradictory intel is not the kind of thinking humans excel at. There's too much room for error. An operator might hesitate too long and endanger an innocent, or he might be too quick on the trigger and violate the rules of engagement. Decisions by different operators would be based on hunches and emotions and at odds with each other. It's inconsistent and inefficient. Machines can do better."

*Worst of all*, Kyra thought, *a human can be broken by the experience of having to decide.*

"If we take these decisions away from people, make it so that individuals are out of the decision-making loop, the result should be less collateral damage and a more humane, more civilized form of warfare."

But all Kyra could think was: *No one would have to do what my father did.*

The process of getting security clearance took a while. Kyra's mother was surprised when Kyra called to tell her that government investigators might come to talk to her, and Kyra wasn't sure how to explain why she took this job when there were much better offers from other places. So she just said, "This company helps veterans and soldiers."

Her mother said, carefully, "Your father would be proud of you."

Meanwhile, they assigned her to the civilian applications division, which made robots for factories and hospitals. Kyra worked hard and followed all the rules. She didn't want to mess up before she got to do what she really wanted. She was good at her job, and she hoped they noticed.

Then, one morning, Dr. Stober, the head roboticist, called her to join him in a conference room.

Kyra's heart was in her throat as she walked over. Was she going to be let go? Had they decided that she couldn't be trusted because of what had happened to her father? That she might be emotionally unstable? She had always liked Dr. Stober, who seemed like a good mentor, but she had never worked with him closely.

"Welcome to the team," said a smiling Dr. Stober. Besides Kyra, there were five other programmers in the room. "Your security clearance arrived this morning, and I knew I wanted you on this team right away. This is probably the most interesting project at the company right now."

The other programmers smiled and clapped. Kyra grinned shyly at each of them in turn as she shook their outstretched hands. They all had reputations as the stars in the company.

"You're going to be working on the AW-1 Guardians, one of our classified projects."

One of the other programmers, a young man named Alex, cut in: "These aren't like the field transport mules and remote surveillance crafts we already make. The Guardians are unmanned, autonomous flying vehicles about the size of a small truck armed with machine guns and missiles."

Kyra noticed that Alex was really excited by the weapons systems.

"I thought we make those kinds already," Kyra said.

"Not exactly," Dr. Stober said. "Our other combat systems are meant for surgical strikes in remote places or prototypes for frontline combat, where basically anything that moves can be shot. But these are designed for peacekeeping in densely populated urban areas, especially places where there are lots of Westerners or friendly locals to protect. Right now we still have to rely on human operators."

Alex said in a deadpan voice, "It would be a lot easier if we didn't have to worry about collateral damage."

Dr. Stober noticed that Kyra didn't laugh and gestured for Alex to stop. "Sarcasm aside, as long as we're occupying their country, there will be locals who think they can get some advantage from working with us and locals who wish we'd go away. I doubt that dynamic has changed in five thousand years. We have to protect those who want to work with us from those who don't, or else the whole thing falls apart. And we can't expect the Westerners doing reconstruction over there to stay holed up in walled compounds all the time. They have to mingle."

"It's not always easy to tell who's a hostile," Kyra said.

"That's the heart of the issue. Most of the time, much of the population is ambivalent. They'll help us if they think it's safe to do so, and they'll help the militants if they think that's the more convenient choice."

"I've always said that if they choose to help the militants blend in, I don't see why we need to be that careful. They made a decision," Alex said.

"I suppose some interpretations of the rules of engagement would agree with you. But we're telling the world that we're fighting a new kind of war, a clean war, one where we hold ourselves to a higher standard. How people see the way we conduct ourselves is just as important nowadays."

"How do we do that?" Kyra asked before Alex could further derail the conversation.

"The key piece of software we have to produce needs to replicate what the remote operators do now, only better. The government has supplied us with thousands of hours of footage from the drone operations during the last decade or so. Some of them got the bad guys, and some of them got the wrong people. We'll need to watch the videos and distill the decision-making process of the operators into a formal procedure for identifying and targeting militants embedded in urban conditions, eliminate the errors, and make the procedure repeatable and applicable to new situations. Then we'll improve it by tapping into the kind of big data that individual operators can't integrate and make use of."

*The code will embody the minds of my father and others like him so that no one would have to do what they did, endure what they endured.*

"Piece of cake," said Alex. And the room laughed, except for Kyra and Dr. Stober.

Kyra threw herself into her work, a module they called the ethical governor, which was responsible for minimizing collateral damage when the robots fired upon suspects. She was working on a conscience for killing machines.

She came in on the weekends and stayed late, sometimes sleeping in the office. She didn't view it as a difficult sacrifice to make. She couldn't talk about what she was working on with the few friends she had, and she didn't really want to spend more time outside the office with people like Alex.

She watched the videos of drone strikes over and over. She wondered if any were missions her father had flown. She understood the confusion, the odd combination of power and powerlessness experienced when watching a man one is about to kill through a camera, the pressure to *decide*.

The hardest part was translating this understanding into code. Computers require precision, and the need to articulate vague hunches had a way of forcing one to confront the ugliness that could remain hidden in the ambiguity of the human mind.

To enable the robots to minimize collateral damage, Kyra had to assign a value to each life that might be endangered in a crowded urban area. One of the most effective ways for doing this—at least in simulations—also turned out to be the most obvious: profiling. The algorithm needed to translate racial characteristics and hints about language and dress into a number that held the power of life and death. She felt paralyzed by the weight of her task.

"Everything all right?" Dr. Stober asked.

Kyra looked up from her keyboard. The office lights were off; it was dark outside. She was practically the last person left in the building.

"You've been working a lot."

"There's a lot to do."

"I've reviewed your check-in history. You seem to be stuck on the part where you need the facial recognition software to give you a probability on ethnic identity."

Kyra gazed at Dr. Stober's silhouette in the door to her office, back-lit by the hall lights. "There's no API for that."

"I know, but you're resisting the need to roll your own."

"It seems...wrong."

Dr. Stober came in and sat down in the chair on the other side of her desk. "I learned something interesting recently. During World War II, the U.S. Army trained dogs for warfare. They would act as sentries, guards, or maybe even as shock troops in an island invasion."

Kyra looked at him, waiting.

"The dogs had to be trained to tell allies apart from enemies. So they used Japanese-American volunteers to teach the dogs to profile, to attack those with certain kinds of faces. I've always wondered how those volunteers felt. It was repugnant and yet it was also necessary."

"They didn't use German-American or Italian-American volunteers, did they?"

"No, not that I'm aware of. I'm telling you this not to dismiss the problematic nature of your work, but to show you that the problem you're trying to solve isn't entirely new. The point of war is to prefer the lives of one group over the lives of another group. And short of being able to read everyone's minds, you must go with shortcuts and snap heuristics to tell apart those who must die from those who must be saved."

Kyra thought about this. She could not exempt herself from Dr. Stober's logic. After all, she had lamented her father's death for years, but she had never shed a tear for the thousands he had killed, no matter how many might have been innocent. His life was more valuable to her than all of them added together. His suffering meant more. It was why she was here.

"Our machines *can* do a better job than people. Attributes like appearance and language and facial expressions are but one aspect of the input. Your algorithm can integrate the footage from city-wide surveillance by thousands of other cameras, the metadata of phone calls and social visits, individualized suspicion built upon data too massive for any one person to handle. Once the programming is done, the robots will make their decisions consistently, without bias, always supported by the evidence."

Kyra nodded. Fighting with robots meant that no one had to feel responsible for killing.

Kyra's algorithm had to be specified exactly and submitted to the government for approval. Sometimes the proposals came back, marked with questions and changes.

She imagined some general (advised, perhaps, by a few military lawyers) looking through her pseudocode line by line:

A target's attributes would be evaluated and assigned numbers. Is the target a man? Increase his suspect score by thirty points. Is the target a child? Decrease his suspect score by twenty-five points. Does the target's face match any of the suspected insurgents with at least a fifty-percent probability? Increase his suspect score by five hundred points.

And then there was the value to be assigned to the possible collateral damage around the target. Those who could be identified as Americans or had a reasonable probability of being Americans had the highest value. Then came native militia forces and groups who were allied with U.S. forces, and the local elites. Those who looked poor and desperate were given the lowest values. The algorithm had to formalize anticipated fallout from media coverage and politics.

Kyra was getting used to the process. After the specifications had gone back and forth a few times, her task didn't seem so difficult.

Kyra looked at the number on the check. It was large.

"It's a small token of the company's appreciation for your efforts," said Dr. Stober. "I know how hard you've been working. We got the official word on the trial period from the government today. They're very pleased. Collateral damage has been reduced by more than eighty percent since they started using the Guardians, with zero erroneous targets identified."

Kyra nodded. She didn't know if the eighty percent was based on the number of lives lost or the total amount of points assigned to the lives. She wasn't sure she wanted to think too hard about it. The decisions had already been made.

"We should have a team celebration after work."

And so for the first time in months, Kyra went out with the rest of the team. They had a nice meal, some good drinks, sang karaoke. And Kyra laughed and enjoyed hearing Alex's stories about his exploits in war games.

"Am I being punished?" Kyra asked.

"No, no, of course not," Dr. Stober said, avoiding her gaze. "It's just administrative leave until...the investigation completes. Payroll will still make bi-weekly deposits, and your health insurance will continue, of course. I don't want you to think you're being scapegoated. It's just that you did most of the work on the ethical governor. The Senate Armed Forces Committee is really pushing for our methodology, and I've been told that the first round of subpoenas are coming down next week. You won't be called up, but we'll likely have to name you."

Kyra had seen the video only once, and once was enough. Someone in the market had taken it with a cellphone, so it was shaky and blurry. No doubt the actual footage from the Guardians would be much clearer, but she wasn't going to get to see that. It would be classified.

The market was busy, the bustling crowd trying to take advantage of the cool air in the morning. It looked, if you squinted a bit, like the farmer's market that Kyra sometimes went to to get her groceries. A young American man, dressed in the distinctive protective vest that expat reconstruction advisors and technicians wore over there, was arguing with a merchant about something, maybe the price of the fruits he wanted to buy.

Reporters had interviewed him afterwards, and his words echoed in Kyra's mind: *"All of a sudden, I heard the sounds made by the Guardians patrolling the market change. They stopped to hover over me, and I knew something was wrong."*

In the video, the crowd was dispersing around him, pushing, jostling with each other to get out of the way. The person who took the video ran, too, and the screen was a chaotic blur.

When the video stabilized, the vantage point was much further. Two black robots about the size of small trucks hovered in the air above the kiosk. They looked like predatory raptors. Metal monsters.

Even in the cellphone video, it was possible to make out the recorded warning in the local language the robots projected via loudspeakers. Kyra didn't know what the warnings said.

A young boy, seemingly oblivious to the hovering machines above him, was running at the American man, laughing and screaming, his arms opened wide as if he wants to embrace the man.

*"I just froze. I thought, oh God, I'm going to die. I'm going to die because this kid has a bomb on him."*

The militants had tried to adapt to the algorithms governing the robots by exploiting certain weaknesses. Because they realized that children were assigned a relatively high value for collateral damage purposes and a relatively low value for targeting purposes, they began to use more children for their missions. Kyra had had to tweak the algorithm and the table of values to account for these new tactics.

"All of your changes were done at the request of the Army and approved by them," said Dr. Stober. "Your programming followed the updated rules of engagement and field practices governing actual soldiers. Nothing you've done was wrong. The Senate investigation will be just a formality."

In the video, the boy kept on running towards the American. The warnings from the hovering Guardians changed, got louder. The boy did not stop.

A few more boys and girls, some younger, some older, came into the area cleared by the crowd. They ran after the first boy, shouting.

The militants had developed an anti-drone tactic that was sometimes effective. They'd send the first bomber out, alone, to draw the fire of the drones. And while the drone operators were focused on him and distracted, a swarm of backup bombers would rush out to get to the target while the drones shot up the first man.

Robots could not be distracted. Kyra had programmed them to react to such tactics.

The boy was now only a few steps away from the lone American. The Guardian hovering on the right took a single shot. Kyra flinched at the sound from the screen.

*"It was so loud," said the young man in his interview. "I had heard the Guardians shoot before, but only from far away. Up close was a completely different experience. I heard the shot with my bones, not my ears."*

The child collapsed to the ground immediately. Where his head had been, there was now only empty space. The Guardians had to be efficient when working in a crowd. Clean.

A few more loud shots came from the video, making Kyra jump involuntarily. The cellphone owner panned his camera over, and there were a few more bundles of rags and blood on the ground. The other children.

The crowd stayed away, but a few of the men were coming back into the clearing, moving closer, raising their voices. But they didn't dare to move too close to the stunned young American, because the two Guardians were still hovering overhead. It took a few minutes before actual American soldiers and the local police showed up at the scene and made everyone go home. The video ended there.

*"When I saw that dead child lying in the dust, all I could feel was relief, an overwhelming joy. He had tried to kill me, and I had been saved. Saved by our robots."*

Later, when the bodies were searched by the bomb-removal robots, no explosives were found.

The child's parents came forward. They explained that their son wasn't right in the head. They usually locked him in the house, but that day, somehow he had gotten out. No one knew why he ran at that American. Maybe he thought the man looked different and he was curious.

All the neighbors insisted to the authorities that the boy wasn't dangerous. Never hurt anyone. His siblings and friends had been chasing after him, trying to stop him before he got into any trouble.

His parents never stopped crying during the interview. Some of the commenters below the interview video said that they were probably sobbing for the camera, hoping to get more compensation out of the American government. Other commenters were outraged. They constructed elaborate arguments and fought each other in a war of words in the comment threads, trying to score points. Some commenters brought up the point, again, that comments on news reports really ought to be moderated.

Kyra thought about the day she made the changes in the programming. She had been sipping a frappé because the day was hot. She remembered deleting the old value of a child's life and putting in a new one. It had seemed routine, just another change like hundreds of other tweaks she had already made. She remembered deleting one IF and adding another, changing the control flow to defeat the enemy. She remembered feeling thrilled at coming up with a neat solution to the nested logic. It was what the Army had requested, and she had decided to do her best to give it to them faithfully.

"Mistakes happen," said Dr. Stober. "The media circus will eventually end, and all the hand-wringing will stop. News cycles are finite, and something new will replace all this. We just have to wait it out. We'll figure out a way to make the system work better next time. This *is* better. This is the future of warfare."

Kyra thought about the sobbing parents, about the dead child, about the dead children. She thought about the eighty-percent figure Dr. Stober had quoted. She thought about the number on her father's scorecard, and the parents and children and siblings behind those numbers. She thought about her father coming home.

She got up to leave.

"You must remember," said Dr. Stober from behind her, "You're not responsible."

She said nothing.

It was rush hour when Kyra got off the bus to walk home. The streets were filled with cars and the sidewalks with people. Restaurants were filling up quickly; waitresses flirted with customers; men and women stood in front of display windows to gawk at the wares.

She was certain that most of them were bored with coverage of the war. No one was coming home in body bags anymore. The war was clean. This was the point of living in a civilized country, wasn't it? So that one did not have to think about wars. So that somebody else, some*thing* else, would.

She strode past the waitress who smiled at her, past the diners who did not know her name, into the throng of pedestrians on the sidewalk, laughing, listening to music, arguing and shouting, oblivious to the monster who was walking in their midst, ignorant of the machines thousands of miles away deciding who to kill next.

# THE MAKING OF MARY

## - *Steven Pirie* -

*To my mother; may she roam amongst the stars*

Sometimes, Gaia comes to Earth as a single snowdrop. Then her roots can drink the soil and her leaves taste the acidity of the rains. Her flower, as delicate as the spring breeze, tests the health of the returning sun. Sometimes, Gaia's a meadowlark, her song a summer melody as she counts the insects of the fields. But, it's always Ruth she returns to. Gaia never feels more at home than when she walks the Earth as Ruth. When she's Ruth, she has Mary. And if ever she needs a reason to keep this world turning, it's Mary.

It's just lately, as Ruth, she's never felt quite so alone.

It's Sunday evening. Ruth stares out to sea. Behind her the cliff looms, before her the waves swell and foam over angular rocks. Ruth stands on the narrow, shingle beach between the land and the ocean. She tastes brine upon her lips, and smells kelp on the breeze. Gulls wheel above her. Ruth's counted them; their numbers are dwindling.

She steps back and shelters from the wind. She feels the weight of rock above her and the churning planet below. Ruth sings a Pagan song of the Earth.

She's not yet sure if the song she sings is a dirge.

It's Monday morning. Ruth's at her desk in the reception of Specs4U on the high street. She hates the name, because to Ruth its truncated nonsense is everything that's wrong with the world. When she answers the telephone, she says: Spectacles For You, how may I help you? And Mr. Tate, the shop manager, tells her off. Specs4U is snappy and quick, he says. It yells *get in, get your new glasses, and get out.* Wham, bam, boom. Spectacles For You is so last year, Ruth, you must move with the times.

Ruth sighs. Some days it feels like she's moved with more times than is good for her. And it doesn't help that she'd rowed with Mary, last night, when Ruth had come home late and walked sand in everywhere. Romantic dinners, Mary had said, aren't so romantic when the candles have burned down to their wick. You do know it was our ten-year anniversary? And she'd stormed off to bed before Ruth could hold her and kiss her and tell her she was right, and Ruth was sorry.

It's quiet first thing Monday. The spectacle-buying public doesn't want their eyes mucked about with that early in the day. Ruth helps out by tidying the rack of two-for-one frames near the door. The cheapest is twenty-five quid. Ruth knows they cost fourteen pence to make, because Mr. Tate told her when he was loud and drunk at the Christmas work's night out. It was just before he'd put his hand on her leg and she'd leapt up saying she needed the loo.

Ruth runs a finger along one of the spectacles' temples. It's a hydrocarbon, cellulose acetate, a molecule that's man-made and not found in nature. And Ruth doesn't have a problem with that in principle—everything in nature is made from combinations of the same elements, so why shouldn't humankind's ingenuity add to that?

Ruth feels the chemical bonds between its atoms. They're strong enough to last until the sun bloats and the Earth is gone. That's where Ruth has issues. Back when she formed the Earth, when she caught rocks tumbling about the newly ignited sun and sent them crashing together, even then she'd made the rule that one civilisation should leave the world as pristine as possible for the next to inherit. Bones, that's all they should leave. Bones, and fossils, and perhaps an air of mystery to ponder upon.

"They're nice, aren't they?" says Mr. Tate.

Ruth's startled momentarily. He's touching her arm, for longer than would seem appropriate in a work-related environment.

"They're...cheap," says Ruth.

"But hard-wearing for the price."

"That's true, Mr. Tate."

"The wife could sit on them and they'd not break." Mr. Tate grins. "I can't say that about most things the wife sits on."

"No, um, yes."

"I'd like you to set up the eye-testing area for this afternoon," says Mr. Tate. "We've a minibus coming in from the old folks' home on Wainwright Street. Get some biscuits in, please Ruth, and some more milk. Oh, and a tin of air freshener."

"What time are they due in?"

"Two-o-clock, so best have an early lunch."

"I will do, Mr. Tate."

Early lunch is in the Grapes across the road. Mary's there—it's her day off—and they both sit quietly at a table in the corner. They pick at sorry baked potatoes. And Ruth wants to say: I was late because the world's falling apart, but Mary wouldn't know what she meant. Then she'll get angry again...When Mary's angry it's Ruth's world that's falling apart.

"I really am sorry about last night," says Ruth.

Mary shrugs. "It doesn't matter. You should've called to let me know where you were."

"I know, sorry."

"I was worried when you were late."

"I'll make it up to you."

"You've said that a lot, lately."

Ruth knows that's true. Through her feet upon the pub floor, Ruth feels the world turn in time and space. In some ways it's delicate like Mary. In others it's robust like, who, like Ruth? And in between it's by degrees; the world isn't going to leave its orbit about the sun. But it is on the brink of change. It's been there before, because Ruth's seen ice ages come and go, and mass extinctions litter the world's history. But this time it feels different, and Ruth's worried.

"Why don't I take you to dinner tonight?" says Ruth. "We could go to that new French place, and afterwards we can go dancing at Annabel's."

"On a Monday night?"

"My treat."

"It could be fun, I suppose," says Mary.

"It will," says Ruth. "It feels like a while since we had _fun_."

"I have work Tuesday."

"We'll phone in sick. Both of us. We'll have the day in bed, and I'll make it all about you."

Later, back at Specs4U, while Mr. Tate is knee-deep in cataracts and barely attached retinas, Ruth stares motionless out through the shop's plate glass window. It's raining, and already there's dusk lurking over the town. The part of Ruth that's Gaia has gone, and Ruth left behind always feels sluggish and empty. And old, so very old, as if without Gaia to prop her up Ruth wilts under the millennia she's seen come and go.

Ruth, or Gaia, or both, is an eagle soaring effortlessly through the smoke-strewn skies over Yellowstone in America. From above, it's easy to see the outline of the super volcano below the ground. Where it belches methane, Ruth rises on thermal updrafts.

Ruth's felt the tremors. They're small but coming more frequently. She still has some time before the big one, but she's keeping an eye on it just the same. She knows there's enough methane, sulphur, and carbon down there to warm the world by degrees. There's enough ash to plunge the world into a mini ice age. Ruth's already thinking what she should do about it.

If anything.

She spirals downward as she mulls that thought. She could do nothing. The world would recover, eventually. She'd built it with resilience in mind. Ten years of winter wouldn't affect Ruth at all. There are other planets in this universe she could winter upon. Of course, some species would go extinct. But Ruth's made that happen before now—pressed reset when things didn't quite turn out how she'd liked. She'd pulled in a comet from the Oort cloud when she felt the dinosaurs had run their race. She could easily do so again.

Except now there's Mary.

Everything's worth saving for Mary.

Everything.

There's still fresh paint smell in the new French place. It taints the taste of Ruth's Mushroom Julienne with a hint of magnolia. The maître de apologises in a thick French accent, even though Mary says he's from Basingstoke and he went to her school.

"We can go somewhere else," says Ruth.

Mary raises a finger. "No, we're here now. I'm hungry; I want to eat."

She eats delicately, Mary, that's what Ruth always notices. The shape of Mary's mouth as she chews was what first attracted Ruth to her. Was it really ten years ago?

They'd met on some march or other—save the whale, or ban the bomb, or something—and Ruth had been drawn to Mary's passion, because it was clear right away that Mary loved the world more than she loved anything. *You want to get a drink after?* Mary had said, and she looked a little coy and embarrassed. *I can tell you about next month's protest.* Ruth shivered, because for the first time she'd felt the rush of hormones, of dopamine and oxytocin, the heady mix making her woozy and light-headed. Right then Ruth would have let worlds collapse for a single kiss of those delicate lips. How had she not allowed these feelings in Ruth before? How had she never allowed Ruth to feel love?

"Tate was all over the place today," says Ruth.

"Oh?"

"We had fourteen pensioners in. They were all lavender bath scrub and honey-and-lemon cough sweets. I could see Tate's eyes watering. He was slumped in the chair when I left. I think he was overcome by vapour rub."

Mary laughs. "Serves him right, the old pervert."

"Can I ask you a question?"

Mary pauses in eating. "Go on."

"Have you ever wanted a child?"

Mary pauses longer. "I think one of us needs a penis for that sort of thing."

"We could adopt," says Ruth. "Or, we could find a donor."

"Yes, well." Mary drinks her wine. "I'm sure there are a million reasons why that's not a good idea."

"And not even one reason why it's good?"

"This is all out of the blue," says Mary.

"I know. I'm not suggesting we drop our knives and forks and head straight down to the sperm bank."

"That's a relief."

"I'm just planting the thought in your head. Will you think about it?"

"I don't know. I don't think it's a good idea."

That night, as Mary sleeps, Ruth walks upon Mars. It's dusk on the foothills of Olympus Mons. The steppes are dark, but for the huge caldera of the volcano towers above her in glorious sunlight. She's alone; there's no life here anymore, not even the last microbes in the rusted soil can survive the naked radiation from the solar winds. Here, with just the odd robotic probe from Earth to keep her company, Ruth likes to come and think.

She looks back at the Earth in the blackening Martian sky. It's a pale blue star caught in the haze of the setting sun. She holds up a palm, and the entire planet can rest on the end of her fingernail. She could crush it between forefinger and thumb if she chooses.

Ruth reaches down and scoops a handful of sand. It's smooth and rounded by dust devils and Mars' fierce winds, and it slips easily through her fingers.

Mars is barren. Like Ruth.

Its lifeless plains are a lesson that not all worlds bear fruit. Before now Ruth's never worried that such an outcome is perhaps a failure. She's always seen beauty in isolation. A rocky world steeped with mountains and shaped by ancient estuaries is as awesome to her as any lush green world like Earth.

So what's all this "do you want a child" nonsense all about?

Venus dips below the ridge on the horizon. The Earth will follow it soon. Ruth's sad because Venus was supposed to be green like the Earth. But she'd stood by as runaway volcanism poured out greenhouse gasses and Venus choked to a slow heat death. It happens sometimes, Ruth tells herself, that worlds fail. She fears the Earth will go the same way should she do nothing about humanity's failings. Earth's future as a living planet is finely balanced.

Is that why she wants a child? To give her a reason to not stand by and let that happen on Earth? Is it not enough that Mary can be that reason? Was it a mistake to fall in love with Mary? Ruth is Gaia, and Gaia is immortal; the Immortals shouldn't have feelings for their Creation. Ruth will be here long after Mary is dust. Why should Gaia care about that? Gaia is about protecting worlds, not those who dwell upon them. Nature is cold. Surely that's the only way it can be.

Ruth shivers. Mars is colder than anywhere on Earth. She hugs her arms against her chest. Mary's arms are warm. Ruth knows that's where she should be. She slips back into bed and spoons Mary. Mary stretches and groans but doesn't wake. Ruth kisses her neck. Within moments, Ruth's asleep. She doesn't dream, because when she's with Mary she doesn't have to.

They grin as they call in sick the next morning. Ruth thinks Mr. Tate might have caught the laughter in her voice as Mary makes faces at her. Women's troubles, they say, because even Mr. Tate fears to delve too deeply there.

"Muesli, or fry-up?" says Ruth.

"Oh, fry-up, I think. Full English."

She's mostly vegetarian, Mary, and Ruth's pleased with her choice. Vegetarianism's all well and good had evolution not made humanity omnivorous. Sometimes, Ruth thinks Mary looks a little peaky and needs a bit of meat in her diet. Sometimes, she slips some in when Mary's not looking.

"I'm sorry about last night," says Ruth.

"What about?"

"About the baby thing. I shouldn't have said that."

"It was just a bit sudden," says Mary. "It came from nowhere."

Ruth shivers. The ice caps are melting. It seems a random thing to think about whilst frying bacon, but Ruth's just felt the planet shake beneath her feet as at the pole an ice field the size of Wales breaks in two. The pole is warming, and not by the return of the sun from winter's night.

"I was wrong to mention it," says Ruth.

"No," says Mary. "If it's on your mind you should say. We've always been open and honest with each other, haven't we?"

Open and honest?

Like Ruth's ever said who she really is. Like when Mary's gorgeous and down between her thighs and doing things only Mary can do, Ruth's ever said: Oh, by the way, I'm of the Gods, Mary. I came with the first stars that lit the universe, because someone had to swirl dust into worlds to orbit around them. Someone had to hurl moons into the new worlds' skies. I sculpted mountains and hollowed basins to fill with oceans and fish and rain. I'm the gulf stream, and the jet stream, and I drive tectonic plates below.

"Breakfast is done," says Ruth. "Do you want tea or coffee?"

"Let's take it into the garden."

"It's a bit cool out there still."

Mary's already on her way out. "It'll wake us up."

Actually, it's quite pleasant outside. The sun is warming nicely. Summer's not far away. The patio Azaleas are already blooming. Early insects drone listlessly about their buds. The signs of re-growth are everywhere.

"We're marching on Saturday," says Mary. "It's a rally on Whitehall to protest against America pulling out of the Paris treaty on climate control."

"Can the government do anything about that?"

"We have to let our feelings be known. It's happening all over the world, so the White House will get the message."

"But will it care?"

Ruth's immediately sorry she's said this out loud. Mary is a wonderful person, and so passionate about her causes, and Ruth wonders if she's too negative towards her sometimes. It's easy to be dismissive, Ruth supposes, when one can hold a wet finger up to the world and feel climate change in real-time. It's all politicised, that's the problem, it's all point-scoring and money-making, it's about vested interests on both sides. For every beautiful soul like Mary, there's a hundred naysayers and manipulators out for what they can get. If half the planet dies, so what? They'll probably be long gone by the time the gulf submerges Texas, by the time East Anglia is an inland sea, by the time the Florida Keys are no more. If the crops fail and millions die, their grandchildren will be fine because they've friends in high places and money in the bank. Money will always take food from the mouths of the poor if need be.

"We'll bang on its doors until it does care," says Mary.

"You know, I think you will," says Ruth.

"Will you march with us? You haven't been active for a while."

Ruth sips tea. She grins. "Maybe I will."

Ruth looks away. They'll have to say goodbye, soon, because Mary will age but Ruth will not. What future is there in a relationship where one of them withers and dies in front of the other who's still in the flush of youth? It will be hard; probably the hardest thing Ruth's ever done. She thinks she should do it sooner rather than later. That way maybe Mary can find someone else, someone who can grow old with her.

"What time does it start?" says Ruth.

"We're gathering at nine to march at ten. If the police aren't heavy on us, we should be at Parliament by noon."

"You know, I'll come. It will be like old times."

"I'll make you a placard."

"Make it a dirty one."

"How about: The World Says Fuck Trump!?"

"Ha, I think he might like that."

There's an asteroid near miss due at ten. Ruth knows it's on a collision course at the moment. It's a rock the size of a football field that will only show up when it ionises in the upper atmosphere. It'll come blind-sided from behind the sun where it will slingshot unseen by NASA or anyone but Ruth toward the Earth. Too late to do anything about it, NASA will say; funding cuts have seen to that. It will land in Washington. Ruth wonders if that will solve Mary's White House problem, but of course the President will be in Air Force One long before the rock strikes.

"You look tired," says Ruth. "You should have an early night."

If Ruth's going to do anything with this asteroid, she needs Mary asleep. She can't very well say: I'm just popping up into space, Mary. It's another deception that hangs over them with all the others, like their own personal asteroid that will one day come crashing down.

Ruth could stop time, she supposes, but to do that she'd have to map the position and movement of every atom in the universe. Who'd want to do that on a damp Tuesday night?

"It has been a long day," says Mary. "I am up early tomorrow."

"I probably won't be long myself," says Ruth.

They kiss goodnight. Ruth holds her even when Mary moves to let go. Maybe it's time to move on. Maybe when she's pushed aside the rock, Ruth thinks she should continue out into the vast sprawl of space. There's no future here, not for Ruth, for Mary, or their adopted child. The planet is dying, no, being killed, there is a difference. Ruth could walk away, could come back in a million years or so and see what new life has sprung forth with evolution playing to a new tune. Maybe it would be a life that loved and nurtured their world and not one that was all take, take, take.

"I love you," says Mary.

Ruth hugs her closer. "I know."

"You're leaving me, aren't you? Is it because of the child business?"

"Go to bed. We'll talk in the morning. I've a lot I need to tell you."

That night, as meteors rain down where the asteroid grazed the sky, Ruth is back at the shingle beach where the cliff meets the sea. She looks down at the tide line. The waters are rising as the ice caps melt. The ice-melt is fresh water, so the salinity of the oceans is changing. It's salt that drives the conveyor currents of the deep ocean, that swirl nutrients around the globe to feed the very basic levels of the food chain. And these currents themselves are negative feedback loops against excessive heating and cooling of the planet. It's a natural thing Ruth built-in at the start. She'd never imagined humanity would put them at peril with their chlorofluorocarbons, their love of fossil fuels and carbon costs. The ocean conveyors will stop flowing once the energy of Sodium and Chlorine ions is gone, and then the world will plunge into a long winter. Or maybe it will turn into another Venus with runaway warming. There're fields of methane hidden below the ice. That's the problem with chaotic systems, they can go either way.

Ruth watches the stars cross the sky. She'd stood here when the world was new, when she'd solidified the rock and calmed the volcanoes and earthquakes. She'd breathed oxygen into the ocean, and twisted the molecules of life into the first blue-green algae blooms that would, one day, become Mary. And she'd waited, because creating Mary couldn't be rushed. It was a delicate process, with many false dawns and blind alleys, because evolution just goes where it goes until it bumps into something. It knows nothing of Marys and their wonders. It was a lonely process, because nothing would do until there was Mary.

Nothing.

Now Ruth must leave. Because she loves her too much to watch her grow old and die. The thought of an eternity without Mary makes Ruth shiver. That's why she wants Mary's child. Ruth wants something of Mary to go on. It's the gene's imperative, is it not? Selfish reproduction at any cost.

Wednesday morning, and Ruth's in Specs4U staring absently out from her desk. Mr. Tate fusses with the new retinal image camera. So far he's taken pictures of his foot, the back wall of the shop, and his left ear. Ruth doesn't care. She's had enough of this drudgery, this game of normality to hide the fact she's anything but normal. She's meeting Mary for lunch, and she intends to tell her everything, never mind the consequence. Even the Gods can live a lie only for so long.

"It's a bit complicated, this thingy-ma-jig," says Mr. Tate. "It keeps taking pictures when I'm not ready."

"Do you know there's arsenic in rice, Mr. Tate?" says Ruth. "Yet rice is a staple food source for much of the world population. Would you feed rice to Mrs. Tate if you knew that?"

"I think it's this blue button that's doing it."

"Do you know there are viruses under the permafrost that are still living but haven't been active for millions of years? No one has immunity to those, Mr. Tate. Such a pandemic they would bring if they're ever released."

"No, hang on, there's a switch here to stop it snapping away. Ah, progress, Ruth, progress."

Ruth needs air. She goes outside on to the high street. It's late morning, and the street's bustling with cars and shoppers. Ruth tastes sulphur dioxide and carbon monoxide from the car exhausts. There's soot, and lead, and Gods knows how many hydrocarbons in the air. And no one else cares. She could stand and shout of the world's end and no one would take notice.

Ruth crosses the road and peers in through the murky window of the Grapes. She sees Mary at the bar. Frank the barman's flirting with her, not knowing Mary's riding the other bus, as Mr. Tate suggested when Mary wouldn't dance with him at the work's Christmas party. Probably doesn't shave under her arms, Mr. Tate had added, and Ruth was sorely tempted to send him to Pluto or somewhere.

Ruth opens the pub door. "Mary," she calls, "I want to take you somewhere."

"I've just bought a lager top," says Mary.

"It's important. The drink will be there when we get back."

"What is it?"

"Hold my hand. This will scare the pants off you. But just remember you're safe. I won't let any harm come to you."

"I'm not sure I like the sound of this," says Mary, "What is it?"

"Close your eyes. Now, open them."

Together they walk upon the sun. The sky is fire. Fingers of plasma snap and flail. The surface churns with the gasses rising and falling. Mary yells, but there's no sound but the rumble of the great engines below, of hydrogen becoming helium in huge storms of energy. Ruth leaps and pulls Mary upward with her into the photosphere. They ride outward on the solar winds. The hiss of photons and x-rays and gamma rays is in their ears. They sail through a golden arch of plasma.

"The universe is filled with hydrogen," says Ruth in Mary's head. "But it was me who pulled it here five billion years ago. It was me who moulded it and condensed it and set it spinning. And it was only a matter of time then before it collapsed under its own gravity, and then there was heat and pressure, enough that fusion may start and the sun might shine. What a day that was when the sun first ignited. I remember it like it was yesterday. Everything begins with a sun. It was like the birth of a child."

They pass Mercury, sun-ravaged and wasted, barely bigger than the moon. They plunge through the clouds of Venus, through winds that crack at supersonic speeds. There's lightning, and thunder that thuds against the ribs and takes their breath. "This rain," says Ruth, "is so acidic it would strip the skin from bone were I not protecting us."

"I don't understand any of this," says Mary. She's vomited, more than once, down her shirt. "Take me back."

"I'm sorry," says Ruth. "I thought if I simply tell you of all this in the pub you'd think me mad. Hell, I know I would. So I thought it best I show you. I want to show you the wonders of the universe. I don't mean to frighten you. Just remember, you are safe; you're always safe with me."

They punch down through the cloud base. The ground is bleached white, a snowfield of methane. "This is global warming," says Ruth. "This is what you're fighting against on Earth. This is why you're right and they're wrong, Mary. Don't ever stop raging against this."

They circle in a lazy arc before plunging upward once more, through the dense cloud and shrieking winds, and out into the bleak, coldness of space. And there's the Earth. It's a pearl against the backdrop of stars. It's fragile and wonderful, and its atmosphere is a thin silver line that hugs its curvature.

"It's my pride," says Ruth. "I've put planets all over the universe, but this Earth is my joy."

They orbit the moon. The dark side is in bright sunlight. "It's beautiful," says Ruth. "Do you know, Mary, that you're only the twenty-fifth human to look directly upon it. In all of human history, only twenty-five people have been here. How wonderful is that? And how dreadful that humanity bickers and fights over nonsense and doesn't return.

"Do you want to see the first footprint on the moon? I was there when they landed. They had no fuel left, so I carried them the last few meters to the soil and settled their lunar module safely on its feet." Ruth grins. "It's not in the history books. But I suppose most of what I do isn't.

"I'm Gaia, Mary, and I'm here in the guise of Ruth because of you. I built all this for you. It's for one, fleeting lifetime; for one perfect person, for one idyllic moment in time and space. Is that wrong of me to want that?"

"I want to go home," says Mary.

"Then we can."

They're in the flat. They sit across the dining table from each other. Mary sips water. Her hand shakes.

"I had to tell you," says Ruth. "I'm tired of the lie. I'll go, if you want, and I won't come back."

"Stay," says Mary. "I need to sleep, if I can. Stay until tonight, and we'll talk more then."

Mr. Tate is worried. He's managed to take a picture of his retina, and he does a happy dance about Specs4U until he looks closely at it. There's a tumour on his left eye. "Now that I think of it, Ruth," he says, "I've had headaches since I danced too close to the ultraviolet lights at the work's Christmas night out."

Ruth studies the image. She looks inside Mr. Tate's head. It's a malignant lump the size of a golf ball, of runaway cell growth and nothing to do with dodgy lights and work's nights out. Ruth reaches in and pulls it out. She takes it all with the precision of the very best surgeon. Mr. Tate yelps but doesn't know why.

"I think it's dust in the camera," says Ruth. "Take another picture to confirm things. I'm sure you're fine."

He does, and then he wants to close early and take Ruth to the pub to celebrate. But Ruth's mind is on Mary. There's bigger cancers on the world that Ruth's already decided not to cure unless Mary comes with her. But she won't force her; if Mary says go then that's what Ruth will do.

"It gave me the shock of my life, for a moment," says Mr. Tate. "I thought I was done for."

"Everyone's done for eventually, Mr. Tate."

"Yes, but we all hope not quite yet."

She's languid and gorgeous, Mary, when she comes barefoot from the bedroom. She's draped in a long shirt and with her hair all over the place. Ruth hugs her and breathes her natural scent. They might make love when they hold each other like this.

"Have you thought about what happened?" says Ruth.

Mary shivers. "I don't even know what happened."

"There's a choice. I can go and let you rebuild your life, or you can come with me and together we can rebuild the world."

Mary grins. "I think you might be some help on our march, Saturday."

"An understatement," says Ruth.

"You can throw moons at them."

Ruth pauses. "So can you."

"I don't know. It's all very...odd."

"I meant what I said," says Ruth. "I really did build it all for you."

"I believe you," says Mary. She fills a kettle for coffee. "But how will it work if I come with you?"

"You can drink your coffee, and then we can go fill the ozone hole."

"We can really do that?"

"We're immortal; we can do anything we want."

Ruth clicks a finger and they're both on a tropical beach somewhere far across the galaxy. There are two suns setting in a golden sky. They make love on the warm sand, and when they're done, they lie back and watch the stars come out.

"Earth is somewhere over there," says Ruth.

"And together tomorrow we really can begin putting it right?"

Ruth kisses her gently. "Together we can do anything we want."

# MOUTHS FILLED WITH SEAWATER
## — Jonathan Cosgrove —

They'd said to keep my distance from bodies of water, but it was an Olympic-sized pool and I couldn't hurt anyone just sitting in the stands, could I? At reception I told them I wanted to check out the female-only classes, see if it was for me. There was only the advanced class on now, the receptionist said, not recognizing me. Good. I wouldn't have been able to explain myself if they had.

The girls' voices bounced joyfully from the water. Each of them looked so alike in their swimsuits, so sleek. I pinched my side thinking of how out of shape I'd become since the water was taken away. The swim caps made them near indistinguishable. I'd have recognized Melody anywhere though.

She was already out of the changing rooms when she saw me. Alone. Her hair still damp. She froze, the door softly closing behind her, and I walked over.

Up close, her skin looked pale. I told her I wasn't there for lessons. She didn't seem surprised.

"What, do I not have the body for it?" I said, gesturing to myself with a smile, trying to be playful. To make her laugh.

She didn't laugh though. Didn't say anything. She looked from me to the pale blue water, then to the cars outside, their lights turning on and disappearing on out the gate. Her eyes kept getting redder the whole time. From the chlorine, I guessed.

I always preferred open seawater but there was something dazzling about chlorine-filled pools, too. It had a lot to do with the smell. Melody was coated in it. She'd showered after class, tried washing it from her body, but it was still there. Lurking. Her hair looked like dying seaweed and when she turned to see if anyone was still here the scent of it gushed inside my nostrils.

The phone was ringing when I got in. I almost didn't recognize the noise. No one had a landline anymore. Even my parents got rid of theirs years ago. Its presence was a part of the deal though.

"Where were you?" It was Aidan, out of breath. He'd got an exercise bike. Had he told me that?

"Out," I said.

"Darina, your curfew is 8.30. I've been calling since 9." I glanced at the cheap plastic clock on the wall, almost eleven. What time had the swim class finished? Eight?

"You know you're meant to be in when I call," he continued.

"I ran into someone," I said, regretting my honesty immediately.

There was a pause as he tried steadying his breath.

"Who?" he said.

"No one you know."

"That worries me."

He was going to adopt his Da-Da voice now. Explain how I needed to behave, or I'd go back.

"Look, this might be your only chance to stay ou– "

"Ugh," I said not really meaning it. There was something reassuring about his predictability. "I'm home, goodnight."

I hung up the phone before he replied.

Melody's exhibition was at the museum the following week. There was a full page about it in the paper, about how she used her art to deal with loss. There was a picture of Melody beside a large multi-media portrait of a familiar looking girl. The caption beneath it said that this was Eboni, Melody's twin.

I wasn't the only girl at the exhibition. Which made sense once I'd calmed down. There were a lot of people, in fact, and at first, I was nervous of someone noticing me but I needn't have worried.

A group of girls my age stood outside the front door in a cloud of clove cigarettes that reminded me of the potpourri Dr. Higgins kept in his office. It was a sickening smell and I clenched my nose between knuckle and thumb as I walked past.

Melody circulated the gallery in an elegant white dress. I didn't go over right away, it was just nice to watch how she moved through people. How their words washed over her as she passed from one group to the next.

I didn't look much different from the other girls there. Drinks held at their chests, free hands adjusting their glasses or tucking hair behind their ears.

Some of the clove cigarette girls came inside, they stared in my direction meaningfully. Perhaps I should have said hi. Coming back, I knew there would be rumours, that people would talk, Dr. Higgins said as much. Melody's art, though, was a reminder of how much people preferred reading sad stories than hearing about them. I didn't waste my breath.

After a couple minutes of wandering I found myself facing the picture from the paper. Eboni's head was inclined to her chest, eyes closed, not asleep but as if catching her breath. Her hair was thick and dark and swirled about her head in threads of black silk intertwined with tendrils of blue reaching for an implied surface. A bouquet of flowers rested between her hands, white petals bobbed up and away; her chest, too, seemed to disperse. From a certain angle you might be convinced she was not sleeping at all but observing the gentle necrosis of her heart.

As she floated in reverie the din of voices dissipated. The gallery's murmur replaced by the throb of water. Her eyes blinked awake. Beneath my feet the floor was gone, replaced by a thick gloom. There were things far below, moving, gliding along the surface of some other world.

Eboni drifted inches away, reached out, and behind her I saw her flowers still rising, and just as a puckered palm caressed my cheek, I stumbled to the wooden gallery floor with a clatter. A few conversations stopped; a man came forward to help me up. I saw Melody quickly turn back to the other room. Shit.

On the wall, Eboni dreamed.

I kept making small advances towards Melody and her group of friends. There were enough people to cloak my movements somewhat but every few steps I would become self-conscious, stop and look about to see if a friend was nearby. The likelihood of this was, of course, zero. I had no friends here.

This staggered approach had not gone unnoticed. Melody would glance around occasionally then back to her circle. Closer, I could see Melody was crying, her shoulders shuddering. It was now or never. I walked towards her with purpose. A very tall red-haired woman I dimly recognized—her name might have been Karen—broke from the group and stepped in front of me. She told me it'd be better if I left.

Melody was completely turned away from me now. One girl put a hand on her and I felt a wave of jealousy. There were more people standing behind the tall girl now, their eyes alert and wary. Around the museum people were beginning to notice. It was time to go.

When I'd gotten onto the street, I texted Melody. Did I mention she gave me her number? Well, I have it.

*Had to leave early, sorry. Your art is beautiful. Hope you feel better.*

She read the message about eight minutes later, but no reply came.

The dream, when I remembered it, was always the same. A female form, someone I felt like I'd known from before the hospital, always slipping beneath the surface of inky seawater. While I sat close enough to help but unwilling to move.

Recently it's been different. The woman is Melody. The water is still dark and oily, but I know we are in the swimming pool. The roles are reversed and it's me trying to keep my head above water. Melody, sits a few feet away, observing my struggle. She can reach me but won't try. I keep thinking, how could you let this happen?

Taking one last gulp of air, I go under. I'm not like the other woman though. I belong down here. I see Melody's legs treading water. I grab hold of her ankle and pull. Together we descend and in the place where no light can find us, I let her go. Her pupils are dark swirling holes blindly probing the depths, her hands and legs searching for anything to touch.

When she's resigned to the emptiness, I swim towards her.

"We can't give out personal information of our clients." The receptionist picked up the clipboard with the sign-in sheet I'd been eyeing and held it to her chest. It had the names and phone numbers of everyone currently enrolled in the class. I didn't need Melody's number but I wanted to know if she was still coming here. She hadn't been to a class in nearly three weeks.

"She's a friend," I said, smiling. "I just want to know she's all right,"

"If she's your friend maybe you could try calling her?" said the woman. Her name tag said Kate.

Things became heated. When Kate's coworker came out from the back room because of the shrieking I was behind the counter and Kate was curled on the floor clutching her face. He seemed familiar.

"Hey! I know you!" the coworker said. I scrambled back over the reception counter and his shouts followed me as far as the automatic doors.

The museum was closed. I cupped my eyes against the window and could see Melody's work was gone. I rapped on the glass-paneled doors, but it was deserted.

I called the number Melody gave me. No answer. I tried again from a payphone. Nothing. No answering machine, just an abrupt end.

I sent a text.

*Everything okay?*

It stayed unread.

I didn't go back to the apartment that night. I walked to the quay instead. The police would know about the swimming pool and by now have contacted Aidan. He'd be calling and I'd feel compelled to answer or unplug the phone and then he'd just come over. He might already be at my apartment. He had spare keys.

I used to spend a lot of time down here. Like a lot of places I hadn't been for years, there was a sweet nostalgia, memories of a person framed blankness.

The tide was in. Boats in need of fresh paint bobbed in the water. I remembered we'd unmoored one, taken it into the night. There was a small island we wanted to visit. It looked like a patchwork of yellow grass from the pier. We never made it.

The water was always peaceful during the day. Deceptive. Only a few feet below the surface lay a quicksand of sludge and shit. I preferred the open water but never swam here. It could swallow you before anyone threw you a lifeline. If they threw you a lifeline. Not everyone knew that.

Ripples mesmerised me for a long time. It used to be so inviting.

Sounds of fishermen woke me. It was still dark. I'd fallen asleep against a metal shipping container, my joints painful and cold in the morning grey. I got up and walked in the direction of my apartment.

Everything seemed fuzzier along the way. I'd just taken my keys out of my pocket when I heard my name.

Aidan. He looked paler than me, eyes puffy from lack of sleep. His car was across the road. He wasn't meant to come here, except in emergencies. It was almost nauseating seeing him outside. I wanted to get away, but he grabbed my hand that held the key before I could do anything.

"Let go of me," I said, unable to break his grip.

"Where were you?" he said, clamping on to my other arm, turning me around. I could knee him between the legs, but he didn't deserve that.

"Nowhere," I said, trying to think of the answer myself. Everything that had come before suddenly slipping away.

"You were at the swimming pool last night," he said.

I'd completely forgotten about that.

"They called the police, Darina. You could have taken that girl's eye out." He was looking at the nails on my right hand. One of them was broken and there was something dried and brown beneath the others.

"I didn't do anything." I shrugged from his grip, and my phone fell out of my jacket pocket. Aidan picked it up.

"When did you get this?" he asked.

I thought it was better if I just didn't say anything. He sighed, handed it to me.

"Have you been in contact with Melody," He nodded at the phone I was now shamefully putting back into my pocket. "I told you it was better to keep your distance."

"When?" I said.

Aidan looked at me, wrestling with something in his head.

"During our session last week," he said.

Down below the surface Melody didn't scream. Or struggle. Her eyes just probed the darkness expectantly. It felt good to be down there with someone, someone to help fear the dark a little less. When her breath ran out she didn't panic. Where others showed despair I saw resolution. She couldn't see me but I smiled. I brought my mouth to hers and gave her more life to breathe.

Her pupils contracted and a beam broke across her face. Something behind me. I turned just as a hand rested on my shoulder. And then I was smiling, too.

The papers said that the body was a woman. That was about the only thing they said. Not how long she'd been in the water, for example. Her hair colour. The police were keeping as many details as they could from leaking out. No cause of death given though assumptions could be made. Aidan called me in for an appointment. Since the swimming pool incident, I was under review but I knew what this meeting was really about.

There were newspapers and magazines in a pile in the waiting room. The girl on reception was new and told me to help myself. She smiled for too long across the desk. A bowl of fresh potpourri sat in front of her. I tried holding my breath but it was pointless. It made me think of the museum, Melody's exhibition. I didn't need to check my phone anymore to see she wouldn't be calling. Not now.

The door opened and Dr. Higgins stuck his head out.

"Come on in," he said.

He'd moved his practice to his home a few years beforehand and it was a lot more casual than his old one at the hospital. His exercise bike stood proudly in the corner where his wife told him to put it because there was no room left in the house. A towel hung unevenly from the handlebars.

A national newspaper lay on his desk, the front page dedicated to some scandal but I knew there was an article in there about the girl they'd found. Pictures of police in high vis jackets down by the quays.

He saw me looking and sighed.

"Well I guess I might as well skip right to that," Dr. Higgins said. There was an inevitability to this conversation that I wanted to run away from. My body tensed and all the breath seemed trapped inside. Was it possible to forget how to breathe?

"Honestly, they can't say anything for certain yet. Water tends to slow decomposition somewhat. Though there's no stopping sea life." His Da Da voice again. Christ, the inevitability. I wanted to scream at him to just say it already. "But they don't believe it's Eboni."

My breath came pouring out.

The quay opened again a week later. The water splashed against the walls of the pier and I remembered a day when my friend dared me to jump in. I would have, but that day felt different. Eventually she jumped and didn't return. There was another day, too, when we'd both sat with our feet dangling in the water. I'd only meant to push her softly but she disappeared beneath the waves and I walked home alone. Or that time we'd dared each other to race to the yellow grass island and back, only she never climbed back up the slippery, metal ladder.

She once told me a story about a town beneath the breakers. She asked me to go with her. She told me not to follow her. I forgot my promise and dived in. Or I didn't. Or that other time. Or when she. Or the day that.

These are my memories. Such as they are.

All I'm left with is the absence.

That feels true.

She might still be out there. If she'd ever been there at all. I might still catch her. Years have passed but maybe. I take off my clothes. A phone vibrates against the ground. My skin tingles in the wind. It looks so peaceful down there. Dirty white petals bob along here and there, I get ready to run.

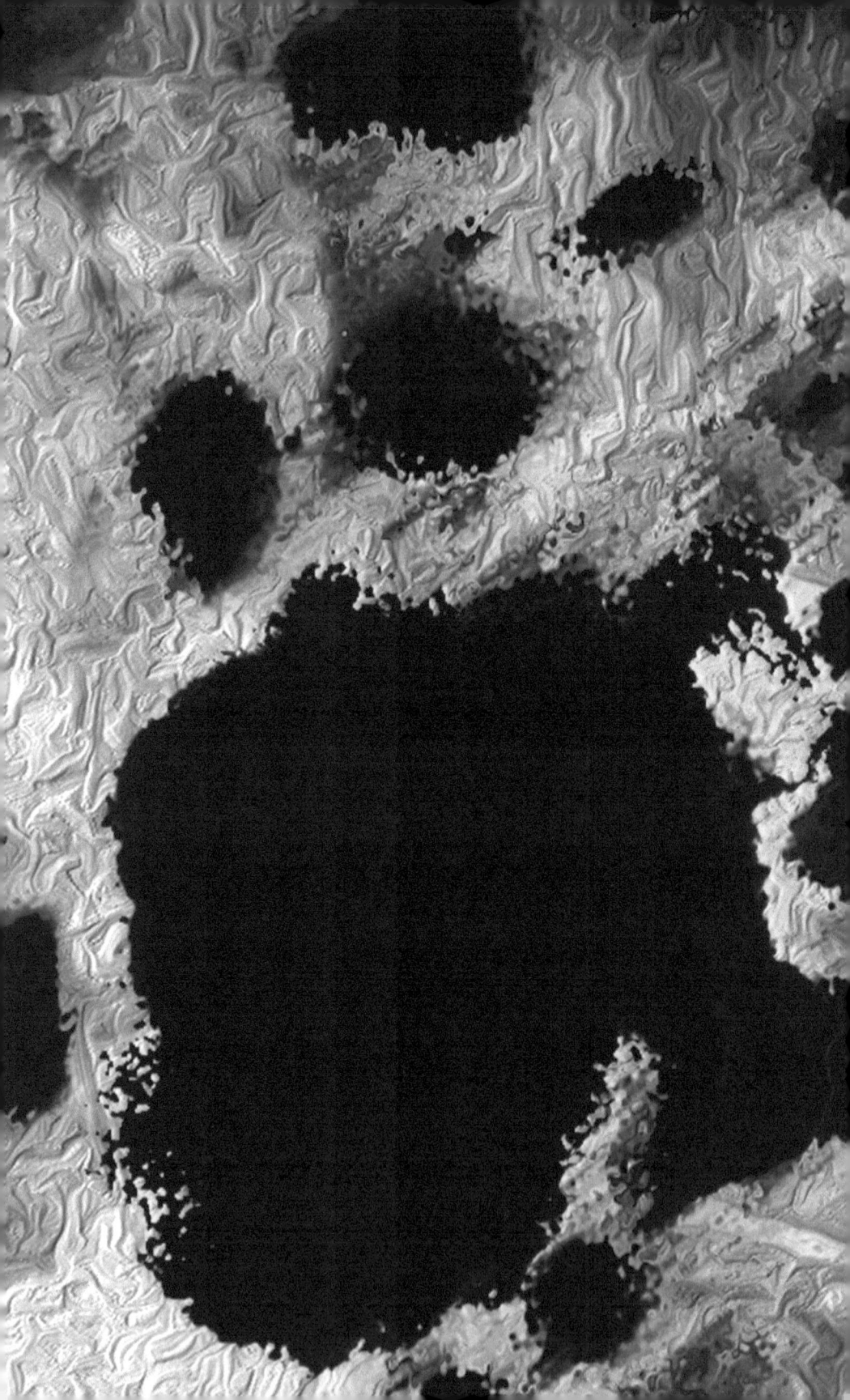

# ROTTEN
## - Carina Bissett -

*An apple a day keeps the doctor away. – English Proverb*

The fluted bowl shimmers like an oil slick in the dim light of the rainy afternoon. I am not allowed to touch it, but I touch it anyway. I trace the ridges of the design, delighting in the ripples of metallic pink bleeding into an acid green. Purchased in the years before the Great Depression, this piece of carnival glass has retained its place of honor on tables set by the women in my family for generations. It has only one function for my mother. She uses it to display her apples. When it becomes mine, I plan on filling it with polished stones.

Each and every day, my mother eats an apple. During her morning ritual, she sorts through the lot, seeking the one that speaks the loudest. My mother prefers the glossy finish of Red Delicious with their flavorless white flesh and saccharine blandness.

If I had it my way, I would spend more time in the forest, munching on the little green globes growing on the gnarled tree in front of my grandmother's house. I delight in their sour bite and crisp texture. My grandmother presses the crop, bottling it to ferment into hard cider. In the last days of autumn, the remaining fruit falls to the ground in rotting piles.

My grandmother says apples are like men. She tells me fresh fruit is boring; it's always better after it has been torn apart and transformed into something else. I wouldn't know.

I'm not allowed to eat my mother's apples. They are hers and hers alone. She polishes them into miniature mirrors reflecting her face. She says those cultivated spheres keep her beautiful. It works too. Men adore her. I watch them watching her. They never see me. I'm too young, too plain to compete with her. She reminds me of this often.

The tempo of the rain increases. The insistent drumming eases my fears of being alone in the quiet darkness. This morning, my mother said she'd be back before lunch, but the clock is ticking down the last hours of the day. I ache in strange places. My stomach rumbles, a plea for nourishment.

One by one, I polish my mother's apples with a mist of breath and a cotton sleeve, but as hard as I try, I cannot find an apple willing to show me my face. They stay silent in their bowl, hoarding their compliments for the woman who loves them more than she loves me. Frustrated and defiant, I pluck the shiniest piece of fruit from the bowl and roll it in my hand, relishing its smoothness and weight before I take a bite.

The sweet rot hits hard. I spit it out and hold the apple up for inspection. A worm has carved a prayer in the pulp. Acid floods my mouth. The apple drops to the floor and I cover my lips, both hands cupped against the revolt.

If I'd looked closer, would I have seen the hole near the stem? If I'd listened harder, would I have heard their words of warning? She would have seen. She would have heard. The apples reflect her image and her image only. A fragment of a laugh whispers through the room. I should have known better.

My stomach cramps, tugs down. I run to the bathroom. Bile erupts, a vile stream of yellow staining the toilet and the floor. My gut throbs and I feel a gush of wet between my legs. I wipe my mouth and look down to see white shorts stained red. A wrenching pain twists low in my stomach. It takes me a moment to realize I'm not a girl anymore. I'm a woman now.

I kick off my shorts and underwear and shove them in the bathroom trash, covering them with wadded toilet paper. Under the sink, I dig through boxes and try to remember my mother's vague comments on the trials of being a woman. I find a carton of tampons, slender sticks full of cotton plugs. I pull the crisp white covering back, revealing pink plastic prepared to flower deep within. Deep in denial, I toss the stick back in the box and clean up with a wet washcloth before heading back to my room with a roll of toilet paper in hand. Determined to hide my transition, I stuff my underwear full of tissue and get dressed in a pair of black jean shorts. Swaddled in secret, I return to the bathroom to empty the trash and clean the toilet. If I'm careful, she'll never know.

*Handsome apples are sometimes sour. – German Proverb*

"Your daughter looks just like you, Layla," says my mother's newest friend. I blush at the woman's observation and pretend I didn't hear.

"Don't be ridiculous," says my mother, anger flickering deep in her eyes.

The towel is all I have to cling to as I scoot into a sun-shaded chair. Chlorinated water drips down my legs and puddles at my feet.

The woman flinches at the barbs in my mother's voice. She backpedals. "I'm going to get another drink. Would you like one?"

My mother shifts on her lounge chair and lifts a hand to wave the woman away. The frowsy blonde's forced smile falters and she stumbles to her feet. Her skin stretches over plump thighs and her stomach folds into rippling rolls as she bends over to shuffle through the bags lumped together on the table. Her body fascinates me. The startling contrast between her pink, lumbering flesh and my mother's firm, tanned form only makes the woman look more awkward.

I can't remember this new friend's name. I gave up trying to keep up with the ever-revolving door of my mother's companions a long time ago. They never last long.

"One apple martini coming right up," the blonde says as she holds up her wallet.

My mother closes her eyes under the shaded brim of her sunhat.

The woman's features pinch into a scowl. My mother never frowns. She keeps her face in a smooth emotionless mask, the product of one of her poisonous secrets. Her new friend never learned that lesson. Wrinkles crease the blonde woman's forehead and feather out from her eyes.

She glances at me. "Do you want anything, Stella?"

I want to tell her that being nice to me will only make my mother madder, but I just shake my head. Layla muzzled me long ago.

The woman sighs and walks away to place her order at the pool bar.

"Stella." My mother's voice is rich and warm. "Come here."

I move slowly, a stone in the pit of my stomach weighing me down. *You stupid little bitch.* The silent words cut more cruelly than the ones she speaks. I want to protest, but I know better. The chair screeches as I push it back.

"Bring the lotion."

I shuffle over, flip-flops scraping against the rough tiles. She watches me, an exclamation of disdain evident in the tilt of a raised eyebrow. *Lumbering cow.* My towel comes undone, slipping down to expose my bony body loosely covered in a brown bikini. She never wears earth tones. She leaves those to me. Her nail polish matches her red lips, which curve in a smile as sharp as a scimitar.

Her accusations bash around inside my head. *Ugly. Bony. Awkward.*

"You don't look anything at all like me," she says. "If I didn't know better, I would think you belonged to someone else."

I wish it was true.

Her French-cut swimsuit gleams white, accentuating her hourglass figure and bronzed skin. She turns over her palm and I pass her the suntan lotion. Before she can begin, a man approaches with two drinks in hand.

"You look thirsty." He offers my mother a martini glass filled with a liquid as green as envy. A round, wafer-thin circle of apple floats on the top. I catch a glimpse of the pentagram in the center, a starburst of seeds.

Her eyes narrow as she assesses him. I know he passes her appraisal when she tilts her head and arches her back. Her attention shifts and she casts her net of seduction, a silvery shimmer spreading out to ensnare a new prey.

"Parched," she says, waving to the empty seat at her side.

He grins and sits, placing the drinks on the side table.

Layla's blonde friend stops a few feet away and stares. She holds a drink in each hand. Her face flushes pink and then she slowly turns to walk back the way she came.

Layla ignores her. "Go play, Stella," she says without looking at me.

I wander over to the sparkling water. A woman frolics in the shallow end with a fearless toddler pushing the limits of his water wings. The rest of the pool is empty, a backdrop for the beautiful people visiting the resort. The cool blue promises a respite from my mother's scathing tongue and hot looks. I raise my hands overhead, preparing to dive. Her laugh arrests me and I freeze, peering across the water to her cabana. She looks straight at me and points. Her companion grins and joins the fun.

Heat flushes my face. I'm afraid to look down, afraid of what I will see. I look anyway. The hand-me-down bikini has betrayed me, riding up across my narrow chest to expose budding breasts. *Underdeveloped little runt.* I shrug off her curse and take the plunge. Her words can't reach me here under the waves. If only I could hold my breath, I would stay down here forever.

*No apple tree is immune from worms. – Russian Proverb*

Today, it finally happened. A man watched me with an appraising look most men reserve for my mother. And then he ruined the moment.

"You must be sisters," he said.

Layla laughed, but I could hear the sharp edge in her voice as she sliced his attention away from me. She pushed me aside and redirected his attention, trapping him with her seductive power in just moments. He didn't look at me again.

I could have despaired, but I figure I've had enough of that in my life. Instead, I went down to the local drug store, lifted a box of hair dye, and went back to the house to orchestrate my transformation while my mother was still away.

Behind the safety of locked doors, I survey the implements arrayed in front of me: one of my mother's new razors, her tweezers, her cherished comb, her sewing kit, and the unboxed hair color, all neat and tidy in shiny tubes. I shed my clothes and scan my image in the mirror. Unlike my mother's overripe voluptuousness, my body fits on a narrow frame. My breasts are small, but high and firm. My legs are long and lean under the shadow of hair she refuses to let me shave. My heart-shaped face hides behind a chestnut curtain hanging to my waist.

I start with the most obvious link between us. I pull her carved bone comb through my hair, watching the pearled handle glint between my fingers. Some of her magic must be trapped between its teeth because my hair responds, lifting in a nimbus that dances in the air. Only then do I smash the ivory fangs, letting the fragments fall to the floor. Sharp scissors slice through the hated mass and I revel in the freedom of finally being unveiled. I sweep the heavy locks aside with a bare foot. Short and spiky, my hair makes my face appear sharper, fey. For the first time since I can remember, I smile.

Eager to expand my newfound freedom, I turn on the hot water and sit on the edge of the tub. Foamy lather spurts out of a pink can and I spread it on my legs, covering the hair in a layer of white. Never having shaved, I am cautious, but eager to shed the dark down. With each pass, black curdles in white, revealing soft skin. I rinse and repeat. Overly confident, I press too hard on the last stroke. The razor slices. As I watch, blood wells from the cut, falling in three large drops to spread across the white tile. My grandmother's lessons are not wasted. Three wishes tumble past my lips in a breathy rush. Ignoring the stinging cut, I grit my teeth and pick up where I left off. With the last of the foam and hair rinsed off, I step out of the tub and prepare for my final act of defiance.

Steam obscures the mirror. I use a towel to clear a window in the glass, but I have only moments to stare at my own reflection before it clouds back over. My mother speaks to this mirror several times a day, but it has never spoken to me. I should have known it was on her side.

Hands encased in plastic gloves, I follow the instructions, mixing color with toner. Guided by touch alone, I apply it to my newly cropped cap of curls released from the heavy burden. The air pricks at my bare skin and cools my saturated hair. Even though I know I should be ashamed, I revel in the feeling of being comfortable in my own body.

A glance at the clock tells me that my freedom is coming to an end, so I crack the door and listen to the silence of the house before dashing across the hall to my room. Shuffling through the clothes in my closet, I find a plain black sheath given to me by one of my mother's friends. It will do.

Back in the bathroom, I rinse the dye out of my hair. The stain swirls in the sink like a deepening bruise left from one of my mother's barbs. I run one of her immaculate towels across my shaggy curls and it comes away marked by my defiance. My resolve slips at the sight of the discolored linen, but there is no going back, so I shrug and let it fall to the splotched tiles covered with severed hair.

Disregarding the modesty of underwear, I slip into the chic dress, a gift my mother allowed me to keep only because she thought I'd never be able to wear it. I reach behind me and pull up the zipper to where it ends in a deep V at the back. I tug the hem down, but it won't go any farther than mid-thigh. Having second thoughts about my wickedness, I reach for the door knob, but flinch when I hear the front door slam.

I freeze. My heart pounds, but I push the fear aside. I am someone else. I am no longer her shadow. With the stained towel, I wipe away the last residue of condensation on the glass and peer into the mirror. This time the mirror speaks.

I no longer resemble my mother. A black tumble of short curls frames a face turned pale by contrast. A delicate pink blush fills full lips under clear hazel eyes. The dress hugs my form, revealing subtle curves from my waist to my hips. The slight mounds of my breasts press against the soft fabric.

"Stella," my mother calls out. "Where are you?"

I stand straight and push my shoulders back, bracing myself for the attack. With a studied grace, gleaned from 15 years of watching Layla, I walk down the hall. My approach causes her to drop a bag of groceries. *Slut.* Ripe red apples roll across the floor. One stops at my bare foot and I lean over to pick it up.

"What have you done?" She chokes on the question. Her mask slips as a frown pinches her forehead.

I roll the apple in my palm, inspecting it for flaws. It's perfect. "Don't you like it?"

"Stella?" Her mask collapses under the weight of the word. Tiny wrinkles appear on her face. A tear slips down her cheek. "Why did you do this?"

"That's easy." I breathe on the apple and polish it on my dress. When I hold it back up, it reflects my face and tells me that I'm the fairest in the land.

I smile and take a bite out of the firm flesh, letting the apple's juice run down my chin. "I got tired of looking like you."

*When the apple is ripe it will fall. – Irish Proverb*

When the weight of winter finally becomes too much for Layla to bear, she drops me off at my grandmother's house in preparation for a vacation in warmer climes. She doesn't want me around to sour her adventure.

"Don't let her out of your sight," she says, not caring that I am standing right in front of her. "She's a wicked, spiteful creature."

My grandmother just watches my mother with her mild dark gaze until Layla's litany of complaints tapers off.

"You'll see," Layla says as she stomps out of the cabin. The door bangs shut behind her.

"Good riddance," says my grandmother.

My shoulders relax even though my mother continues a scathing reproach only I can hear. *Ugly bitch.* Even after the car rolls down the long gravel driveway, her words whisper in my ear. *Stupid cow. Cunt.*

My grandmother turns her attention to me and grins. Her teeth are sharp and white behind her blood-red lips. "Now where shall we start?"

I hesitate and stare out the window. Large snowflakes swirl through the air in a thick flurry of white. A frosting of ice silvers the stark black limbs of the trees. Silence spreads in the space between us. Although the fire crackles and shares its generous heat, a chill skates across my spine.

My grandmother has never resembled the other grandmothers I've meet in friends' homes. I know she must be old, but her skin shows only the lightest hints of age. In fact, she doesn't look old enough to be a mother, let alone a grandmother. Her body is long and trim like mine, but she walks with a grace I've yet to learn. Her long hair resembles hammered silver just on the verge of turning liquid. When she moves, the heavy mass floats behind her like a fairy cape. And in the dim illumination of the fire, it appears to be edged with molten red.

"Your heart is too tender, my dear." My grandmother opens a cabinet and retrieves a little glass coffin from the shelf. "Let's put it somewhere safe, shall we?"

I find my voice. "Will it hurt?"

My grandmother's smile broadens and her eyes glitter like black stars. "Only for a moment."

She reaches out to embrace me, one arm wrapped around my waist, the other buried deep in my chest. In the space between one breath and another, my heart flutters in her palm. All of the bitterness, the rage, the pain locked away panics in a flurry of fervid emotion. And then it is done.

She releases me and gently places my heart in the glass box. "There now. Isn't that better?"

Everything is the same, but different at the same time. Now that the last of my mother's power over me has been stripped away, I can hear so many things: snowflakes brushing against the frosted windows, the fiery dance of sparks in the hearth, the crush of heavy boots pressing through snow, a human heartbeat moving closer and closer toward the cottage.

The rap of a fist against wood startles me out of a fugue.

"It appears there's a wolf at the door," my grandmother says. "How marvelous."

A strange hunger gnaws at my insides.

My grandmother pats my cheeks. "Wolves love my cider," she says as she turns my face from side to side in the cradle of her hands, searching. "The beasts are notorious for having a sweet tooth."

"Cider?" The hunger grows, leaving me hollow.

Apparently satisfied, she releases me and steps aside. "Have a good time, my dear." My grandmother plucks her favorite wool cape from its hook. She fastens it at her throat and draws the red hood up to cover her hair. "And try not to make a mess."

She leaves with a stealth born from a life filled with secrets. The latch on the back door snicks shut, but I know the man lingering on the front porch will not be able to hear what I can hear. How could he? Poor thing.

The knock comes again, louder. "Is any one home?"

This time I answer.

*An apple never falls far from the tree. – English Proverb*

The water ripples and rolls as I shift my weight in the tub. The petrified remains of the wolf's heart rest between my breasts. I have taken to long soaks after that long winter night, but it doesn't matter how many baths I take or how long I stay submersed; there is no washing away the stain of my nature.

Fragmented memories drift in my mind as I float in the rose-scented water, but I push them aside and concentrate on breathing. Bubbles follow the slopes of my body, rising and falling with each breath. The water starts to chill and I reluctantly sit up, hand clenched around the bloodstained stone the size of a man's heart. The blackness refuses to give up its hold, no matter how many times I scrub it, but I run my thumb over the stain anyway.

*Monster.*

I cock my head in the direction of the master bedroom, but the sounds of my mother's perversions have quieted. Layla and her young lover must be taking a break. Grateful for the reprieve, I slip out of the tub and dry off. The mirror comments on my sleek form and I smile.

A door shuts and the hall floor creaks. I freeze and listen to the steps coming down the hall. Layla has been avoiding me, so I know it's her huntsman who pauses at the door. After a long beat, the footsteps continue down the hall toward the kitchen. The grandfather clock in the living room chimes twelve.

I release a breath I hadn't realized I was holding. Earlier in the evening, I heard Layla bragging about stealing her newest lover from a younger woman. She had been inordinately proud of the acquisition of this rugged bounty hunter. Now her prize is walking around alone in the house.

Dishes clatter in the kitchen and I realize I don't have long before he will return to her. In a hurry, I sift through assorted beauty products for rose lotions and powders. Layla once told me roses belong to the apple family. The scent of roses sours on her skin, but the floral notes complement me perfectly. My grandmother told me so. I finger comb my damp curls and pinch my cheeks until they bloom. Before I can have second thoughts, I wrap myself in one of

Layla's cast-off robes. The shimmering pattern settles around me, revealing dwarfed figures trapped in the weave of scarlet, sapphire, and saffron.

The carpet tickles my feet as I glide down the hall. I pause in the kitchen. The only piece of clothing on the man's body is a pair of jeans that hang low on his hips. The muscles on his back ripple as he sorts through the refrigerator. I rock back on my heels and enjoy the view of this huntsman who was brought down by Layla's wiles.

He pulls out a milk carton and shuts the refrigerator door with a bare foot. Even though the kitchen is dim, I can tell the exact moment he sees me. He freezes in place, the milk carton crushed in his grip.

Sensing an advantage, I edge closer and drop the bloodstained stone among the apples cradled in the lurid carnival glass. They scream and wail in despair, but the huntsman is deaf to their warnings.

"Did you find everything you need?"

"I was just making a snack." He shifts his weight and relaxes, watching me watch him.

"I'm hungry too." I twist the satin sash holding my robe closed.

He opens his mouth as if he is going to say something, but then appears to think better of it.

"Where's Layla?" I ask, even though I already know the answer.

"Sleeping."

I think of Layla's pill drawer and smile. She isn't the only one with knowledge of poisons.

He watches me with a mixture of fear and lust. I decide to accept both. With a tug, the sash unties and the robe falls open. I shrug off the silky material and let it pool in a kaleidoscope of color around my feet. An understanding passes between us.

"She said you were heartless." He sets the milk carton on the counter.

"Did she?" I smile with the knowledge that my heart is safe in its glass casket, hidden deep in the woods.

"She said you were sleeping."

"I'm awake now." A coy glance reveals the knowledge I desire. He belongs to me now.

This is how I know it's time to move on.

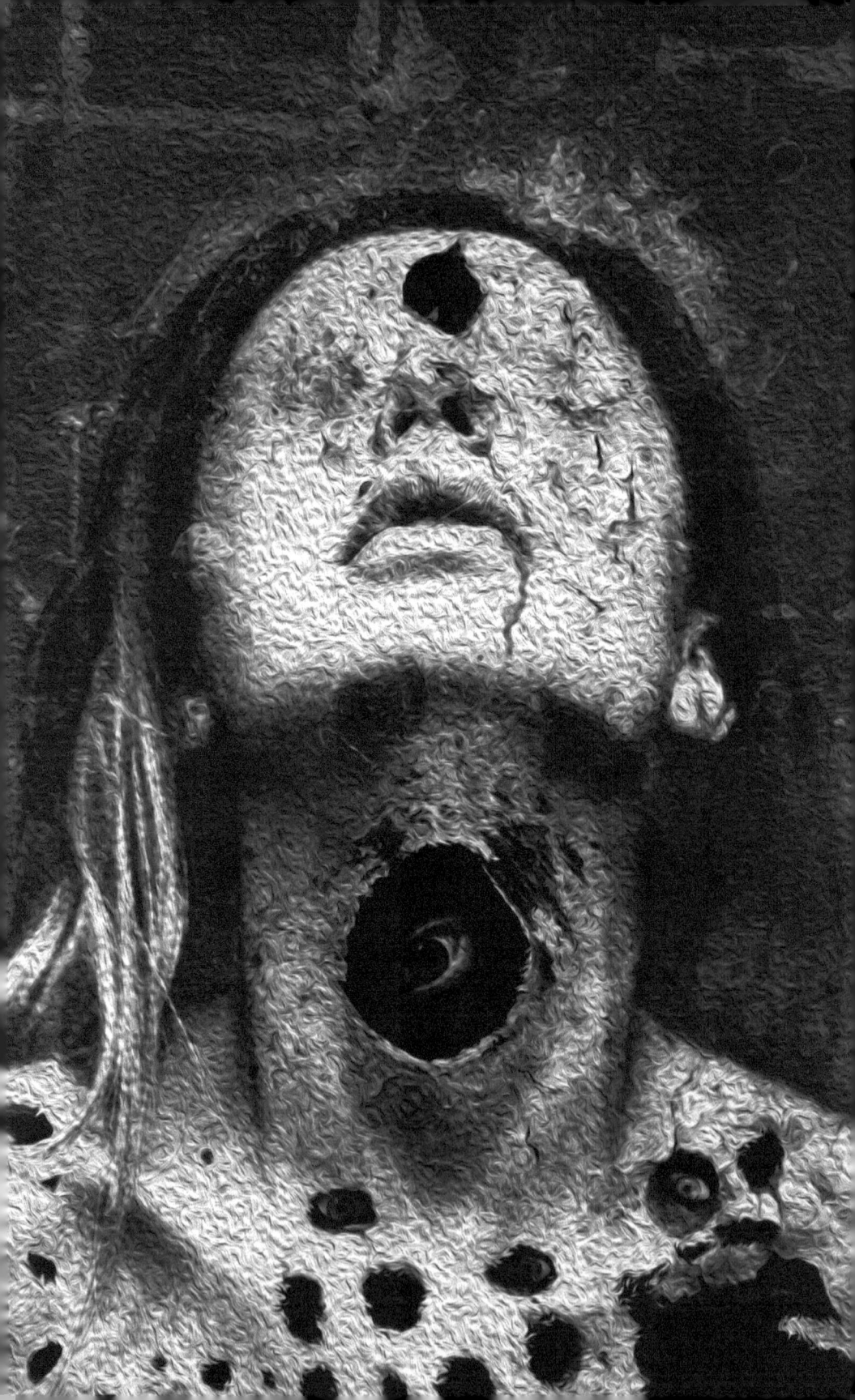

# About the Authors

LINDA D. ADDISON is an American poet and writer of horror, fantasy, and science fiction. Addison is the first African-American winner of the HWA Bram Stoker Award®, which she won four times for her collections *Consumed, Reduced to Beautiful Grey Ashes* (2001) and *Being Full of Light, Insubstantial* (2007) and *How To Recognize A Demon Has Become Your Friend* (2011) and *Four Elements* (2014). In 2016 Addison received the HWA Mentor of the Year Award and in 2018 she received the HWA Lifetime Achievement Award.

CHRISTOPHER BARZAK is the author of the Crawford Award winning novel, *One for Sorrow,* which was made into the Sundance feature film, *Jamie Marks is Dead.* His second novel, *The Love We Share Without Knowing,* was a finalist for the Nebula and Tiptree Awards. His third novel, *Wonders of the Invisible World,* is a Stonewall Honor Book. He is also the author of *Before and Afterlives,* which won the Shirley Jackson Award for Best Collection. His most current novel is *The Gone Away Place.* He grew up in rural Ohio, has lived in a southern California beach town, the capital of Michigan, and has taught English outside of Tokyo, Japan. Currently he teaches fiction writing in the Northeast Ohio MFA program at Youngstown State University.

JIMMY BERNARD is a writer born and raised in Antwerp, Belgium. He's got an office job and is a professional shower singer. Most of his time is spent writing or reading, and, of course, haunting his wife with his latest horror story idea. Luckily, he's a great sushi cook to make up for it.

CARINA BISSETT is a writer, poet, and educator working primarily in the fields of dark fiction and interstitial art. Her short fiction and poetry has been published in multiple journals and anthologies including *Hath No Fury, Gorgon: Stories of Emergence, Mythic Delirium, NonBinary Review,* and the *HWA Poetry Showcase Vol. V* and *VI.* She teaches online workshops at The Storied Imaginarium and she is a graduate of the Creative Writing MFA program at Stonecoast. Her work has been nominated for several awards including the Pushcart Prize and the Sundress Publications Best of the Net. Link to her work can be found at http://carinabissett.com.

JOHN BODEN lives a stone's throw from Three Mile Island with his wonderful wife and sons. His work has appeared in *Borderlands 6, Shock Totem, Splatterpunk* and *Lamplight.* His first published book was the not-really-for-children children's book *Dominoes.* Followed by *Jedi Summer With the Magnetic Kid* and *Walk the Darkness Down.* He has also written collaborative novellas: *Detritus in Love* with Mercedes M. Yardley, one with Chad Lutzke called *Out Behind the Barn* and *Rattlesnake Kisses* and *Cattywampus* with Bob Ford. His next book, *Spungunion,* will be published by Fungasm Press in early 2020. There are more things in the works.

JONATHAN COSGROVE is an Irish writer of dark fiction. As a child, he convinced his mother's best friend that he'd been born in America, despite the fact she'd visited him in the Irish hospital where he was born. Since then he's been trying to write just-as-convincing stories. When not grappling with words he grapples at Brazilian jiu-jitsu. His fingers are in constant agony. Find him as @jjingo_gaijin on Twitter and Instagram.

DANIEL CROW is a 27-year-old journalist and writer with degrees in Linguistics and International Relations who is currently based in Tel Aviv. He has been passionate about writing ever since school years, with Stephen King and Neil Gaiman among his favourite authors. Inspired by the tales of the past, he seeks to bring out the mythical in the present, pitting his character against children of the unknown and unfathomable. "Draugen," his first short story in English and a modern take on the Norse myth of the draugs, was published in *Allegory* e-zine volume 35/62, and is set to come out again in an anthology by Mortal Realm. "The Ocelot," a short story exploring the mythos of the voodoo, is slated for the Monsters *We Forgot* anthology by Soteira Press.

NACHING T. KASSA is a member of the Horror Writers Association. She has over nineteen short stories published (the most recent, "The Face," is in the anthology, *Campfire Tales*) and she's written two novellas. She lives in Eastern Washington State with her husband, Dan, their three children, and their dog.

TODD KEISLING is a writer and designer of the horrific and strange. He is an author of several books, including *Devil's Creek, Scanlines, The Final Reconciliation,* and *Ugly Little Things: Collected Horrors,* among other shorter works. He lives somewhere in the wilds of Pennsylvania with his family where he is at work on his next novel. Share his dread on Twitter (@todd_keisling) and Instagram (@toddkeisling) or check out his website www.toddkeisling.com for more information.

GRANT LONGSTAFF is from Gateshead; a small, suitably dismal town in the north east of England where nothing much happens. He had no choice but to write fiction. He now lives in Glasgow. You can find him on Twitter @GrantLongstaff or visit his website www.grantlongstaff.co.uk for more information.

JENNIFER LORING'S short fiction has been published widely both online and in print, appearing alongside Graham Masterton, Joe R. Lansdale, Elizabeth Massie, Ramsey Campbell, Kealan Patrick Burke, Steve Rasnic Tem, and Clive Barker. She holds an MFA in Writing Popular Fiction with a concentration in horror fiction and is currently working toward her PhD in Creative Writing. Jenn lives with her husband in Philadelphia, PA, where they are owned by a turtle and two basset hounds.

KEN LIU (http://kenliu.name) is an American author of speculative fiction. A winner of the Nebula, Hugo, and World Fantasy awards, he wrote *The Dandelion Dynasty,* a silkpunk epic fantasy series (starting with *The Grace of Kings*), as well as *The Paper Menagerie and Other Stories* and *The Hidden Girl and Other Stories.* He also authored the Star Wars novel, *The Legends of Luke Skywalker.* Prior to becoming a full-time writer, Liu worked as a software engineer, corporate lawyer, and litigation consultant. Liu frequently speaks at conferences and universities on a variety of topics, including futurism, cryptocurrency, history of technology, bookmaking, the mathematics of origami, and other subjects of his expertise.

LINDA J. MARSHALL lived in a van beside the Colorado River in Utah where she kept company with a carp named SuckPop. Later, she lived in the Mississippi Delta where she met many of the great, old Blues Musicians. Teeming with stories, she's writing them in Oklahoma, where her son thinks his wandering mom is kind of cool.

KELLI OWEN is the author of more than a dozen books, including the novels *Teeth* and *Floaters,* and novellas such as *Waiting Out Winter* and the *Wilted Lily* series. Her fiction spans the genres from horrific thrillers to psychological horror, with an occasional bloodbath, and an even rarer happy ending. She was an editor and reviewer for over a decade, participated on dozens of panels, and spoken at the CIA Headquarters in Langley, VA regarding both her writing and the field in general. Born and raised in Wisconsin, she now lives in Destination, Pennsylvania. Visit her website at kelliowen.com for more information.

DINO PARENTI is a writer of dark literary and speculative fiction. He is the winner of the first annual Lascaux Review flash fiction contest and is featured in the Anthony Award winning anthology *Blood on the Bayou.* His work can be found in *Pantheon Magazine, Menacing Hedge, Pithead Chapel,* as well as other anthologies. He is a fiction editor at *Gamut Magazine* and a member of the HWA. His short-fiction collection, *Dead Reckoning and Other Stories,* is now out with Crystal Lake Publishing.

STEVEN PIRIE lives in Liverpool, UK, with his wife and son. He spends his day shuffling about moaning and groaning, as currently he's awaiting surgery for a hernia repair. It's possible the wife and son might lynch him before then. He loves to write humour, and has had some success with two humorous fantasy novels published by Storm Constantine's Immanion Press. His short stories tend to be a little more dark and gritty, although there's often levity lurking just below the surface. He has a website at stevenpirie.com. Occasionally, he even updates it.

ARMAND ROSAMILIA is a New Jersey boy currently living in sunny Florida, where he writes when he's not sleeping. He's happily married to a woman who helps his career and is supportive, which is all he ever wanted in life. He's written over 150 stories that are currently available, including horror, zombies, contemporary fiction, thrillers and more. His goal is to write a good story and not worry about genre labels.

MERCEDES M. YARDLEY is a whimsical dark fantasist who wears stilettos, red lipstick, and poisonous flowers in her hair. She is the author of *Beautiful Sorrows,* the Stabby Award-winning *Apocalyptic Montessa and Nuclear Lulu: A Tale of Atomic Love, Pretty Little Dead Girls: A Novel of Murder and Whimsy, Detritus in Love,* and *Nameless.* She recently won the prestigious Bram Stoker Award for her story *Little Dead Red* and was a Bram Stoker Award nominee for her short story *"Loving You Darkly."* Mercedes lives and creates in Las Vegas. You can find her at mercedesmyardley.com.

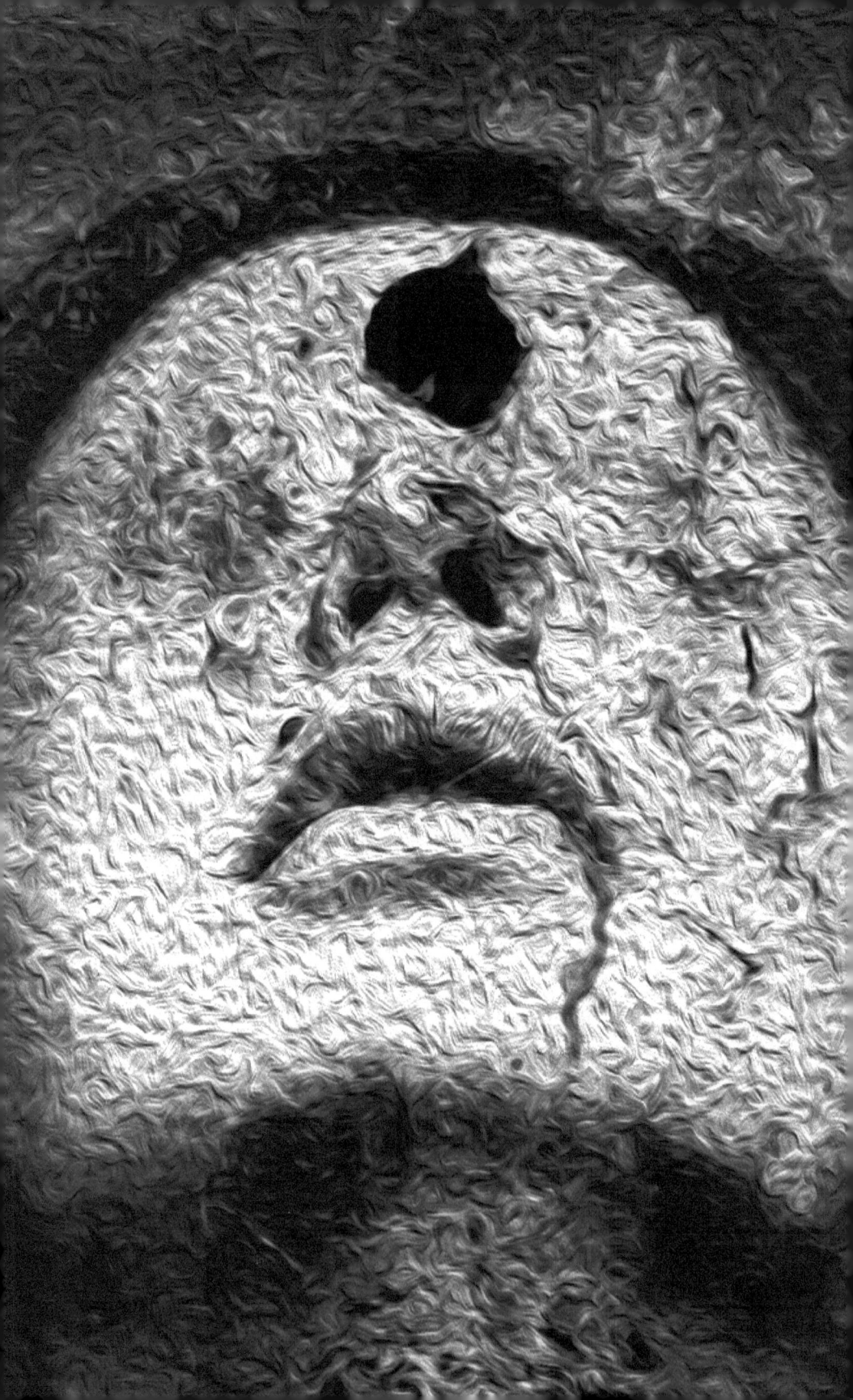

# THE END?

*Not quite...*

Check out these other titles by Mercedes M. Yardley:

*Pretty Little Dead Girls: A Novel of Murder and Whimsy*
*Nameless: The Darkness Comes*
*Apocalyptic Montessa and Nuclear Lulu: A Tale of Atomic Love*
*Little Dead Red*

Or check out other Crystal Lake Publishing titles for more Tales from the Darkest Depths.

# ANTHOLOGIES

*Shallow Waters Vol.3*, edited by Joe Mynhardt
*Tales from The Lake Vol.5*, edited by Kenneth W. Cain
*Welcome to The Show*, edited by Doug Murano and Matt Hayward
*Lost Highways: Dark Fictions From the Road*, edited by D. Alexander Ward
*C.H.U.D. Lives! – A Tribute Anthology*
*Tales from The Lake Vol.4: The Horror Anthology*, edited by Ben Eads
*Behold! Oddities, Curiosities and Undefinable Wonders*, edited by Doug Murano
*Twice Upon an Apocalypse: Lovecraftian Fairy Tales*,
edited by Rachel Kenley and Scott T. Goudsward
*Tales from The Lake Vol.3*, edited by Monique Snyman
*Gutted: Beautiful Horror Stories*,
edited by Doug Murano and D. Alexander Ward

If you've ever thought of becoming an author, we'd also like to recommend these non-fiction titles:

## NON - FICTION

*It's Alive: Bringing Your Nightmares to Life,*
edited by Eugene Johnson and Joe Mynhardt
*The Dead Stage: The Journey from Page to Stage* by Dan Weatherer
*Where Nightmares Come From: The Art of Storytelling in the Horror Genre,*
edited by Joe Mynhardt and Eugene Johnson
*Horror 101: The Way Forward,*
edited by Joe Mynhardt and Emma Audsley
*Horror 201: The Silver Scream Vol.1* and *Vol.2,*
edited by Joe Mynhardt and Emma Audsley
*Modern Mythmakers: 35 interviews with Horror and Science Fiction Writers
and Filmmakers* by Michael McCarty
*Writers On Writing: An Author's Guide* Volumes 1,2,3, and 4,
edited by Joe Mynhardt.

Hi readers,

It makes our day to know you reached the end of our book. Thank you so much. This is why we do what we do every single day.

Whether you found the book good or great, we'd love to hear what you thought. Please take a moment to leave a review on Amazon, Goodreads, or anywhere else readers visit. Reviews go a long way to helping a book sell, and will help us to continue publishing quality books. You can also share a photo of yourself holding this book with the hashtag #IGotMyCLPBook!

Thank you again for taking the time to journey with Crystal Lake Publishing.

We are also on...

Website: www.crystallakepub.com
Books: http://www.crystallakepub.com/book-table/
Twitter: https://twitter.com/crystallakepub
Facebook: https://www.facebook.com/Crystallakepublishing/
Instagram: https://www.instagram.com/crystal_lake_publishing/
Patreon: https://www.patreon.com/CLP

Or check out other Crystal Lake Publishing titles for more Tales from the Darkest Depths. You can also subscribe to Crystal Lake Classics, where you'll receive fortnightly info on all our books, starting all the way back at the beginning, with personal notes on every release. Or follow us on Patreon for exclusive content and behind the scenes access, bonus short stories, polls, interviews and, if you're interested, author support.

With unmatched success since 2012, Crystal Lake Publishing has quickly become one of the world's leading indie publishers of Mystery, Thriller, and Suspense books with a Dark Fiction edge.

Crystal Lake Publishing puts integrity, honor, and respect at the forefront of our operations.

We strive for each book and outreach program that's launched to not only entertain and touch or comment on issues that affect our readers, but also to strengthen and support the Dark Fiction field and its authors.

Not only do we publish authors who are legends in the field and as hardworking as us, but we look for men and women who care about their readers and fellow human beings. We only publish the very best Dark Fiction, and look forward to launching many new careers.

We strive to know each and every one of our readers while building personal relationships with our authors, reviewers, bloggers, podcasters, bookstores, and libraries.

Crystal Lake Publishing is and will always be a beacon of what passion and dedication, combined with overwhelming teamwork and respect, can accomplish: unique fiction you can't find anywhere else.

We do not just publish books, we present you worlds within your world, doors within your mind from talented authors who sacrifice so much for a moment of your time.

This is what we believe in. What we stand for. This will be our legacy.

Welcome to Crystal Lake Publishing.

www.ingramcontent.com/pod-product-compliance
Lightning Source LLC
Chambersburg PA
CBHW050256110726
47898CB00007B/2430